SCORPION RISING

SCORPION RISING

Marilyn Todd

This first world edition published in Great Britain 2006 by
SEVERN HOUSE PUBLISHERS LTD of
9–15 High Street, Sutton, Surrey SM1 1DF.
This first world edition published in the USA 2006 by
SEVERN HOUSE PUBLISHERS INC of
595 Madison Avenue, New York, N.Y. 10022.

British Library Cataloguing in Publication Data

Todd, Marilyn
      Scorpion rising
      1.   Claudia Seferius (Fictitious character) - Fiction
      2.   Rome - History - Empire, 30 B.C. – 284 A.D. - Fiction
      3.   Detective and mystery stories
      I.   Title
      823.9'14 [F]

      ISBN-13: 978-0-7278-6375-1 (cased)
      ISBN-10: 0-7278-6375-4 (cased)
      ISBN-10: 0-7278-9169-3 (trade paper)

This title, as with all others from Severn House, is printed on acid-free paper.

Typeset by Palimpsest Book Production Ltd.,
Polmont, Stirlingshire, Scotland.
Printed and bound in Great Britain by
MPG Books Ltd., Bodmin, Cornwall.

This is where I live. So this book is dedicated to everyone who lived here before me, from Neolithic man to the Gauls, the Romans who bridged the river, the Crusaders who built the fortress, the Knights Templar, the priests who turned the castle into a seminary, even the Germans who occupied it during the War. But most especially to my gorgeous little tortoiseshell, Tuppence.

In the centre of the world, between earth, sky and sea, at the point where the realms of the universe meet, is a place from which everything the world over can be seen. There Rumour lives, in a home she has chosen for herself on a hilltop. Night and day the house lies open, for she has given it a thousand apertures and incalculable entrances, with never a door to barricade her thresholds. The whole structure is of echoing brass and there is no quiet within, no silence in any part, and yet there is no din. Only murmured whisperings, like the sound of the sea's waves heard at a distance, or the last rumbles of Jupiter's thunder. A host inhabits these halls. They come, they go, a shadowy throng. And a thousand rumours, false mixed with true, stray this way and that, while confused words flit about, pouring their stories into idle ears, while others carry off the tales they have heard. And the story grows, each teller adding to what he has heard – and Rumour sees everything that goes on in heaven, in earth and on the sea . . .

Ovid
(43BC–AD17)

One

'Good morning, madam.' Claudia's lanky Macedonian steward bowed dutifully. 'I trust you slept well.'

Claudia's eyes swivelled round the atrium, taking in every marble column and each exquisite fresco, noting every detail from the gold that rimmed the fountain to the elaborate mosaic it was set in, and quite frankly couldn't imagine *anyone* not sleeping well when all this was theirs.

'Like a baby, Leonides, like a baby, except I didn't need burping.' Dear me, was that a smile that almost escaped from his mouth? 'Now then, are the litter bearers outside?'

That was the trouble with these big town houses. No windows faced onto the street, making a perfect buffer from noise, smell and burglars, but of course it meant one had no idea what was happening on the outside.

'Ready and waiting, my lady.'

'Excellent! Then I shall—'

'Before you go.' He leaned down and spoke quietly. 'There's a gentleman to see you.'

'At this ungodly hour of the morning?'

'He's been here since cock-crow, madam.'

'This is June, Leonides. The cocks crow exceedingly early.'

'So I'm told.'

Yes. *Definitely* a twitch of a smile. 'Did this early bird give a name?'

'He made no conversation at all, other than to state his appointment with the Merchant Seferius, though I detected a slight Spanish accent, if that helps. Shall I show him into your office?'

'No. You can show him the door.'

For one thing, Claudia had no outstanding appointments with Spaniards or otherwise, and for another, the Ides was

1

a public holiday. No one in the Empire was conducting business today, especially – what did Leonides say he'd called her? the *Merchant Seferius*. As the bearers set her litter down on the Capitol, she decided she wouldn't give the vulgar little upstart the time of day after an insult like that. Dear Diana, business might not be booming, but there were enough chauvinistic pigs around Rome without adding to her burden.

Outside the Temple of Jupiter, the Guild of Flute Players were gathering for their annual festival. Theirs was an important role in society, and whether at public sacrifice or private funeral, their melodies drowned out any sound which might carry bad omens, and when it came to marriage rites, birthdays and triumphal marches their playing enlivened the day. It was only fair they be honoured with their own banquet.

Shaking knife-sharp pleats into place, Claudia thought back to the Vinalia, when the Guild of Wine Merchants celebrated at their festival with wine tastings, feasting and dance. Being a woman, of course, she wasn't invited, though it hadn't stopped her from turning up. Dammit, Seferius wine was good stuff. Those bastards had no right to demand she relinquish the business.

Dressed in long festive robes and colourful headbands, the cream of flute-playing society prepared to stage their spectacular on the steps of the temple. Here, at least, as the widow of an eminent wine merchant, Claudia was entitled to a good seat – though with her dark flashing eyes and even darker glossy hair, she invariably secured a better one. Today was no exception and thanking the little bald man who hoped to make her his mistress but would have better luck building a snow-horse in August, she reflected that she'd inherited the enterprise perfectly legally and for heaven's sake, there was no law to prevent women from being in trade. At least. She ran her fingers down the pleats of her gown. Not yet . . .

Having tried persuading her to sell up and then failing, the Guild turned to dirtier tactics – and still failed. Currently they were lobbying the Senate for a change in the law, but if that didn't get passed, they wouldn't give up. It stuck in their craw that some flibbertigibbet was making a success

2

of her late husband's business, and whether out of pride, greed or envy, they would not be denied. Claudia sighed. What the Guild didn't know was that they had in fact succeeded. It was true, she mused, as the flautists produced one haunting tune after another. The best way to make a small fortune is to start with a large one. Her affluence was no more than an illusion held together by implication and swagger. Claudia Seferius was broke.

It was midnight by the time the festival finally wound down, and as she closed the door on the rumble of night-time delivery carts, the silence in the house came as a relief. The slaves were tucked up, even the birds in the aviary had tucked their heads under their jewel-coloured wings. The only sounds came from the occasional spitting of the oil lamps that hung from the candelabra, the gurgle of the fountain and Leonides snoring softly as he lay sprawled over a couch in the atrium, where he'd fallen asleep waiting for his mistress to return.

'As a guard dog I'd want my money back,' she tutted, stepping over his feet. 'But at least you got rid of that odd-bod Spaniard.'

'He did not,' an accented voice swirled out of the shadows. 'That odd-bod Spaniard is still waiting.'

Claudia spun round. 'Well, it's a fine night and the honey-suckle's sweet,' she retorted, and look, not a hint of quiver in her voice. 'I'm sure he won't mind waiting a bit longer. In the street.'

'That, I am afraid, is out of the question. My name is Gabali, and I still have the outstanding matter of our appointment to deal with.'

Had she thought about it, she would have imagined him to be typically Iberian – stocky, with long hair, beard, and his long tunic looped up into what could only be called drawers – and, since he'd dismissively referred to her as the 'merchant' Seferius, she would also have expected him to be oily and slick, with a medallion or three to attest to his manhood. Instead, her visitor was lean, modest, with penetrating brown eyes set in a thin pointed face and hair which she could only describe as longer than a Roman's but shorter than a Gaul's, with a shine you could kohl your eyes in.

3

She smiled prettily. 'Which I would be only too happy to deal with as well, Gabali, were it not for the fact that I have no appointments outstanding.'

'No,' he agreed, 'but I have.' He moved towards her. 'As you say, the night is warm, the honeysuckle sweet. Shall we take a walk in the garden?'

Claudia glanced at her sleeping steward.

'I wouldn't, if I were you,' the Spaniard said mildly.

'Are you threatening me?'

'More than thirty people sleep in this house, including your own private bodyguard.' He smiled. 'I would have to be mad.'

A ripple of ice fluttered the length of her spine. How long had he been watching? she wondered. How long had it taken him to acquire such intimate details of a world that was not visible from the street?

'It's late, I'm tired and you're leaving,' she snapped. As with the Guild, it was all about bluster.

'You might want to hear me out before you throw me out,' he said, and how come that sounded like an order? Either way, Claudia realized that this man would not simply melt away.

'You have three minutes to satisfy my curiosity, Gabali.'

A flicker of amusement kindled in his eyes. 'Three minutes to satisfy a woman? Personally, I do not think that is enough, but you Romans. Tch, tch. Always in such a rush.' The light died. 'Do you know a warehouse in Santonum in Aquitanian Gaul?'

'I know several.'

Now that the new province was becoming established, trade and peace flourished, as did as a taste for luxury goods. Thanks to the Emperor's ban on viticulture, the tribes were unable to manufacture wine of their own, but were forced to rely (as the wily Augustus intended) on imports. For that reason, Claudia reasoned that it might as well be her wine they swilled as anyone else's.

'During my visit to Aquitania last autumn, I made quite a few contacts in the province's capital,' she told him.

'Let's talk about one by the name of Sualinos,' Gabali murmured, dabbling the fingers of his left hand in the fountain.

Oh dear.

'Like I said. Several contacts. I would need to consult my records on that one, so if you'd care to make an appointment—'

'Suppose I save you the trouble?' The Spaniard cracked his knuckles, and for a man who claimed it would be madness to make threats, he was doing a bloody good job. 'You contracted to ship Sualinos one hundred and thirty-four amphorae of wine, each containing eight gallons, for a total cost of two thousand seven hundred sesterces, including shipping, at fifty per cent in advance and the balance upon delivery.'

Credit where it was due. This Gabali was a stickler for detail.

'Standard terms,' she said lightly.

'Hm.' He steepled his fingers against his lip and smiled at her through hooded eyelids. 'But what is not standard, I think, is that Sualinos received a message, telling him that the ship had been raided by pirates.'

Claudia forced her lips into a reciprocal smile. 'Sadly, Aquitania is not considered a primary destination for exports, and though I believe it's the Emperor's intention to protect supply routes as of next year, one still runs the inevitable risks.'

'You don't seem very concerned about the loss.'

'Insurance, Gabali. That's what insurance is for.'

'Indeed.' He nodded slowly, and why did she have a feeling she'd just walked into his trap? 'Insurance.'

As he paced the atrium, Claudia considered how much dodging the Guild's dirty tactics had cost her. More than she could keep tally of, certainly, which meant offsetting those losses with a number of measures which might not, strictly speaking, be termed legal. She looked upon this as a mere stumbling block, a hurdle to be overcome, but somehow the State viewed tax evasion in a rather different light. In fact, three unsmiling tax officials paid her a visit just last month, she recalled, and left her with a straight choice.

Pay up or be exiled.

With no cash in the coffers, there was only one way to settle the dispute, recompense the State with Seferius wine; it was an arrangement the State was perfectly happy with, but it left nothing to ship to Suo-what's-his-name in Santonum. Swindling Gauls wasn't intentional, but let's face it, Aquitania was three hundred miles away, that hoary old tale about the ship being raided by pirates hadn't failed her in the past, and just look at the advantages! Suo-what's-his-name's thirteen hundred and fifty sesterces put smiles on the faces of numerous creditors. The threat of exile popped like a bubble. And having her wine served at State banquets wasn't doing Claudia's reputation any harm, either.

'Let me tell you about another man.' Gabali stopped pacing. 'A man known throughout Aquitania as the Scorpion.'

'Funnily enough, his name cropped up several times during the course of my visit last autumn,' she said. 'Some sort of fanatic, as I recall.'

These types were commonplace throughout the Empire. Disgruntled militants who thought they were heroes, or else failures in search of fame and attention, each and every one of them claiming they could single-handedly free the conquered territories by uniting the tribes against Rome. Of course, not one of these deadbeats ever found fame or glory, and usually there was some personal axe to grind at the root of their disaffection. In the Scorpion's case, it was shunning. His very own tribe had voted this loser invisible – meaning that, in their eyes, he didn't exist.

'Spearheading an uprising seems a pretty effective way to make yourself visible again.'

'Do not underestimate this man, Merchant Seferius. The Scorpion, he is dangerous. As cunning as he is ruthless, no one betrays him and lives. Especially,' he added quietly, 'young widows who double-cross him without conscience.'

Shit.

'Are, um – are you saying Sualinos is the Scorpion?'

'It is one of his names, yes.' The Spaniard turned his head sideways and looked at her from the corner of his eye. 'And I, as it happens, am *his* insurance.'

Shit, shit and double shit. Claudia ran her tongue over her lips. If she sold the gold plate that she used to entertain her richest clients, she might be able to raise a quarter of what she owed, and the contents of her jewel box would probably bring it up to the half. But then word would get out that she was panic-selling, and what was left of her business would crumble to dust at her feet—

'I will not be intimidated, Gabali.' She clasped her hands firmly behind her back lest he saw that she already was. 'If your scorpioidal boss feels hard done by, he has my sympathy, but it's not incumbent on me to make restitution for piracy. However.' She flashed what she hoped was a generous smile. 'On this occasion, I am prepared to split the insurance settlement.'

The Spaniard walked towards her on the softest feet she'd ever heard. 'Please do not insult my intelligence. There were no pirates, therefore there is no insurance.'

She swallowed. 'He wants the full fifty per cent back . . . with interest?'

Thirteen hundred and fifty times twelve per cent divided by—

'No.' Gabali drew a deep breath and held it. 'He did not send me here for the money, Merchant Seferius. Like I said earlier, and I'm sure you were listening, no one betrays the Scorpion and lives.' He held her gaze with his penetrating brown eyes. '*Now* do you understand the nature of this appointment?' He paused. 'The Scorpion sent me to kill you.'

Two

The night was warm, the honeysuckle was sweet and Claudia was oblivious to both. Sinking down on a marble bench in the garden, she was unaware of Hercules striding through the constellations or Boötes the Herdsman prodding his celestial cattle. She did not hear the owl hoot from the oak tree next door, or smell the sweet blossoms of the myrtles in flower, or notice whether the moon was waxing or full.

She sat, rigid and mute, while her mind whirled like a mill race.

'Surely the Scorpion isn't going to kill me for thirteen hundred stupid sesterces?' she asked, though there had been no disguising the quiver that time.

'Thirteen hundred and fifty,' the assassin corrected, 'and do you not imagine that people have been killed for less? Uniting the tribes to push Rome out once and for all requires fundraising on an enormous scale, and the type of criminals the Scorpion employs need to be kept in check by something more than a spank on the bottom. Come.' He'd held out his arm. 'Let us take that walk in the garden.'

How much time had passed since Claudia had linked her elbow through his? Seconds? Minutes? A lifetime—?

'You were wise not to wake your steward,' he said, leading her to a seat beneath an acacia.

Claudia already knew that. Instinctively, she had realized that if she'd raised the alarm, he'd be left with no choice. Not tonight, not tomorrow, but some time he would come back and fulfil his contractual obligation. She shivered. Gabali wasn't the type who fed off the fear in his victim's eyes as they died. He was calculating, clever and detached, not sick. Had he not wanted something else from her, she would already be dead . . .

8

A faint light appeared in the sky over the Viminal Hill. Any minute now, roosters would start crowing and she realized with a jolt that the Spaniard had been in her house for twenty-four hours. Apart from a faint hint of stubble, he was as fresh as the dew.

'What do you want, Gabali?'

Her legs were weak, her heart pounded like thunder and there was something wrong with her breath. But she had to know . . .

'What do you need from me?'

His stillness lasted for an eternity, or maybe a heartbeat. Then he knelt down to face her, his penetrating eyes at a level with hers.

'Help,' he said carefully. 'There is a college of priestesses near Santonum known as the Hundred-Handed, a revered and powerful order, not unlike the Druids—'

'With the same attitude to human sacrifice?'

A muscle contracted in the Spaniard's cheek. 'When I kill, I kill cleanly,' he said. 'There is no question of sending you to be burned alive inside the wicker man, or indeed enjoying any of the other hospitalities that are practised in some of the remoter regions of Gaul.'

He rose, smoothed his hair back from his face and ran his fingers down the delicate leaves of the acacia.

'The Hundred-Handed wield the same spiritual influence as the Druids, except they interpret the cycle of life as a five-pointed star which they call the pentagram. The tips represent birth, growth, maturity, decline and death in sequence,' he said, 'but the difference is, the priestesses do not believe in gods like the Druids. They preach worship through nature and advocate peace in all things.'

'Sounds very noble.'

'It is.'

'But?'

Gabali turned his face away. 'One of the initiates, a girl of a mere twelve summers, was found murdered close to the sacred boundaries of the College. Her name was Clytie, she was killed on the spring equinox and her murder has never been solved.'

There was no point in asking where this was leading.

9

Claudia stared at the Spaniard's straight back and wondered why a day in midsummer should dawn so chill.

'The priestesses aren't celibate,' he continued, 'but no man is permitted to set foot inside the precinct, not even the tribal Chief, and thus, since no proper investigation was conducted, Clytie's killer remains at large.'

'Call me slow, Gabali, but I don't see where I come in.'

'No? I was rather thinking that if you were to talk to the priestesses—'

'Excuse me, this *is* Gaul you're talking about?'

'Yes.'

'And you haven't forgotten that we're in Rome having this conversation?'

'No.'

'Or that I'm not a priestess?'

'No.'

'Or that I'm unfamiliar with the Gaulish language?'

'I assure you, I have not forgotten any of those things.'

'Well, I'm glad we cleared that up. Do carry on.'

'Thank you.' He bowed. 'Clytie's death was similar to previous murders that plagued Santonum two years before, but then a group of vigilantes caught the brute kneeling over his victim with his hands round her throat. I won't go into details. Sufficient to say, this monster was put to execution.'

'You think it was a miscarriage of justice?'

'I do not.' Gabali was clear about that. 'Although Clytie's arms were arranged like this,' he positioned his own in an outstretched position, 'her hair fanned out and her face painted—'

'Like the previous victims?'

'Like previous victims, *si*, but this time the body was not found in the town, there was no sexual assault and no signs of strangulation. Little Clytie bled to death from cuts on her wrists— Are you all right?'

'I'm . . . fine.'

From inside the house, skillets clacked in the kitchens as breakfast was cooked, the sound of heather brooms could be heard sweeping the cellars and the smell of freshly baked bread filtered out from the ovens. With every ounce of self-control she had left, Claudia thrust the memories of her mother's drained corpse back into the dark pit where they belonged and concentrated on staying alive.

'You obviously don't feel there's a copycat killer on the loose, either,' she said, because why else would he be proposing this bizarre exchange?

'That is the story Beth, the Head of the College, is putting about, but me, no. I do not believe it.'

As daylight turned the leaves from dull grey to green and the first blackbird began to sing, Claudia wondered why she'd thought her wine business important.

'Gabali, you seem a level-headed sort of chap, let me ask you a question.' She swivelled round on the bench to face him. 'Why me?'

He shrugged. 'I'm assuming you don't want to die.'

Fair point. 'Then let me ask you another question.' She stood up and walked across to where he was standing. 'What's to prevent you from killing me, once I've discharged my obligation?'

Blackmailers don't stop once they've got their claws into their victim, and she was unlikely to be useful for anything else. Also, he said himself the Scorpion was a ruthless thug and that no one who double crosses him lives.

'Because I give you my word.'

'Which, as an assassin and extortionist, is worth what, exactly?'

He ran his tongue under his upper lip. 'In their thirteen years of Roman occupation, the Aquitani have not confined themselves solely to the import of wine and olive oil. In the past, of course, their slaves comprised fellow Gauls, captured in raids or taken as trophies of war.' His mouth twisted up at one corner. 'But thanks to you Romans, a whole new global market in human flesh has opened up.'

'Including Spaniards.'

'The Andalus yielded an especially rich harvest, *si*. I have the distinction of being one of their earliest exports, and never let it be said the Hundred-Handed don't move with the times.'

'I thought you said men weren't allowed in the College?'

'That's right, they're not.' Gabali plucked a late cherry

from the tree and munched carefully. 'They live in a compound on the hill behind the College, where they're set to tending the livestock, brewing and general maintenance work.' He spat the cherry stone into the centre of the fish pond. 'We work like dogs but are kept as stallions, if you follow my meaning.'

'The Hundred-Handed might be a matriarchal society, but they still can't manage to father their own children?'

'It seems we have some uses,' he said, with a lopsided grin, and whilst Claudia could see how he might be bitter, she understood why the priestesses had picked him. 'Once the children are born, they're placed into communal custody, where they're raised by those women who, for one reason or another, didn't qualify for the fifty elite, so you see, even the mothers don't spend time with their own children, much less the poor fathers.'

Oh, sweet Janus. 'Clytie was your daughter?'

'Those bitches wouldn't let me near her when she was alive,' he said thickly, 'but I'm damned if I'll let them betray her now that she's dead.'

It was a convincing argument, Claudia thought. Had it not been for the fact that he killed people for a living and was as trustworthy as his scorpioidal boss—

'I make no promises,' she told him bluntly. 'I'll happily go back to Aquitania' – as though she had a choice – 'and ask around at the College, but I can't guarantee finding your daughter's killer, much less bringing them to justice.'

'If you find the killer, I will see to the justice part,' he murmured. 'As to the rest, all I ask is that you do your best and, as a woman, you will have a better chance of finding the truth.'

Claudia doubted that.

'What about the Scorpion? If he knows I'm not only alive, but on his patch—'

'Do not worry about the Scorpion, Merchant Seferius. You will be perfectly safe in Aquitania.'

Claudia doubted that even more.

'Can I hope you will be packed by midday?' he asked in a manner that brooked no negotiation.

'My dear Gabali, I shall be packed in an hour,' she breezed back. Because this Spanish assassin might be a mine of information and a pedant for detail, but what he couldn't possibly have gathered from watching her house was that Claudia Seferius didn't just play rough, she played dirty.

And strangely enough, excelled in both.

Three

In the centre of the world between earth, sky and sea, at the point where the realms of the universe meet, the whisperings slowly came together. Swirling jointly in excitement and confusion, they jumbled through the halls of falsehood, rumbled down the trail of dreams, until finally they tumbled through the gates of confidence as truth.

Unlike Rumour, Truth carried conviction.

Carried on the soft warm wings of night, she soared over bright, shiny basilicas and painted stone tribunals without stopping, for there was no one to listen to her there. On and on she flew, past fountains, statues, bathhouses and barracks, watching broad metalled roads below give way to narrow rutted tracks as six-storey tenements fragmented into single-storey thatch. With every rolling hill and wooded river valley that she passed, Rome became more and more distant. For though the conquerors pulled on the oars of administration and finance, it was the Druids that steered the spiritual tiller.

And so it was here, to the lands under the Druids' dominion, where human sacrifice placated the black gods of vengeance and the powers of darkness were summoned and harnessed, that Truth swooped and imparted her wisdom.

'Nonsense!' Dora slammed the table with her fist. 'In all my sixty summers, I've never heard such rubbish!'

'We don't even allow men in the compound,' Fearn protested. 'How on earth are we supposed to suck their minds clean while they sleep?'

Beth ran her hand over the table shaped in the form of a pentagram around which the five women sat and studied the reflection of her silver robe in the shine. 'It's human nature to fear what we don't understand.'

'But *witches*!' It was a wonder the thatch stayed on the roof when Dora's fist crashed down a second time. 'Never in our history have we laid a single claim to sorcery or magic!'

'Fabrication walks hand in hand with fear,' Luisa pointed out.

'But who started this wicked fiction?' That's what Fearn wanted to know.

Beth pushed her chestnut hair back from her face and gazed around the half-timbered hall, whose rafters of ash were interwoven with hazel and whose basket-weave walls were hung with dried flowers and carved, painted plaques.

'The issue is not how the rumours started, it's how we scotch them,' she said.

Without windows, the only light came from the scores of candles dotted round the hall, and the only sounds that intruded were the soft coo of a pigeon on the roof and the occasional bubble of the scented infusion in the brazier.

'By ignoring them,' Dora retorted. 'Slurs are no different from hearth fires, Beth. They fizzle out soon enough for lack of attention.'

'That only holds true up to a point,' she replied. 'For personal insults, I agree. Ignore it. But, Dora, this accusation has the backing of the Druids.'

'Whose power is waning,' Luisa said.

'And for which they only have themselves to blame,' Fearn added, rubbing the arm of her wickerwork chair. 'They live apart from society—'

'So do we,' Beth pointed out.

'Indeed we do, my dear, but the Hundred-Handed don't believe themselves superior to their fellow Gauls.'

'It's why we don't embroil ourselves in local politics,' Dora said. 'Who are we to pass judgement on others?'

'An attitude which seems to be working against us right now.'

'Why?' Dora spread her large hands. 'If setting themselves apart makes the Druids *more* mystical, rather than less, why shouldn't the same apply to us? Let our very remoteness work in our favour, that's what I say.'

'I agree,' Fearn said, nodding. 'By ignoring these preposterous allegations, the communities that rely on the forest will come to realize that in an impermanent world, nature is constant, while the gods of the Druids are bloodthirsty, capricious and vengeful.'

'Our healing springs will also speak for us,' Luisa added confidently. 'People will soon see that the Hundred-Handed reflect the steadfastness of nature.'

'Will they.' Beth sighed. 'Rome has opened minds as well as trade routes,' she said. 'People no longer accept authority without question.'

'Which is exactly why the Druids' influence is on the slide,' Luisa said. 'The Aquitani have stopped running to them for guidance on every petty issue, and people have grown stronger in character because of it. That can only be a good thing.'

'Unless we are proved to be witches,' Beth said. 'The disbanding of this College will undermine the concept of independent thinking more effectively than any Roman law once the Druids show the Aquitani that, left to their own devices, they put their faith in monsters.'

Dora snorted. 'Are we really saying we're so damned powerful that we can bring down the Druids?'

'Or be responsible for building them up to the force they once were?' Fearn asked.

Beth watched a spider climb up the wall, reach a plaque and fall back down. She waited until it began to climb again.

'We've heard Growth's views.' She patted the arm sitting beside her, draped in linen dyed the colour of gorse. 'Fearn here believes that the goodness of nature will prevail over whatever malevolent gods are thrown in our path.' She turned to Dora. 'Maturity – and I think we can all agree on this – is *firmly* of the opinion that in ignoring the rumour, the fire will go out, while Decline,' she smiled at Luisa, utterly resplendent in red, 'puts her trust in the powers of healing.'

The spider fell back onto the floor. This time it did not attempt another ascent, but scuttled under the table. Beth crushed it under her foot.

'As the Birth point on the pentagram and Head of this Order, you know my view. I believe closing our eyes to the accusation of witchcraft is dangerous in the extreme, because, as someone far cleverer than me once said, for evil to triumph, it only needs for good men to do nothing. However.'

She swivelled in her chair to face the woman sitting on her right, whose robe was black as night.

'The one opinion we haven't heard today is Ailm's.'

The narrow, watchful eyes of the Death Priestess tapered to mere slits and through the coo-coo-coo of the pigeon on the thatch, the fragrant contents of the brazier bubbled gently.

'If Rumour whispers into credulous ears,' she said eventually, 'credulous minds are bound to put their trust in her wisdom.'

'Is that it?' Dora turned her head away in disgust. 'Is that the extent of your input? Trotting out some trite old saw that might sound deeply intellectual to those who know no better, but is meaningless in its actual content?'

'You asked,' Ailm said.

'*I* didn't,' Dora corrected, with a glare at Beth.

'Ailm.' Beth refused to meet her friend's eye. 'Ailm, this is serious. As Head of the Order, I have three votes. Right now, the pentagram is deadlocked.'

'Then instate a fairer ballot.' The Death Priestess stood up and swept towards the door, her skirts billowing like the wings of a bat in her wake.

'*Ailm!*' Beth brought her palms down on the five-pointed table with the full weight of her position. The boom stopped the priestess in her tracks. 'The voting system is part of our heritage. It underlines the College hierarchy and reinforces the Head of the Order's authority. Remember, only the five pentagram priestesses are entitled to vote. Our decision affects the whole of the College.'

'There's nothing in the rules that prevents us from canvassing the opinion of the rest of the Hundred-Handed, though.'

'Apart from time,' Luisa said. 'If we opened a debate to the remaining forty-five, we'd be opening a floodgate of hot air and the whole point of the pentagram is that we, as the governing committee, act swiftly.'

'And . . .' Dora sniffed. 'Decisively.'

'Not only that,' Fearn said, 'even if we mooted every issue

under discussion before the rest of the Hundred-Handed, why stop there? If it's democracy you're pushing for, Ailm, you'd have to include the Initiates of Light, whose very training is to prepare them to step in once the next priestess dies.'

'How could you possibly then exclude those women who didn't qualify for Initiatehood,' Luisa asked, 'but who oversee the nursery, the cooking, the cleansing of holy spaces and such like?'

'Indeed,' Dora said. 'That only adds another couple of hundred, and why not poll the novices while you're about it? Or aren't children entitled to a say in their own future under your precious voting system?'

'Ailm.' Beth pulled the meeting back on track. 'Ailm, the College stands accused of witchery and you know the Druids' attitude to that.'

'The Druids have no power over us,' Ailm retorted, 'and anyway, we're under Rome's protection now. Let them put their money where their mouth is.'

'Rome!' Dora pushed her chair back from the table. 'How can they possibly protect us out here? Ailm, you're a fool. A selfish, narrow-minded, short-sighted fool—'

'How dare you, you who—'

'*Enough.*' Beth stood up. 'Ailm, I'm sorry but Dora's right. Rome would willingly send its legions to our aid, but for how long? They can't stand around these woods for ever, and the Druids are like cats outside a mouse hole. They'll wait weeks, months, years if necessary, but far more likely they'll pounce before the Governor has even had time to read our petition.'

'The first Rome would see of our plight would be the smoke from the razing of the College,' Fearn added bitterly.

'We'd be dead within the week,' Luisa said.

'Only the lucky ones,' said Dora.

'And since you protect the Death point on the pentagram,' Beth said, 'you must see why your vote is crucial on this issue.'

'Once again.' A hard light glinted in Ailm's eye. 'You are not pinning the future of this Order on me.'

As she marched through the door to leave it swinging on

its hinges, the others shielded their eyes from the sudden rush of sunlight. Disorientated, perhaps, by the scents from the infusion, a butterfly flew into the hall, the undersides of its wings reflecting metallic in the flickering candlelight. Had the butterfly been Rumour, and had it flown in at the start of the meeting, it would still have been unable to carry off a tale. It would still have been no wiser about what had taken place between the Hundred-Handed.

Because from start to finish, the entire exchange had been conducted in silence.

Not one spoken word had passed between the priestesses.

Four

Snuggled in a broad bend of the River Carent amid a backdrop of soft rolling hills, Santonum was the obvious choice for the province's capital. Spanning the crossroads of the major north–south and east–west arteries, the river here was deep enough, and wide enough, to allow single-masted, shallow-draught ships to sail the thirty-odd miles to the coast without trouble. Dense forests supported a creditable boat-building industry, hill quarries yielded limestone for construction and the game in the woods was enough to satisfy even the most ardent huntsman's demands.

It was a town Claudia had hoped and prayed never to return to.

'Great Jupiter on Olympus, what's that?'

She indicated an animal that looked like a donkey, brayed like a donkey, was hitched to a cart like a donkey, only this beast was enormous, black and shaggier than the average yak.

'It's a donkey, madam.'

'No, no, Junius, I know a donkey when I see one and you aren't making an ass of me with this.'

'I would never dishonour you with sarcasm,' her bodyguard replied solemnly, but then again, when was he anything else? 'It is a local breed, much prized hereabouts for its strength and—'

'Please don't say beauty.'

Its ears were the length of a fully grown fox. You could use those teeth to mark graves.

'I was about to say hair.' Junius prodded the padded seat of the gig as it bounced over the solid stone bridge that led to Santonum. 'It makes for warm and comfortable stuffing.'

'I thought you Gauls opted for the austere life?'

'That's Spartans, madam, and besides, would a nation who embraced austerity *choose* to wear red and yellow check pantaloons?'

With anyone else Claudia would have thought he was cracking a joke. Bless him, Junius couldn't crack his own funny bone.

'I don't trust that Gabali,' he added under his breath.

'Although one can't help noticing that you waited until he'd dismounted before making that observation,' she quipped, except teasing Junius was like kicking a kitten. No matter how tempting, in the end you just couldn't bring yourself to do it. 'Don't worry about the Spaniard,' she told him. 'You invest your energies in doing what you're paid to do, namely guarding my body, and I'll handle the trust side of things.'

'That's the problem,' he said. 'How can I protect you, when men aren't allowed anywhere near the College? Worse, you forbade the rest of your bodyguard from leaving Rome—'

'We've been through the reasons why I didn't bring a large entourage with me.'

None of which were valid, of course, but it wasn't for Junius to know that Gabali had insisted Claudia travelled lightly. *Less risk of your coming to the Scorpion's attention if you slip in quietly*, he'd said, and on balance that seemed a damn good incentive.

'The fact remains that you're exposed and vulnerable, madam, and I don't like it.'

He didn't like it!

'There are rumours,' he said, geeing up the mule with a flick of the whip. 'At every inn we stopped at in Aquitania, the kitchens have been full of rumblings about how the young men of the tribes are growing restless under the peace.'

'That's what kitchens are designed for, Junius. Gossip.'

'This goes a lot deeper than that,' he said. 'Old tales are being dredged up. Past glories, in which a united Gaul sacked Rome then went on to destroy much of Greece.'

'Including Delphi, if my memory serves me correctly.'

'It does,' he said, with a tight-lipped nod. 'And the feeling among the young warriors is that there's no reason why history should not repeat itself. Under the right leader, they're convinced Gaul will rise again and be more powerful than ever before.'

'And this hero wouldn't happen to have a nickname, would he?'

Do not underestimate this man, Merchant Seferius. The Scorpion, he is dangerous. As cunning as he is ruthless, no one betrays him and lives.

She pulled her veil low over her face as the gig passed under the soaring stone archway and forced herself not to even glance towards the wharf where the Scorpion had his warehouse.

'His tribe sentenced him to be shunned because they believed his behaviour was unpatriotic and therefore detrimental to the welfare of the people,' Junius said. 'But instead of making him humble and contrite, his zeal found favour and support among the disenchanted, and if I may be so bold, madam, this is not a good time to be a Roman.'

'How?'

From beneath the veil, Claudia surveyed the stacks of sawn timbers piled up on the dockside, the constant flurry of activity between rope-makers, sail-makers and black-smiths, the sacks and barrels stacked alongside great blocks of limestone awaiting embarkation as porters, clerks and chandlers cupped their hands to their mouths and yelled to make themselves heard above the hammers from the boat-yards and the beating out of lead.

'How can they *possibly* be disenchanted in this thriving economy?'

One, moreover, that was set to grow further.

'Pride,' he said simply. 'Their fathers were warriors, who have scars to prove it. The sons have nothing to testify to their courage.'

Didn't pride in not leaving widows to raise their children alone count? she thought. What about pride in having a good trade at their fingertips? Of being instrumental in creating a healthier, safer, more prosperous environment?

'You're both a slave and a Gaul, Junius, how do you feel?'

Colour flooded his neck right up to the roots of his thick

sandy mop. 'I apologize if I ever have given you cause to question my loyalty,' he said stiffly.

'You haven't, not for a moment, and that's why I ask.'

Because that was odd in itself. Shadows couldn't glue themselves tighter than this boy to his mistress. Every time he accompanied her, his eyes were twin beams of piercing blue vigilance and his hand hovered constantly over his dagger. Had it not been Junius, she'd have thought the lad was besotted, but what twenty-three-year-old with those strapping good looks wastes his life mooning over a woman who's not only five years his senior, but his owner to boot? All the same, it was strange that he hadn't bought his own freedom, even though he'd earned the chance several times over, and stranger still that Claudia had never seen him flirting with girls, much less asking one out. Yet household gossip insisted his inclinations didn't veer towards his own sex and, as she observed him from the corner of her eye, corded muscles bulging out of his Roman-style tunic, she decided it was just as well every Gaul wasn't like her young bodyguard or the race would be facing extinction.

'If you're asking me whether I sympathize with men who have become wheelwrights instead of warriors, then the answer is no,' Junius said. 'It's a man's duty to provide for his family and keep them safe, and sometimes, regrettably, it becomes necessary to go to war to do that. But, in my view, madam, wealth is the best security a man can bestow on his family. It buys physicians when they fall sick, education for the children, servants to fetch water from the well and gives them a roof over all their heads for life.'

'I'll drink to that.'

A girl doesn't drag herself up from the gutter not to appreciate the rewards, and she was just about to compliment him on his passionate defence when she realized he hadn't finished.

'But if you're asking me whether I condemn young men for wanting to be warriors, the answer again is no.' He gaze fixed on a point in the distance. 'It is man's nature to fight,' he said. 'To prove himself the best in the pack.'

Except not all the hounds can be top dog. What happens to those who don't make the grade? All in all, she decided, as the cart clopped through the artisan quarter, teeming with potters, coppersmiths and caulkers, being a woman was by far the best deal. Because what on earth was the point in having eyelashes if you couldn't flutter them in an emergency?

'So working for me gives you the best of both worlds. You get to fight—'

'When you're not tethering me like a billy goat.'

'– and as head of my bodyguard,' she ignored the sulking, 'you're top of your own little pack, too.'

An explanation for his odd behaviour at last!

Slowly, the city opened out to lush water meadows that nourished sheep, crops and long-horned cattle, and as Junius steered the gig off the main road and through the Santon countryside, memories of last year flooded in. When Claudia was ten, her father marched off to war and never came home. That campaign had been here, in Aquitanian Gaul, and, determined to discover whether he was dead or whether he'd simply abandoned her, she'd come in search of the truth. The truth hurt. The only discovery was that the answers are rarely those which we'd choose. Keep the memories, she thought bitterly, keep them by all means, but keep them where they belong. Precious, blurred, but most importantly in a place where they cannot be sullied. Firmly locked in the past . . .

But Gabali had left her no option. Thanks to him, she was plunged back into the nightmare, deeper even than before.

Santonum was where he'd been brought as a captive, bought as a slave, it was here that his daughter had died. Gabali and Santonum were one. He was linked to the town through tragedy twice over – and who could imagine his emotions, disembarking in chains (younger even than Junius was now) knowing his family were dispersed across Gaul, maybe even the Empire, and that he'd never see them again. What hopes had still blazed in Gabali's heart? Dreams of a future with a wife, children, grandchildren would have shattered like glass when he'd been bought up by the College. How had he felt once he'd escaped the harpies' clutches, only to end up in servitude to a misguided fanatic?

At what point, she wondered, had the assassin in Gabali been born . . .?

As Junius coaxed a reluctant mule round a steep hairpin

bend, her thoughts drifted to the task the Spaniard had forced upon her. To listen to him talk about the Hundred-Handed – which he'd done at length during the journey here from Rome – their ideals sounded noble enough. Fifty priestesses, each responsible for a different aspect of nature, preaching peace and spiritual harmony since according to their beliefs nature was a living personification of the universe. Birth, he added, was the most important aspect of the pentagram and for that reason Beth – the Birch Priestess – topped the College hierarchy, the silver birch being the first tree to cover new ground in the forest and thus symbolic of all new beginnings.

'The very word *beth* means silver birch,' he'd explained.

As the stately birch stood guard over the first month of the year, so her job was to ensure a propitious birth to that new year, commencing at the winter solstice.

'Then the roles are hereditary?'

'More a rota basis.' Gabali had fixed Claudia with his penetrating brown gaze. 'When a priestess dies, the oldest Initiate steps forward, adopting her predecessor's name as well as her responsibilities.'

Not necessarily the gentle, soulful creatures people might imagine, then.

Once the children are born, they're placed into communal custody. His soft Andalusian accent echoed round the Santon woods. *They're raised by those women who, for one reason or another, didn't qualify for the fifty elite, so you see, even the mothers don't spend time with their own children, much less the poor fathers.*

And yet, though isolated, the Hundred-Handed were hardly an insular and archaic society. They used men for sex, moved with the times when it came to the purchase of foreign slaves, and held considerable sway over much of Aquitania. So how, she wondered, as the gig made its descent down a steep, winding hill, could so powerful and so feminine an influence have stood back and let a child-killer go unpunished? Especially when that child was one of their own?

'Sorry, driver.'

A young man with a shock of prematurely grey hair, tight-fitting pantaloons and thoroughly disarming grin stepped from behind the barrier that blocked the road.

'This is as far as non-College men are allowed.'

In his right hand he clutched a short sword in a loose but professional grip, while his left thumb hooked itself in his belt in a manner far too casual to be coincidental that his dagger just happened to hang adjacent.

'The name's Swarbric, my lady – ' he stepped neatly in front of her bodyguard to help her dismount – 'and it's a pleasure, believe me, to escort you the rest of the way.'

'The lady Claudia will need a translator,' Junius said through gritted teeth.

'The lady Claudia will lack for nothing here.' Swarbric didn't take his twinkling eyes off her. 'Especially a translator.' And just when she thought his grin couldn't widen further, more strong white teeth were revealed. 'The Hundred-Handed communicate in silence.'

'Are you serious?' she asked.

'Am I ever anything else?' He performed a broad and sweeping gesture that put his pants seams in serious jeopardy. 'This way, if you will.'

Claudia hefted a crate out of the gig, from which a blue-eyed, cross-eyed demon vented its fury in a series of hissing snarls. 'Do all the sentries flirt as wildly as you?'

'Since I'm the only sentry, I suppose the answer's yes,' Swarbric replied, taking the wooden crate as though it was a pell of parchment. His voice, she noticed, held a slight Teutonic accent.

'You . . . you're the only guard?'

'Quality outweighs quantity every time,' he said cheerfully. 'And this is one nasty temper your cat has on him, if you don't mind my saying so.'

'Her,' she corrected, following him down the steep incline. She really *didn't* want Drusilla disbarred from entry as well. 'And this seems as good a time as any to let her out. As I recall from our previous visit, there's something about Gaulish mice that makes her mouth especially water – Jupiter, Juno and Mars!'

So busy flipping the lock as her mind tried to wrap itself round Swarbric's revelations about the Hundred-Handed's code of silence that Claudia hadn't taken stock of her surroundings. Until now.

'This is . . .'

'Incredible, yes.'

Swarbric nodded in a way that suggested everyone who came here needed their sentences finished for them.

'That's the beauty of the place.' He waved his short sword airily. 'You can't see it for the trees as you come down the hill. The gorge always catches visitors off guard.'

Her eyes transfixed on the arrow-shaped cliff that rose out of nowhere, a hundred almost vertical feet. This isn't a gorge, she wanted to say, a gorge rises on both sides, but before she could form the words, her attention was diverted to the rush of water that, like Minerva springing fully-armed from Jupiter's thigh, gushed directly from the foot of the cliff. She watched it bounce into a pool, white and foaming, before dancing its way through flower-filled meadows lined with willows until it disappeared round a bend and was swallowed up by the woods.

'The Hundred-Handed call it paradise,' the sentry said, following the direction of her gaze.

'I can see why,' she acknowledged, though a miss was as good as a mile. The valley radiated beauty, tranquillity and calm in bucketloads. But a child was killed here. Rebellion was swelling. Paradise this was certainly not. To the left of the spring she noticed two caves in the rock face. One had been decked with garlands of honeysuckle and wild roses, the other with garlands of yew.

'There you go, my lady Claudia,' Swarbric said, performing a dashing, some might say theatrical, bow at the edge of the small wooden footbridge. 'If you need anything while you're here, anything at *all*, that hut's where you'll find me.'

He pointed to a small, round building whose thatched roof was barely visible through the trees.

'Night and day, I'm at your ladyship's service – and if you lot don't come down this instant,' he added in a loud voice, shooting a broad wink at Claudia, 'you're going to be in seriously big trouble.'

There was a scuffle from the branches in the oak tree behind, then three girls aged between ten and fourteen dropped to the floor, their skirts tucked into their knicker cloth to reveal muddy knees and badly scuffed sandals. Same flaxen hair, same pale complexions, same graceful deportment, the girls could have been sisters.

'I swear you have eyes in the top of your head, Swarbric.' The oldest shook her skirts loose before brushing the dust off the little one's shoulders.

'You won't tell on us, will you?' pleaded the middle one, whose face seemed comprised of nothing but blue eyes and dimples.

'There's nothing to tell,' the third member of the flaxen-haired trio sniffed, with a toss of her plaits. 'We were only climbing the branches to learn about squirrels.'

'Nuts,' Swarbric laughed. 'Now run along, all of you, before I chop off your thick bushy tails.'

At the swish of his sword, the girls raced down the path, squealing at the tops of their voices. He turned to Claudia.

'Don't forget, now.' With sparkling eyes, he tugged an imaginary forelock. 'If you need anything . . .'

'The hut. Yes.'

Claudia glanced back over her shoulder at the thatch peeping out through the woods and wondered if this dashing German was really offering what she thought he was offering, but by the time she'd turned, he was gone. Not a sign, not a sound, not even a girlish squeal cut through the stillness, and now even the gig had disappeared back up the hill, taking her bodyguard with it. It was just her, alone, in the valley . . .

She stared at the footbridge. It wasn't too late. She could turn round, right now, march back up the hill and hitch a lift on a cart to Santonum . . .

Slowly, her eyes followed the perpendicular precipice. Had this arrowhead of rock not been commandeered by the Hundred-Handed, it would have made an excellent fortress, and perhaps it was the military connection, or maybe it was the liveliness of that beautiful flaxen-haired trio, but as she walked slowly across the footbridge, Claudia imagined she was in very much the same frame of mind as Julius Caesar when he'd crossed the Rubicon a decade before she was born.

She hadn't known Clytie, those priestesses disturbed her, Gabali only *said* he'd protect her from the Scorpion's sting

– and where the hell in the Empire was any time a good time to be Roman?

But there was no turning back.

Clytie's lifeblood had been drained out of her like water from a jug, her body daubed with paint and arranged as though she was some outlandish exhibit to be analysed and studied at leisure. Uh-uh. Death demands respect, and to put a little girl on display was callous and demeaning. Dammit, no one deserves to be gawped at in death. Not you, not me, not even the son-of-a-bitch who killed without conscience, and most definitely not a twelve-year-old child who'd had her life and her future snatched from her.

Dignity was the only thing Clytie had left.

Now the bastard had stolen that too.

No town in the Roman Empire reflected progress quite like the capital of Aquitania. Here, timber roundhouses gave way to limestone where shops offered every luxury from parchment to onyx to rare aromatics. Instead of having to quench their thirst with a swill of cheap beer, shoppers were invited to cool off in the shade of elegant colonnades and appreciate the artwork of the frescoes while they refreshed themselves with fine wines and nibbled on delicacies such as fatted dormice and garlic-stuffed quail. In wide cobbled streets, richly caparisoned horses displaced the huge shaggy beasts that tried to pass themselves off as donkeys, and chariots rattled by on thin iron tyres, rather than heavy carts lumbering along on creaking timber wheels. Legionaries tramped, dispatch runners jogged and over it all, the incense from a dozen marble shrines mingled with barbers' exotic unguents and the scents of oils wafting out from the bathhouse.

In effect, Santonum was Rome's shop front. It advertised opulence and sophistication with the slogan *This could be yours, if you work with us* and backed up its claims with a rash of theatres, public sewers and hippodromes. *Support us and aqueducts could be pumping sweet water to* your *door* was the message, and the message was getting home. Through the twin transport links of road and river, the populace was growing richer by the day, and thus nobody noticed one more young merchant leaning against the wall of the basilica. Not handsome, not ugly, not short and not tall, his clothes neither flashy nor dull, the young man watched the bustle of lawyers and clerks, lackeys and scribes with a predator's eye, pausing from time to time to nod the occasional greeting as he stroked his neatly clipped beard. As he did so, the sun glanced off his seal ring, making it appear as though its scorpion engraving was scuttling.

As the herald called the third hour after noon, the crowd was too busy going about its own private business to notice that a second man had joined him. Slightly older with penetrating brown eyes, a thin pointed face and hair which could only be described as longer than a Roman's but shorter than a Gaul's, and with a shine you could kohl your eyes in.

'It is done.' The newcomer spoke with a faint Andalus accent.

'Any problems?'

'No, sir.'

'No – how shall we say? – complications that I need to be made aware of?'

'None whatsoever.'

The young merchant nodded. 'Excellent work, Gabali.' He untied the drawstring purse from his belt and it chinked as he tossed it across. 'I knew I could rely on you.'

'Appreciation is always appreciated.'

'Good, because there's one more thing.'

'Sir?'

'Now that you've lured Claudia Seferius to the College, I need you to smuggle me in as a slave. Is that possible?'

'There's a slave auction scheduled for tomorrow and the Hundred-Handed desperately need to augment their workforce.' He spread his hands. 'If you can furnish a set of forged transfer papers, I can have you in that line-up first thing in the morning.'

'Gabali, your sense of enterprise never ceases to amaze me.'

The young merchant blew on his scorpion ring then buffed the shine on his tunic.

'Now let's get the hell out of here, because I tell you, my friend,' he slanted the Spaniard an affectionate smile, 'the gum holding this beard on is really making my face itch.'

Five

Craning her neck upwards from the bridge over the spring, Claudia was unable to glimpse any activity up on the plateau. For a secretive sect this was hardly surprising, but somehow she was disappointed not to be seeing dozens of women in white, floaty robes swanning about bearing lustral bowls here, pouring libations there and singing paeans to Mother Nature. Perhaps the birdsong was paean enough.

'Can I help you?'

Claudia turned, but once again there was nobody there. Just the river that danced through the flower filled meadows, the cliff, the caves and the woods. It was a trick of the wind, of course. Or the valley's acoustics—

'Down here,' the voice said, with a tug on her robe. 'I'm Gurdo,' he added cheerfully. 'I have healing powers, you know.'

She looked at the dwarf, clad in green plaid pantaloons and matching shirt, and decided that wasn't so much a twinkle in his equally green eye as mischief.

'What? You don't think little people can cure you?' He tutted. 'This here's the Cave of Miracles, lady. Cross my palm with gold, tell me what ails you, and between me and the healing springs, we can fix it.'

He beckoned her into the cool of the cavern decked with roses and honeysuckle, where, rather than gushing out of the rock, water trickled through a fissure in the soft white limestone into a basin hewn out of stone before being channelled to a place where the oil lamps that twinkled in niches carved out of the rock didn't penetrate.

'How much gold?'

The cave smelled of comfrey, rosehips, yarrow and horehound. All of which had acclaimed healing properties.

'I might have small hands, but together they make a large cup. See? Fill that to the brim and in exchange I'll give you a grail of this water. Your ailment will be gone by the dawn.'

'Probably not as fast as my gold.'

'Oh, so you're a cynic as well as an invalid? Lucky me.' He crossed militant arms over his chest. 'Now do you want to be cured, or don't you?'

'Yes,' she said, 'I want to be cured.' According to Gabali, it was the only way into the College. 'But I thought physicians were supposed to exercise charm and have a good bedside manner.'

She'd seen lions in the arena less hostile than Gurdo.

'Listen, lady, I'm the guardian of these springs, not a physician, and frankly, what I do with my charisma's my business. Besides. I told you. Dwarves possess curative powers.'

'Since *when*?'

'Since you Romans started putting us to death for being malformed.'

Claudia laughed. 'You and I, Gurdo, are going to get along very nicely, but pull that extortion-and-menaces act one more time and I shall hold your money-grubbing head under the water for forty-five minutes and see whether you possess lung power as well.'

'I suppose you don't care that you've hurt my feelings?'

'Oh, so you're sensitive as well as a bully? Lucky me.' She crossed militant arms over her chest. 'Now are you going to cure me or not?'

Gurdo tipped his head back and roared. 'You know, Lofty Legs, you could be right. We might be friends yet.' He wiped the tears from his eyes with the hem of his sleeve. 'What's wrong with you, anyway?'

Claudia hadn't thought that far ahead, but whatever made people flock to this cave, it wasn't going to be cured by a mug of water, that was for sure. Still. Faith can move mountains, so the saying goes. In this case, faith drizzled out of the mountain like tears but the principle, she supposed, was no different.

'You don't look ill,' he added, peering at her unblemished skin, bright eyes and shiny hair.

She peered back at the little dandy, rocking on his heels and with his long hair tied back in a queue. 'I have a pain in the neck.'

'Now that I can believe.'

It was true. It came in the form of the Security Police, who didn't view her battle for financial survival in quite the same light as herself. Something to do with fraud and forgery not being all it was cracked up to be when it came to legal technicalities, she believed. And, unless she missed her guess, arrest warrants, handcuffs and trials figured in their equation as well.

'Joint problems comes under the category of laying on of hands – nah, don't look so worried. Not mine.' A stubby finger pointed directly upwards. 'Mavor's the woman for that. Now you wait here, Lofty Legs. Make yourself comfortable, help yourself from the fountain, do whatever you want – only don't go in there, right?'

He pointed to where the channel of water disappeared into darkness.

'Out of bounds,' he warned, 'and that's why this is the Cave of Miracles, lady. Not just this spring. This is the only cave in Aquitania with two mouths, one for us humans, one for the spirits. *You keep away from that part.*'

'I wouldn't dream of coming between you and your charisma,' she said sweetly, but he'd already stumped off.

'Don't mind him,' a youthful voice chuckled.

A spiky dark haircut popped itself round the cave mouth and Claudia thought, First dwarves, now elves.

'Dad works on the theory that if he was so wicked in his last incarnation to be reborn as a dwarf, he might as well enjoy being nasty.'

'It's one of the few pleasures that cost nothing,' she agreed.

That was another thing about these Gauls. Reincarnation. If life was so tough, why keep repeating it? But then theology was never Claudia's strong point.

'Tell you what else he says.' The youth laid down the pile of kindling in his arms and mimicked Gurdo's voice and stance. 'Pod, boy, don't you never go to bed angry, you hear me? You bloody well stay up and fight like the rest of us!'

'*Pod?*'

'Dad said I was always full of beans as a nipper.' The elf grinned so widely that his cheeks dimpled up. 'The name kind of stuck.'

'And your mother?'

'Me mother?' He brushed his hands down his woodsman's tunic as though trying to brush off a memory. 'No more than wind at the door, that's what I reckon.' He pointed to where the stream disappeared round the bend. 'Gurdo found me wandering beside the reed beds over yonder, seven summers old, I was, there or abouts, and what with me having no memories of me own and no one coming forward to claim me, he raised me himself.'

That would make it ten years since Pod was adopted, but why no memories? Was it an injury that wiped them clean? A trauma? Or was this artless imp simply a congenital liar?

'So you think you can burn charcoals with your chattering now?' Gurdo's voice carried along the path even though the dwarf himself was out of sight.

'What he lacks for height, he makes up for in cunning,' Pod confided in a theatrical whisper. 'That crafty bugger can see round corners!' Aloud he shouted, 'Pod off!' as he gathered up his kindling, and was still beaming from ear to ear as he sprinted off with a litheness that would make a polecat jealous.

Gurdo hove into sight, accompanied by a creature whose hair blazed red and wild, whose breasts were full and thrusting, and whose hips swayed to a rhythm that was anything but virginal. Had Claudia been a man, she imagined her jaw would have dropped to her collarbones and stayed down there for a week. Well, well. She knew the priestesses kept men enslaved for sex, but even so. This was not how she'd imagined the Hundred-Handed!

'I hear you have a pain in the neck?' Mavor asked kindly.

'You have no idea.'

It stood six feet tall, boasted dark wavy hair and came complete with a baritone voice. Not that Claudia thought about the Security Police in that way, of course. *If* she ever thought about Marcus Cornelius Orbilio, it was in the official sense and had nothing to do with the way his hair flopped over his forehead in times of emotion or the little pulse that

34

beat at the side of his neck. In fact, she could hardly recall what he looked like, much less remember that musky sandalwood unguent of his. With just a hint of the rosemary in which his patrician tunics were rinsed.

'Does it hurt here?'

'Ouch.'

For heaven's sake, do these aristocrats ration their principles? I mean, why was *he* the only patrician who didn't feel it beneath him to join the Security Police? And was Rome so starved of criminals that he needed to traipse halfway round the world just to catch defenceless young widows in the act of forgery and fraud? Surely it wasn't beyond Orbilio's talents to find a real felon to hound?

'What about here?' Mavor's fingertip gently probed the next vertebra down.

'Worse.'

Unfortunately, persecution had its rewards, and what supreme irony that was. It was because of Claudia's visit to Santonum last autumn that the Governor had offered him promotion in the first place, and talk about a vicious circle.

If she hadn't come here last September, she wouldn't have contracted her wine to the Scorpion. If she hadn't contracted her wine to the Scorpion, Gabali couldn't have blackmailed her into investigating Clytie's murder. And if Gabali had no leverage against her, she wouldn't have ended up next door to the only man in the Empire who could consign her to penniless exile at the snap of his finger.

This circle wasn't vicious, it was positively sadistic.

'And here?' Mavor asked.

'Ooh-ow.'

The redhead sucked in her breath. 'I hate to be the bearer of bad tidings, but yours is not a condition that can be cured overnight. Those backbones will need several days of massage and manipulation, so on behalf of the College of the Hundred-Handed,' she patted Claudia's hand as she linked her arm with hers, 'I offer you hospitality and the hope of a full and speedy recovery.'

Speedy, thought Claudia, was the word. The quicker she solved Clytie's murder, the less likely she'd be caught up in rebellion, the lower her likelihood of attracting the Scorpion's attention, the faster a child killer was brought to justice.

And if leaving Santonum also happened to put three hundred miles between her and that pain in the neck, then so much the bloody better.

Scribes were scurrying about the Governor's palace like ants as that pain in the neck strode down the colonnade. The bitch, he thought. The absolute bitch. Orbilio glowered at one of the marble busts, sending daggers to his ex-wife. How could she? She knew damn well the divorce was absolute. That she, who'd run off with a sea captain from Lusitania, had no further claim on his money. But ho ho, now Marcus Cornelius had been promoted to Head of the Security Police in Aquitania, guess who decided the settlement was unfair and was demanding a full half of his estate?

Committee rooms sped past. Voting halls. Archives.

You bitch, you leave a national scandal behind in your wake and because you know I don't want it resurrected – not here, not in Gaul – you use it as an excuse to squeeze me for every sesterce you can bloody well get. He nodded absently at one of the secretaries, red-faced and puffing, with a quill behind one ear and rolls of parchment stuffed under his arms. Well, you can go to hell, you damned bloodsucking vampire. Marcus Cornelius Orbilio isn't funding *anybody's* personal gravy train, and it had nothing to do with the money. Goddammit, it was the principle and by Croesus, he was buggered if she was going to make a fool of him twice.

Taking the marble stairs two at a time, he knew they'd married too young, of course, and that was the heart of the trouble. Like most patrician marriages, it was a contract drawn up when both parties were toddlers, politics being everything to the aristocracy these days. Even so. If only she'd *talked* to him, for gods' sake. It wasn't as though either of them had ever made the other happy, and he'd have willingly given her an annulment or whatever, had she discussed it. Instead she elopes, her family disown her and yours truly becomes the butt of all jokes.

'You could neutralize that in an instant,' his brother had cautioned, in a rare moment of fraternal affection. 'Quit that ridiculous job in the Security Police and take up law like the rest of us, Marcus. It's what Father wanted, for his sons to continue the noble family tradition, and you'd make a bloody fine advocate, too.'

'Maybe so,' he'd told his brother, 'but don't you think it's more noble to be catching murderers and rapists than trying to get them acquitted? Or doesn't their guilt bother you?'

His brother's reply had been something along the lines that there was no place for vocation among the patrician class, that the notion of job satisfaction was idealistic and selfish, and sucking up here and making the right noises there went with the territory, if a chap ever hoped to take a seat in the Senate. To which Orbilio's reply had been something along the lines that blood might be thicker than water, but if his brother genuinely believed that he must be thicker than both, at which point family relations deteriorated to the extent that even his divorce seemed cordial in comparison.

At the top of the stairs he turned right, past painted battles in which horses reared, their eyes rolling sideways as their riders shielded themselves from a shower of spears while the dead and the wounded were trampled beneath their hooves. And to think he'd hoped life would get better! Dammit, Rome *still* gossiped about his ex-wife's infidelity. His family *still* sneered at his chosen career. And the only woman he'd ever loved wanted nothing to do with him!

He'd taken this job in Gaul to wash Claudia out of his system, and that had turned into a joke, too. Within days he realized he could no more put her out of his mind than he could turn back the tide or make the sun rise in the north, and lately he'd even stopped trying. He would go to sleep with her image engraved on his eyelids, and when he woke up those dark flashing eyes and wild tangle of curls were still all he ever wanted to see. She radiated that heady combination of beauty, independence and self-centredness that set her apart from every other woman he'd known. Claudia Seferius knew what she wanted then set about getting it without even paying lip service to the word compromise.

She broke every single rule in the book – not to mention a good many laws. She lied and she stole, she fiddled and forged.

And he'd marry her today, if she'd have him.

Taking a salute from a legionary beside a statue of an impossibly youthful Augustus, his attention was caught by a movement from the corner of his eye. Among the bustle of bean-counters and pen-pushers, three more shouldn't have attracted anyone's notice. So why his? As the legionary marched off, Marcus bent to adjust his bootlace and now he realized what it was about this particular trio. Whilst there was nothing furtive about their movements, there was nothing purposeful, either. And whilst the Governor's palace also served as the administrative seat for the province's capital, no one ever sauntered around as though they were on a picnic. There was communication between the three, too. A nod here, a raised eyebrow there. Together it added up to an uncomfortable feeling, but he was wary of calling the guard. For one thing, they were embroiled in a skirmish in the main hall, where some drunken fanatic was shouting anti-Roman insults whilst brandishing a very rusty bent sword. And for another, suppose they were the Governor's guests mooching about? Members of a trade delegation from Burdigala on the Gironde, for example? Or official messengers awaiting orders?

Nevertheless, it could do no harm to watch them, he supposed. And once again, his gut served him well. Hidden behind the statue, he saw the three men stop outside the Governor's office, glance round then draw daggers from inside their tunics. Marcus turned to summon the guard, but even as he spun round, he realized the drunk downstairs was a deliberate diversion. The guard was nowhere in sight. While his own dagger was lying on the top of his desk . . .

Surprise was his only weapon.

Charging into the room, yelling and screaming at the top of his voice, he managed to at least kick the knife out of the first one's hand. As it spun harmlessly into a corner, the Governor's thirty years of army training kicked in. He over-turned his desk in the path of the second assassin, while his scribes scrambled to disarm the third. But having been thwarted of their original purpose, now the men's priority turned to escape – and the only thing standing between them and their freedom was a patrician with high ideals.

As fists collided with flesh, Orbilio heard the clatter of hobnailed boots up the stairs and the reassuring jangle of breastplates and greaves. All they had to do was hold out for another few seconds, and as one iron hand tried to snap his collarbone in half and another squeezed his testicles to a pulp, he took comfort that one of the scribes was swinging a stool by a leg and was aiming straight for Orbilio's attacker.

Unfortunately, his attacker chose that moment to slip in a pool of his own blood.

And as the stool crashed down on Orbilio's skull, his last thought before unconsciousness claimed him was, There has to be a better way of making a living.

Six

'My dear, we are so very pleased to welcome you,' Beth said, taking both of Claudia's hands in hers, and to be fair, her delight did not appear to be feigned. In fact, now Claudia looked closely, it seemed to be mingled with a certain amount of relief.

Which was mutual.

'Not as pleased as I am to hear you speak a language I understand,' she replied.

Accustomed to precincts adorned with glistening marble, gleaming bronzes and braziers twice the height of a man belching out thick clouds of incense, the simplicity of the College would take some getting used to, she supposed, but the effect was neither rustic nor dull. There were no temples, of course, and no shrines. But in place of soaring columns and gaily painted stone, half-timbered longhouses with thatched roofs cast welcome shade. And where statues and altars would normally be surrounded by officials scurrying back and forth as they petitioned the gods on behalf of the pious, made sacrifices here, read omens there and generally oversaw the swearing of oaths, trees rustled in the breeze, grass softened the crunch of leather soles and birdsong replaced the flutes that piped away evil spirits. There was no need to purify their enclosure, of course. That had been done three centuries before, when the Hundred-Handed founded this College. Since then, nothing unwelcome could get past their portals.

'Swarbric implied yours was a silent order,' she added.

'Oh, if only!' Beth's laugh was as warm as her chestnut brown hair and as light as her soft, silver robe. 'But he's right up to a point. We often let our fingers do the talking.' She flicked her finger joints in a series of rapid movements.

'It's this ciphering that gave rise to the name "Hundred-Handed".'

Fifty priestesses pointing and jabbing with both hands simultaneously? Claudia could see how that would fire the imagination, and she had to admit the system was faultless when it came to conveying information from one side of the precinct to the other, for example. No running back and forth, no wasting of time, no fear of messages getting muddled through a third party. Whisk-whisk-whisk, message sent.

'With sign language, there can be no mistaking the intention,' Beth said. 'Though that is not the reason we use it. Once words are written down, they become frozen, and as you know, my dear, once something freezes it dies.'

'So this way your language never dies?'

'The meaning never dies,' she corrected, leading her guest to the tip of the arrowhead, where a stone bench offered uninterrupted views over the valley. Spellbound by the rolling hills and the meadows ablaze with wild flowers, Claudia could have been staring into infinity. Far below in the distance, sheep bleated.

'Thoughts, stories, experiences, ideas, they never lose their dynamism, don't you see?' Beth's enthusiasm was contagious. 'They remain fresh. Never withering. Never wavering. As constant as nature herself.'

'But never changing, either.' The theory was sound, but in real life ideas needed to evolve, or stagnation stifled them. 'Without innovation,' Claudia said slowly, 'the world they live in dies instead.'

'Nature gives us stability through its perpetuity, my dear, but I never suggested it doesn't change. No one year is ever like the next.'

Each priestess monitored her own aspect of nature, she explained, and thus it was together, as a body, that the Hundred-Handed assessed what impact any changes they observed might have for the future.

'Fearn, for example, sits at the Growth point on the pentagram and she is the Alder Priestess. As the month under my protection begins at the winter solstice, so hers begins at the spring equinox, but nothing in nature is isolated. Alders grow close to water and if there's a drought, they suffer. So in turn do the crops, the fruits of the forest and those creatures who are sustained by the life in the forests. By working in concord and correlating the information, we effectively become weather forecasters, farmers, prophets and healers rolled into one.'

Claudia stood corrected. 'Are all the Hundred-Handed named after trees?'

Beth laughed. 'Heavens, no! Our duty is to every living being on the earth. It's only the twelve months of the year that have priestesses named after the trees that protect them. Mavor, for instance, watches over birds. Others are responsible for the heaths, the meadows, the wetlands, wild beasts and fishes, even the wind and the moon.'

Across the bowl of the valley, lizards basked on stones, chicks huddled in their nests, dappled fawns hid motionless in the bracken. But while June might be a time for calm and leisure for them, for others it was a month of frantic activity. Watching bumblebees buzz, grasshoppers rasp and swallowtail butterflies take to the wing, Claudia wondered what effect Drusilla's tax on the rodent population would have on the College's painstakingly correlated data.

'Talking of the spring equinox,' she said mildly, 'I gather you suffered a tragedy?'

'Ah, little Clytie.' Beth shook her head sadly. 'On the day when dark and light become equals and the world can rejoice in balance and harmony, something wicked like that happens. Poor Pod.' She sighed. 'Imagine the shock of finding her body laid out like that.'

Claudia didn't imagine Clytie got a lot out of being butchered, either.

'Her killer's still at large, though?'

'Unsatisfactory though the situation is, I'm afraid that is true, but two years ago a monster stalked the town of Santonum, strangling women then ritually arranging their bodies and painting them. This crime bears too many of those hallmarks to be a coincidence, and I have every confidence that between Rome and the Tribal Chieftains this copycat will be unmasked.'

But at what cost? Claudia wondered. *At what cost?*

'Assuming it is a copycat,' a voice behind them boomed.

Of the three priestesses walking towards the tip of the arrowhead rock, the eldest wore a robe the colour of ripe acorns. Her stout arm was linked with a woman clothed in linen the colour of gorse that contrasted prettily with her raven-black hair. The third, dressed top to toe in black, tagged behind taking small tight steps.

'Dora,' the woman in brown boomed by way of introduction. 'The Maturity point on the pentagram and bloody pleased to see you, I must say!'

Another one who was openly relieved, Claudia noticed. Although the light in Dora's eyes seemed to encompass satisfaction as well.

'This is Fearn,' she said, introducing the Alder Priestess Beth had mentioned just now, the Growth point on the star. Interestingly, there was no mention of the third member of the group. 'I'm sorry, Beth,' Dora swept on, 'and as much as I hate to disagree with you once again, darling, your argument about the copycat doesn't add up.'

Even though it was as if the third priestess didn't exist, there was no doubting which point of the pentagram Ailm represented, or which was her sacred tree. And if it was true that dog owners grew to resemble their pets, then the same must be said of the Hundred-Handed. As dark and inscrutable as the transition the Death Priestess watched over, the berries of the yew tree were as beautiful as they were deadly. Dora, on the other hand, stood for the tree that dominated the impending summer solstice, a symbol everywhere of courage, endurance and strength. As Beth had grown as stately as the birch she represented, so Dora had become the sturdy, dependable oak, and looking at her matronly stance and welcoming bosom it was easy to picture the other women flocking to her with their problems, just as she could see Dora dropping whatever it was she was doing to listen. Conversely, though. Claudia pursed her lips. The heartwood of oak can also grow so hard that it becomes impossible to drive a nail into it . . .

'My theory makes much sounder sense,' Dora was saying.

'She believes Clytie was the victim of someone who wondered what it would feel like to take a human life,' Fearn explained in a voice as rich as the hue of her gown. 'A would-be warrior perhaps.'

Claudia goggled. 'Who chose a twelve-year-old child as a soft target?'

'The whole thing was clumsily done,' Dora said bluntly. 'As was plain from the lividity marks on her body, not to mention the lack of blood in the spot where Pod found her, Clytie died in one place and was moved post mortem.'

Ailm said nothing, but her hands remained folded in front of her waist, while her dark narrow eyes kept darting from Beth to Dora and back. In the uncompromising light of the afternoon sun, Claudia noticed that the rich peat tones of her hair had been artificially aided and the first hint of age spots on her cheeks discreetly touched up with white lime.

'I just pray that whoever killed Clytie has been cured of his damned curiosity,' Dora said.

Claudia blinked. How old would the Oak Priestess be? Fifty-five? Sixty? It was hard to tell, since plumpness had rounded out most of her wrinkles, but she was old enough to have learned compassion! And what of Fearn? A child had died on the spring equinox, the very day that her sacred gorse took office for the month, and whether farmer or priest, blacksmith or beggar, this was an important moment in everyone's calendar. How could she not be touched by the sacrilege? And why did Death not have a word to say on the matter? Most of all, though, how could Beth, of all people, discuss this butchery without passion? Yet looking at her handsome face and straight carriage, there was nothing hard about the head of this order. She was simply resolute. Living proof that, unlike the Druids, the power of the Hundred-Handed was enforced through respect rather than fear.

'Also,' Fearn said, 'the painting was amateurish in the extreme.'

'That's because men tend not to know a lot about the application of cosmetics,' Beth replied, smoothing her gown over hips that a woman half her age would be proud of.

'Precisely my point.' Dora nodded forcefully, but then Claudia didn't imagine that woman was half-hearted in anything. 'And since there was no sign of sexual interference, which is the usual motive for such killings, until someone proves otherwise, I remain convinced that the arrangement of Clytie's body was a clumsy attempt to make it look like a replication of previous murders.'

Claudia thanked Jupiter that Gabali hadn't been privy to this conversation. Who knew what the assassin's reaction might be? Because he was wrong, she realized. The Spaniard was wrong. When a child was born into this society, it wasn't simply a matter of being placed into communal care. *The worst part was that it was raised with a communal psyche.*

'How do you choose who fathers your children?' she asked, changing the subject before her gorge rose at their insensitivity.

'Looks are an important consideration,' Beth said, stating the obvious, because from the moment she'd clapped eyes on Mavor, Claudia realized that all the women in this College were stunning.

'Other factors play a part, too,' Fearn said, with a toss of her raven-black hair.

'Strength. Intelligence.' Beth added to the list. 'Health, of course.'

'As it happens, there's a slave auction in Santonum tomorrow,' Fearn said. 'You're welcome to come along, if you like.'

Dora cast a sharp glance over her shoulder, where coils of smoke rose out of the trees on the hill, testifying to the presence of men who lived their lives behind a high palisade.

'About bloody time we augmented the workforce. Half the roofs are an absolute disgrace, the willows are long overdue cutting and the husbandry's on the verge of neglect.'

Beth leaned towards Claudia. 'Now you understand why I wish Swarbric was right and this Order *was* silent,' she whispered.

Claudia smiled, but the smile did not reach her eyes, and as she stared out over the bowl of the valley, something knotted deep inside and began to twist and tighten.

It was much later that she identified the knot as fear.

In the centre of the world, between earth, sky and sea, at the point where the realms of the universe meet, Rumour welcomed her old friend warmly.

Settling herself in a comfy chair, Falsehood poured herself a glass of poison and whispered all her lies into the ears of the children of Truth.

Sipping contentedly as her tales twisted in the telling, warped in their imparting and distorted in their repetition, she stared into the Mirror of Complacency.

And watched the Druids drink them in.

From his vantage point high on the cliff, the young man who had whispered those falsehoods followed the flight of a hunting bird and his heart soared with it. Thanks to him, rumours were spreading on wings every bit as sturdy, multiplying tenfold as his tales of witchcraft and sorcery filtered through the Druid priesthood.

To his right, the sun began to slide towards the horizon, but it was not on the sinking disc that the Whisperer's gaze was fixed. Watching the bird glide above the plateau where the Hundred-Handed had their College, he smiled to himself. The Chieftains talked about Rome putting an end to intertribal warfare, to isolation, to raids on livestock, raids on women, to going cold and hungry in the depths of winter, starving when the rains swamped the grain – ach, but these were old men. Greybeards, who'd grown as soft as the food their rotting teeth sucked on. As soft as the living they'd carved out for themselves under their corrupt regime. What did these old men know?

Tightening the strings on his leather wrist grips, the Whisperer straightened the bandana around his neck and wondered how they dared label him a traitor when they were the real traitors to Gaul. He only had to look back to his childhood. Running through meadows full of hay where the Records Office now stood. Climbing trees that had been felled long since to make way for a public bathhouse. Rolypolying down a hill that been turned, of all things, into a theatre. From a simple cluster of artisans making a living to the beat of their own drum, Santonum had become the jewel in the Occupation's provincial crown – and the Chieftains praised it. They actually *praised* those concrete eyesores that fouled a once-picturesque skyline. Applauded the wide cobbled roads that disfigured the landscape and, worse, roads which were now defaced with an ever-growing line of marble sarcophagi that housed the corpses of foreign intruders.

Watching the hunter soar above the twisting contours of the hills, the Whisperer snorted. Chieftains prattled on about wealth bringing prosperity to the tribes, but how? They claimed that before Rome the potters and metalsmiths had had to scratch hard to make ends meet, but at least their graft had been honest because how, in all conscience, could life under the shadow of the eagle ever be better than freedom? How did the creaking of winches down on the quay improve anyone's quality of life? How could the crack of a charioteer's whip be an asset to the Aquitani Nation? And what about when night fell. When silence descended over their precious new wharf, where did those hypocritical old farts think the sailors went then? Into town, that's where they fucking well went. Polluting the air with their dirty foreign tongues, making whores of the local girls, and who knew what villainy the bastards were plotting? What blasphemy they could be spreading?

With the setting sun beating on his neck, the Whisperer attuned his ears to the high-pitched whistles that told him the hunting bird was keeping in close contact with its nestlings, and he spat. Traitor, patriot, what difference did it make, it was only a word. A name. And how many times had he changed *that* since the tribe cast him out? He buffed his ring down the side of his pantaloons. It was a man's identity that mattered. What he held true to his heart.

Those greybeards had sold their own people out, and if the tribes were too weak and too stupid to see what was happening – and sentenced those who spoke up to be shunned – then someone had to stand up for what was right. Someone had to give the tribes their spirit back before it was broken completely. They needed to be shown that the Romans were not overlords to be feared, but flesh and blood, who screamed when their bodies were sluiced with tar and set alight in the night. Who gushed blood when a broadsword hacked off their heads as they slept. Who fell when the slingshot caught them square on the temple.

It had reached the point now, though, where ambushing patrols wasn't enough. Defacing milestones wasn't enough.

Even sabotaging the likes of granaries, wells and bridges wasn't enough. The rot needed to be stopped before it infected the Nation and tranquillity could be restored to the landscape. It wasn't too late to have the water margins ring with the bleating of sheep again, instead of the clatter of hobnail boots.

'You can't reverse progress,' the Chieftains insisted, 'any more than you can make the sun rise in the north.'

Who couldn't? Measureless eyes followed the bird as it glided on unflapping wings. Was it progress that the legions, with their fancy uniforms and sophisticated ways, had turned the women against their own tribes? Fuck, no. Progress didn't produce mongrels through intermarriage that diluted the purity of the Aquitani, and the Chiefs could bleat about the benefits of fresh blood all they liked, the truth was, those half-breeds were vermin. Pests to be exterminated before they bred further, and killing the little bastards was doing the Nation a favour.

Luckily for the Aquitani, enough brave hearts still beat among the tribes to see the truth for what it was, and he nodded in satisfaction, recalling the heat that had fired in the veins of the warriors as they vowed on their oaths to smear their faces with the blood of their enemies and drive the eagle out of this land, ripping up the stones from their roads, tearing down their buildings and giving the riverbanks back to the cattle.

But it wasn't purely the physical aspects that troubled the Whisperer. Under Rome, the thinking had gone soft as well, and one only had to look up there, to the smoke spiralling upwards through the trees, to see the evidence of that degeneration. It was said that the power of the Druids was waning under Rome, now that people no longer turned to them for guidance. Fuck that. It was the power of *men* that was being eroded – and those bitches on the plateau were living proof.

The lies and the falsehoods he'd fed to the Druids were no more than they deserved. Bloody bitches. The Hundred-Handed had it coming and that was a fact. High time someone redressed the balance and put women back in their place.

Against a backdrop of the setting sun, the bird whistled and wheeled. Confident, skilful, sure of itself, it surveyed its territory with unblinking eye and soared without one feather fluttering on its chestnut-brown wings.

'We'll show them!' one of the warriors shouted, rattling the medallions of dead soldiers that hung from his belt. 'We will show these pretenders what the Aquitani are made of!'

'Aye!' cried the others. 'We have weapons, war chariots, horses, siege engines! What are we waiting for, lads?'

But just as Rumour needs an anchor to attach itself to lest it withers away into nothingness and dies, so War needs a commander.

'Patience, my friends,' the Whisperer had counselled. 'Our stocks and supplies are limited reserves. We must use them wisely.'

Food, clothing, bandages, even armour don't last for ever, he'd told them, and a direct assault on Rome would deplete precious reserves in no time.

'But we've set traps—'

'– dug pits—'

'– sharpened spikes—'

'Which we will use carefully and to our advantage,' he'd assured them. 'But to charge down on Rome would only invite disaster. We must fight the enemy on our terms, my friends, and in a way we can win.'

Think of Rome as a beehive, he'd said. United, they work in harmony and the swarm is invincible. But make them angry . . .

'How do we do that, though?' the young hotheads demanded. 'How do we make Rome angry enough to make them lose their discipline?'

'Women and children,' he said simply. 'We slaughter their babies, we slaughter their wives, their daughters, we slaughter everyone who's placed themselves under Roman protection, and by the axe of the Thunder God, we cut them down without mercy.'

Grief and fury, outrage and anguish were enough to make anyone's self-control crumble. Especially when those strikes were aimed at the innocent and came totally out of the blue.

Not a traitor. The Whisperer notched a three-feathered arrow into his bow. A *patriot*.

Without a sound, the eagle plunged to the earth.

Seven

Immersed up to his chin in hot scented water, Marcus Cornelius groaned. Most people go to sleep counting sheep, but due to a distinct lack of woolly ruminants, he'd tried counting bruises instead. Eventually he gave up, partly because there were too many and partly because he was never going to nod off with that thumping great hammer pounding his brains out. So he'd lain awake through the wee small hours, which ought to have been dark but were punishingly bright, wondering which gods he'd offended this time. He made a mental note to placate them all.

Stretched out in the bath, fragrant with myrtle and hyssop, he felt the first twinge of divine forgiveness. Sod's law stated that it would be him, one of the good guys, who was rewarded for saving the Governor's life by being clonked on the head with a footstool and he supposed he should be thankful that the scribe hadn't been armed with a knife. These pen-pushers were more dangerous than they looked.

Attendants materialized in and out of the steam, topping up the bath with hot water and adding extra phials of healing oils. Orbilio thanked them and closed his eyes again. In fairness, yesterday's sorry interlude hadn't been all bad. Between the Governor, his scribes and himself, the would-be assassins had been prevented from escaping and if he was feeling somewhat the worse for wear after that encounter, imagine what it would be like for them. Gauls who worked with Rome to make life safer and more prosperous for their own people were honoured with citizenship, should they choose to accept it. The three men who'd been lugged off to the dungeons hadn't been given that option, and, since they weren't citizens, torture tended to be Rome's preferred method of interrogation. It wasn't necessarily the most effec-

50

tive way of obtaining information. But in some cases (the attempted assassination of the Governor, for instance) it proved the most satisfying.

Holding a sponge somewhat gingerly to the goose egg on his skull, he reckoned the Governor would probably make political capital out of the attempt on his life. Personally, Orbilio hadn't been convinced that creating a new branch of the Security Police here in Aquitania would serve any real useful purpose, knowing the Governor only set it up in order to make it seem the province was in safe hands from within as well as without.

Orbilio had seen himself as nothing more than a pawn in those politics, which wasn't a problem in the short term, but the squad's success took them both by surprise.

Without the army's bureaucracy getting in the way, crime-fighting was free to take a much broader approach, and since prevention was every bit as important as solving, the Governor had also given Orbilio a liberal budget for rewarding informers. One of the more pleasant adjustments, since in Rome he'd tended to pay them from his own pocket! But it was like he'd always said, pay informants well and you get good results in return, and one only had to look at the present situation to see the benefits. Without financial incentives, it was doubtful that news of this latest uprising would have come to his ears, much less intelligence regarding the sheer number of disenchanted warriors that there were among the various tribes that made up the Aquitani Nation. Instead, thanks to a few overpaid informants, he was well abreast of the Scorpion's activities and—

'Mother of Tarquin!' He jumped, as a woman's figure loomed through the swirls of hot steam. 'This is the men's bath!'

'Constantly nit-picking, Orbilio, that's your trouble.'

'*Claudia?*'

'Yes, and I know what you're thinking.'

'I doubt that.'

'You thought I was in Rome and behaving myself, but as you can see, I'm here – good grief.' Suddenly a mass of unruly curls were peering over the rim of the bath. 'How many of them jumped you?'

'Forty-two.' Marcus belatedly covered his embarrassment with the sponge he'd been holding to the bump on his head. 'Claudia, do you mind? I'm naked.'

'People in baths usually are, but don't worry. I've seen your wife-pleaser before and, impressive though it is, Marcus, I promise to keep a close rein on my self-control.'

'I could make it a widow-pleaser,' he offered.

'Don't flatter yourself, Orbilio, it's not that impressive.'

'Did you come three hundred miles just to insult me,' he laughed, as she settled herself on the tiles, 'or do you simply enjoy startling me out of my wits?'

'In an ideal world, both, but since time is not on my side, I need your help – and quite frankly, Marcus, that spluttering is not remotely amusing.'

'I rather think that depends whose perspective we're dealing with here.' Claudia? Asking for – remind me again – *help?* 'Could you pass me a towel, please?'

'Typical. That's all you ever think about, me, me, me.'

When she threw her hands in the air, he caught a whiff of her intense Judaean perfume. Dear god, how he'd missed that smell—

'Now for heaven's sake, Orbilio, will you stop playing games and tell me, are you coming or not?'

Conscious of the reckless jolt in his loins, he thought she had no idea.

'Slow down, will you.' His head was hurting enough. 'Claudia, what exactly is it you want?'

'The Governor said you saved his life.'

'I may have played a small part in—' Wait a moment. 'Why would the Governor be telling *you*?' The average petitioner waited weeks for an appointment, and even then they were palmed off with a minion.

'Because I introduced myself as your ex-wife, of course.'

Orbilio wondered whether it was too late to change places with the assassins down in the torture chamber.

'And be honest, Marcus, who better to take care of a man who's been battered to a pulp and give him the rest and convalescence that he needs than his deeply repentant ex-wife?'

If *only* that scribe had hit him harder.

'Why is it I have a feeling that "rest and convalescence" is the one thing I won't be getting?'

'There you go again. Negative, negative, negative, when all I'm asking is a tinksy little favour.'

He drew as deep a breath as his ribs would allow. 'I'm scared to ask, but go on.'

She made herself comfortable on the edge of the bath and traced the dolphin mosaic with her finger. 'You know the Hundred-Handed?'

'The priestesses who communicate silently through signs?' That twinge earlier wasn't divine absolution. It was the gods warning of impending retribution. 'Yes, I know them.'

'Good,' she said, 'because I won't bore you with the details. Suffice to say I'm staying there to investigate the murder of a twelve-year-old novice called Clytie, a case I'm sure will have come to your attention, being identical to a series of murders that took place in Santonum two years previously, even though you weren't in the hot seat back then.'

Similar, he thought. Not identical.

'Have you been sniffing hemp seeds?' he asked, and under the circumstances that wasn't an unreasonable question.

'Orbilio, which part of the phrase "time is not on my side" don't you understand? Do you seriously think I'd risk limp curls and runs in my make-up if this wasn't urgent?'

For the first time, something close to alarm rippled through him.

'Has another girl been killed?'

Claudia shifted position. 'To say the Hundred-Handed lead an unnatural existence is an understatement. They breed their own servants, and I mean that quite literally. They keep men as slaves in a stud up on the hill, they don't let the fathers anywhere near their own children—'

'All societies keep slaves,' he reminded her gently. 'Including our own.'

'Who at least receive an allowance, which is theirs to spend as they see fit, even to the extent of owning their own slaves if they want, or saving up to purchase their freedom!'

'Am I imagining this, or is there more steam rising from you than there is from this water?'

'Marcus, these women take babies away from their mothers to be raised in a commune, brainwashing them from the earliest possible age, and although they're charming, friendly and well intentioned on the surface, I tell you, that College breeds poison.'

'What has this to do with Clytie?' he asked, steering the conversation back on track.

'For one thing, she was killed three months ago on the spring equinox, yet the priestesses don't seem remotely bothered that the killer's still free. In fact, the head of the College dismisses the death as a copycat killing and is perfectly happy to sit back and wait for another victim to die before someone else does her job for her and puts paid to the butchery. While the alternative viewpoint seems to be that this murder was nothing more than an experiment by a young warrior curious to know what it felt like to take a human life and then trusting to providence that the sick bastard's worked it out of his system. Don't pretend to me that that's normal behaviour.'

'Unusual,' he agreed, 'and to our way of thinking it might seem a tad callous, but in their minds, remember, the killing of beasts in the arena is mindless and barbarous, and the sect don't understand it at all.'

'Actually, I don't really understand that bit.'

'Me neither, but we've drifted away from the point. Claudia, the Hundred-Handed live very separate lives from the rest of society. Their philosophies are bound to have mutated over the course of time.'

'Morals. You mean morals, Orbilio, and they haven't mutated, they've bloody well disintegrated.' She wagged her finger at him. 'Something is going on up there, I can smell it. We need to find out what that something is and put a stop to it before anyone else dies.'

'Have you considered the possibility that the priestesses are simply idealists?' he asked. 'That they've become so wrapped up in their hierarchies and titles and worship of trees that they've lost sight of— What do you mean, we?'

'What everyone else means by the word. You and me. Us. Look, do you want a grammar lesson or are you going to put some clothes on and come with me?'

54

'Where to?' he asked warily.

'There's a slave auction starting on the quay any second. We – that is, you and I, us, both together – have just a few minutes to get down there, and actually you'll be perfect, covered in those lovely fresh bruises.'

'Perfect for what?'

'Isn't it obvious?' she tutted, tossing him a towel. 'To undertake any kind of investigation, you need access, and really, what better excuse for a late addition to the auction block? A strong, handsome young slave who tried to escape, was beaten for his pains but whose master wants rid of the troublemaker? And for heaven's sake, shut your mouth, man. You're reminding me of a goldfish.'

On the small writing tablet beside Claudia's bed, a metal stylus carefully engraved two words in the soft yellow wax.

I know.

Tempting as it was to rifle through the clothes chests and belongings, the author of the note resisted the urge. There was plenty of time yet, and the cross-eyed, blue-eyed dark Egyptian fiend that protected them with its bared fangs and arched back tended to give weight to the argument.

The door closed with barely a whisper.

Eight

Declining Fearn's offer to hang around the slave auction, Claudia opted for watching Marcus get snapped up by Dora then returning to the College to investigate Clytie's death. There were several good motives propelling that action, the most obvious being that if Beth was right and this was some sick copycat, it was vital to track him down before he claimed another victim. Conversely, should Clytie have been killed for a reason, the quicker Claudia picked up the spoor before the trail cooled completely, then so much the better. Admittedly, after three months, the spoor would have lost much (if not all) of its scent, but at the back of her mind there was another case to be made for solving this murder and taking the next boat back to Rome.

Dammit, she really *must* cover her head next time she went out, because the sun was clearly stronger than she had thought. Janus in heaven, of *course* her heart pounded like a kettledrum when she saw him. What criminal's wouldn't, when reduced to beg favours of the Security Police? And of *course* her breath would have been coming quick and shallow. In that steam, how could it not? And good gracious, the tightness in her chest was what any young woman would have experienced, faced with that amount of raw naked masculine muscle.

No, no. Definitely time to solve Clytie's murder and bugger off back to Rome, she decided, skipping down the wooden steps towards the caves. Because to feel that level of sympathy for the very man who was intent on stepping into the Senate on the back of her felonies meant heatstroke was deceptively potent. Though now she thought about it, and dammit *knowing* he'd be a prize asset to the College, she really ought to have hung a higher price tag round

Orbilio's neck. The derisory little sum that she'd pocketed in the end would barely cover her outstanding account at the bloody cobbler's . . .

Inside the cave, it was cool but not dark. Lamps inset in niches hacked out of the stone lit the interior as brightly as noon, and the scent of the roses and honeysuckle that decked the entrance mingled with the bunches of healing herbs that hung from the roof and whose fragrance had been released by a light crushing of leaves between fingertips. Claudia helped herself to a ladle of water from the stone basin that was fed by the constant trickle from the rock, and was just about to pour herself a second when she realized that the sound she'd assumed to be part of the spring was actually the sound of weeping.

The acoustics inside the cave were confusing, and it took a moment before she realized that the sobs came from outside, where the rocks at the entrance kicked back an echo.

'Oh sweet Janus!'

The woman lay on the ground where she had fallen, her fringed skirt up over her knees, the bruise on her shin already swollen and angry. And the reason she couldn't get up by herself was because she was heavily pregnant.

'Don't move.' Claudia scrambled over the rocks towards her. 'Stay right where you are, I'll go and get help, I just need to make sure you're all right first.'

'Go away,' she sobbed, pushing Claudia away. 'Leave me alone.'

'I certainly will not.'

Apart from the banged shin, there appeared to be no other damage and her stomach lurched, because that meant it was internal.

'Where were you when you fell?' she asked. Dammit, these boulders were *huge*.

'I didn't slip,' the Gaulish girl blubbered. 'I came here to be alone, so go away and leave me in peace.'

'My dear woman, if I thought you were in peace, I'd be gone before you could blink. But.' Claudia made herself comfortable on the ground next to her. 'Since you've gone to a lot of trouble to crawl into this space, curled yourself up like an animal and are obviously intent on creating a water course that not only makes the one inside the cave look like a tap-drip but will probably throw Gurdo out of a job in the process, I'm sticking to you like a wart until you tell me the problem.'

The smile was feeble, but it was a smile nevertheless.

'See for yourself,' she said, handing over a crumpled piece of parchment.

Claudia straightened it out the best that she could, and although tears and ink were not the best of companions, she eventually deciphered the gist.

While you let your horse starve, someone else is bringing him oats.

'Is that it?' She ripped the note into shreds and threw them into the air. 'You're risking your baby, your health and your happiness on someone else's resentment and jealousy?'

The girl blinked. 'You – you don't think it's true, then?'

Claudia had absolutely no idea whether she was married to a saint or a scoundrel, but she did know that an atmosphere of mistrust and anxiety isn't the best start to a newborn life.

'Mischief-making, pure and simple,' she said crisply. 'My advice is to go home and forget it.'

'But suppose it is true? Suppose he has been—'

'Does your husband spend a lot of time preening himself?'

The woman's head shook tentatively. 'N-no.'

'Is he habitually late? Does he enjoy humiliating people? Is he reckless, feckless, unreliable and ruthless?'

'*My Borrix?*'

'There you are, then.'

It didn't follow, of course, that nice boys didn't stray. But serial adulterers followed a tediously consistent pattern and since 'her Borrix' didn't fit the profile, Claudia had been taking no risk. Whereas the mother-to-be had been reassured beyond measure.

'Thank you,' she gushed. 'Oh, thank you so much.'

Drawing the line at having her hands smothered in kisses, Claudia helped the girl to her feet. 'Come on, I'll give you a hand over these rocks, and then I suggest you and your Borrix take a stroll round the village, arm in arm so everyone can see you're devoted. Especially the author of that spiteful missive.'

Spurned lover, jealous mother-in-law, barren neighbour filled with resentment, who knows?

'How can I ever thank you?' the girl sniffed.

'By leaving before you give birth at my feet,' Claudia laughed, but as she watched her waddle off, the fringe of her skirt swinging jauntily, she was aware that the laughter was false. Seeing the woman curled up like that had given Claudia quite a shock. The Clytie factor, she supposed, and again she was struck by the close link between beauty and tragedy. For the birds still sang and the sun still shone. And the seasons continued to turn—

Her thoughts were interrupted by the sound of two sets of footsteps approaching from opposite directions.

'Sarra!' Pod's voice contained pleasure as well as surprise. 'Looking for Gurdo? He's away collecting his herbs this time of a day. You'd best give him an hour.'

Behind the boulders, Claudia watched a girl of the same age as the tousle-haired elf smile coyly back. Thanks to the acoustics, every word carried clearly.

'I wasn't looking for Gurdo,' Sarra said. 'I . . . was just taking a walk.'

Not the most convincing of liars, Claudia thought, as another blushing exchange passed between them. Either she expected to bump into the young woodsman or Sarra kept passing this way until she did.

'I was hoping to pick a few mallow to go with these,' she murmured, indicating the spray of pure white dog roses she held in her hand. 'But I can't seem to find any.'

'I know a spot where they grow real thick.'

Sarra's blush deepened to the pink of her robe, and, in the dappled shade of the trees, her long, silky hair shone the colour of primroses in spring. 'Perhaps you'd be kind enough to point that place out to me, then, Pod?' She pushed a loose tendril hair behind her ear and still didn't make eye contact with the young elf. 'If it's no trouble, I mean.'

'Better than that, I can show you.'

Though Sarra still stared at her roses, her lower lip trembled. 'I'd like that,' she whispered. 'I'd like that very much, but – suppose someone sees us together?'

'What will they see?' The depth of his grin dimpled his

cheeks. 'A simple woodsman helping a girl from the College? Sarra, if it was Swarbric, it wouldn't pass notice.'

Blue eyes met his at last. 'That's because Swarbric's a slave and you're a free man,' she said quietly. 'Pod, you know the penalties for fraternizing with non-College men, and there's you to think of as well. You'll be cast out. Shunned. Oh, Pod, the Hundred-Handed will vote you invisible and—'

'Then let's *be* invisible!' He rushed forward and took both her hands in his, heedless of the roses' thorns. 'Sarra, I know these woods. I know a glade we can meet where no one will see us—'

'No, no, I can't. Even if we did manage to hide out of sight, there's no telling whether someone might hear—'

'Suppose we found another way to talk?' The youth's eyes danced as he flicked his fingers. 'No one can overhear that.'

'Holy heaven!' Her eyes turned to saucers of horror. 'Where did you learn to talk with your hands?'

'From watching you.'

'Oh, Pod, if they ever find out you can cipher—'

He silenced her protests by placing one finger gently over her lips. 'Tomorrow,' he whispered. 'Tomorrow afternoon, when everyone'll be busy with the solstice preparations.'

Even from behind the rock, Claudia could see the girl was shaking and she did not think it was from fear.

'Very well, then,' Sarra said at last. 'If you're sure?'

'I'm sure.' The youth placed a light kiss on her lips, then another, then a longer, much deeper one. 'But you have to admit,' he said, finally pulling away, 'I've picked up your sign language pretty well.'

He gesticulated a few more words with his fingers and despite herself, Sarra laughed. 'I suspect you meant to call me an angel, but you've just labelled me an old bat! This,' she said, swishing her fingers, 'is the cipher for angel.'

She was still smiling as she disappeared round the curve in the path, trailing her spray of white roses and quite oblivious to the fact that those blooms which had survived the crushing embrace had lost at least half of their petals. Several minutes passed before Pod finally tore his eyes away from the empty track, yet when he turned round, Claudia noticed that the expression in them was harder than granite.

So then. Pod was a free man, she thought, watching him sprint off down the path to make up for lost time. Another point she would need to raise with Gurdo, but since the spring's belligerent guardian wasn't here, she decided to wait on a wide flat rock beside the stream that was surrounded by iris and willow. Out of sight, beyond a bend in the river downstream, the babble of women washing laundry mingled with midsummer birdsong, while the gurgle of water glugging round rocks merged with the droning of bees. And yet, as she lay face up to the sun, there was little peace in Claudia's heart.

I know.

She'd found the note the minute she returned from Santonum, and whoever wrote it hadn't bothered to flip the hinge of the wax tablet shut. They'd wanted her to see the message straight away – but who knew? What did they know? And how could they possibly know that Claudia was investigating Clytie's death? Yet:

I know, the note read. *I know.*

Two little words, but enough to chill her through to her marrow. Keeping secrets was not always wise. In fact, in a close, tight-knit community such as this, where mysteries were mandatory and rituals inscrutable, and where conspiracy already bubbled, knowledge could be a dangerous thing . . .

'We used to sit and make daisy chains on this rock,' a small voice piped up. 'In fact, until Clytie died here, it was our favourite spot.'

Spinning round, Claudia came face to face with the same beautiful flaxen-haired trio that Swarbric had castigated for climbing trees.

'Clytie died *here*?'

'You can still see the stains from her blood.' The little novice pointed to a series of smudges in the porous white limestone. 'I'm Aridella, by the way.'

'Vanessia,' the oldest one said, bobbing a curtsey.

'And I'm Lin,' said the one that was all blue eyes and dimples. 'It means pool.'

The girls were so alike that Claudia supposed it wasn't beyond the realms of possibility that three of the women had picked the same fair-haired hunk to father their children.

Since the Hundred-Handed held none of the usual concepts of individual possessions and family bonding, believing in communal ownership, she saw no reason why this philosophy shouldn't extend to the men they took to their beds, since share and share alike was the College's ethos. But sharing can't always be easy, she thought. Not where emotions are concerned.

'We'd come down after tutoring,' Aridella said, and an image of four little girls lying face down on the warm stone flashed before Claudia's mind. Three little blonde heads plus a brunette in her father's image pressed tightly together as they giggled and chattered, swapping jokes and homework in the manner of little girls everywhere.

'At least, when we weren't in detention,' Dimples muttered, with a roll of her enormous blue eyes.

A quick glance at the rope dangling from an alder over the stream brought back memories of the flaxen-haired trio dropping out of the oak tree, their skirts tucked into their knicker cloths, their knees grubby and skinned.

'Aren't novices allowed to have adventures?' Claudia asked.

'Officially, no,' Vanessia said, taking one of Aridella's plaits and tying it neatly. 'We're supposed to devote ourselves to the Wisdom, because it's our holy obligation to learn Nature's lore and store the knowledge inside our hearts.'

'It's our purpose for this reincarnation,' Lin added earnestly.

'But provided nobody gets to hear about it—'

'You mean Beth?'

'Any of the Hundred-Handed,' Vanessia said, tugging the second plait into order. 'We're accountable to them all, but providing they don't catch us in the act—'

'And no one reports us—'

'And as long as we still learn our lessons—'

'– then nobody minds.'

'You must miss Clytie a lot,' Claudia said, but instead of three blonde heads nodding in unison, a shutter came hurtling down. Vanessia dropped the plait without tying the ribbon and the girls stared at their feet.

'Don't you?' Claudia prompted.

'Yes, miss,' they chorused in a dull monotone.

'Of course, it was a long time ago.' Three months at their age must seem like a lifetime. 'But I wonder . . . do any of you remember Clytie slipping out that particular night? Perhaps you saw someone talking to her the day that she died?'

Three pairs of eyes stared steadfastly at the ground, then Lin muttered something about not feeling well and going to bed early, while Aridella couldn't remember anything about it at all.

'It was just a normal day,' Vanessia said, shrugging one shoulder. 'What's to remember?'

'I don't know,' Claudia replied. 'But since the spring equinox is one of the four big events in your calendar, and considering novices play a major role in the festival, I thought *something* about it might have stuck in your memory. Apart from the fact that your friend died.'

Vanessia's lower lip trembled. 'I must have got the days muddled up,' she said, and the other two nodded eagerly, desperate to grasp at the lifeline.

'Me, too.'

'And me.'

As one they turned and belted back across the meadow, and Claudia reflected that it wasn't simply the one life that had been destroyed on the spring equinox. Three others had been shattered as well – but then wasn't it always the way? Wasn't it bloody well always the way? Staring at the rock where she'd sat without even sensing its tragedy, Claudia hugged her arms to her chest. What happened here, Clytie? What were you doing so far from the College, and at night all on your own? Who on earth lured you away from the compound?

Without warning, Claudia was suddenly the same age as Vanessia. It was a warm day, warmer than this, and she was returning home to the apartment that her father had left four years before. A day like any other, she recalled. No money, no food, no furniture even, since that had been sold so her mother could drink herself into the oblivion that was all Claudia had ever known. Oh, yes, a day like any other.

The sound of the slums reverberated across time. The bawling, the yelling, the barking of dogs. The unmistake-able stench of boiled cabbage, stale sweat and, above all, hopelessness that was trapped in the air. Slipping in cat pee, tripping over broken toys, she is climbing the six flights of stairs the same as she has done every day for the past four-teen years of her life. She opens the door, calls out hello, receives nothing back in return, which is no great surprise. Her mother is always dead to the world before noon. What is unusual, however, is finding her mother surrounded by blood, blowflies and the stink of cheap wine—

Unable to control the shuddering, Claudia tugged at a clump of bright yellow trollius and laid them at the place where a twelve-year-old girl with her whole life ahead of her had bled to death from the same wounds she'd seen herself, a long time – a lifetime – ago.

Gaping red mouths, calling silently for help from two wrists . . .

What the hell were the Hundred-Handed covering up? She sniffed angrily. Even in their upside-down world where duty outweighed family, where love was dispensed like so many bread rolls and equality was as cold as the frost, Beth struck Claudia as the sort who might tolerate lies and half-truths perhaps through omission, but somehow she didn't imagine the head of the College condoning out-and-out falsehoods. Yet that was exactly what that lovely little flaxen-haired trio had done. They had lied. Lied through their exquisite white teeth.

Shoving her hair out of her face with the back of her hand, she thought, Their friend was dead. Killed right here, on this stone.

What did those children fear more than the truth?

Sunlight slanting through the willows cast dappled shade on the meadow, and as it gurgled over the rocks the stream sparkled like glass. Fresh from pupation, a fritillary supped from the pale pink blooms of the bramble, dragonflies patrolled their favourite stretches of water and yellow wagtails darted from stone to stone in search of flies. Claudia stared into the crystal-clear water. It seemed inconceivable that a child could have been murdered in a place so lovely, so peaceful, and on the day of the spring equinox, too. A day, like Beth said, when the whole world rejoices in balance and harmony, decking their houses with gorse and celebrating with dancing, with feasting, with music – but was the date relevant? Would the fact that Clytie was the only brunette among the little quartet have been a factor? In other words, had the girl been chosen at random – or had she been picked out for a reason?

'Looking for fish for your supper, Lofty Legs?'

Gurdo marched purposefully round the bend in the stream. In his left hand he held monkshood, hedge hyssop and hellebores. Under his right arm was tucked a bunch of osiers.

'These tiddlers?' Claudia straightened up from where she'd been dabbling her hands in the water, though strangely her mother's blood never washed off. 'Even the herons leave them alone.'

Dark eyes glittered with cunning. 'Angling for a bigger fish, are we? Well, let me tell you, size isn't everything, lady, which reminds me.' He grunted. 'How's that pain in the neck?'

She pictured Orbilio being fitted with pantaloons in place of his long patrician tunic, set to work mending roofs or (if I dedicate a bracelet to you, Minerva?) mucking out the pigsty or the stables.

'Coming along very nicely,' she said.

'That Mavor does a good job on joints,' Gurdo said, rinsing the dirt off his herbs in the fast-flowing water. 'Between her and the Cave of Miracles, we don't see many dissatisfied customers.'

Claudia studied the herbs he'd been gathering. Medicinal herbs, even though his job was purely guardian of the spring. And noted that each plant was deadly in the wrong hands.

'And even then, I'm sure you charm them out of lodging a complaint,' she said smoothly. 'What's in the other half of the cave?'

'None of your business.'

'Did I say it was?'

The dwarf tipped his head back and hooted. 'Pity you hadn't contracted some lingering sickness that'd take several months to put right. I'm kind of getting used to having you around. But if you must know, the second mouth leads to the Cave of Resurrection deep inside the mountain.'

Claudia turned and peered into the twinkling lights that

lit up Gurdo's half of the cavern, where floral bouquets hung from hooks in the rock and where water oozed from the rock into stone channels. A matter of just a few feet from total, Stygian blackness.

'Resurrection, not reincarnation?'

His dandified shoulders shrugged. 'Same thing. The soul's immortal, Lofty Legs. When that lovely body of yours eventually dies, your soul passes into another.'

'In that cavern?'

Gurdo chortled. 'Babies come from gooseberry bushes, lady, not holes in the rock.' His expression quickly became serious again. 'I'm warning you, though, don't go in there. That entrance, see? That's reserved for the spirits. There's a passage there that leads straight to the Underworld.'

Claudia watched a kingfisher dart upstream and thought that often the run-up to the summer solstice was bedevilled by storms. No sign of them so far. But the sense of oppression was building.

'Reincarnation isn't immediate, then?'

'If you're asking whether the soul flies in the dark side and flits out the other, this is the Cave of Miracles, not Impossi-bloody-bility. Souls aren't bats, you know. These things take time.'

The spirits buzz round the cave like silent, invisible bees, Gurdo added, waiting to lead the souls of the dead to the Underworld to be judged, while the spirits passed time weaving shrouds on looms made of stone.

'How much time?' she asked. 'Is three months long enough for a twelve-year-old soul to hang around before it is reborn?'

'Clytie?' Gurdo's eyes darted to the rock beside which she stood. To the bouquet of yellow globe flowers. 'Lady, for that you'll need to talk to someone a lot more experienced in the spiritual line of work than a guardian of springs.' His face was devoid of emotion as he shook the drips off his herbs. 'Can't speak for the fish in this stream,' he said carefully, 'but there's an awful lot of eels, though.'

'Eels?'

'Right slippery things, and just when you think you've caught one, blow me, it's slid straight through your fingers.' He clucked his tongue. 'You want to watch out for them eels, Lofty Legs.' Then he chuckled. 'Ah, but they're beauties to look at.' He winked. 'A real treat for the eye.'

Was that a warning, she thought as he marched off, his ponytail swinging jauntily? Or wasn't he referring to the priestesses at all, but was suggesting *she* was the beautiful but untrustworthy creature?

Beyond the meadow, the forest opened out into oak, ash and hazel, chestnut, apple and holly. Each tree was sacred to the Hundred-Handed for different reasons – rowan was a charm against evil, hawthorn released love, ash was the tree of rebirth. On a more practical side, their wood turned everything from cradles to clogs, charcoal to wheels, and where hawthorn-blossom tea was good for the heart, the juice of the rowan gargled sore throats away and willow bark reduced fever and pain.

Twelve sacred trees, one for each month of the year.

They furnished everything from dyes to whistles via divining rods and brooms, they provided heat, shelter and food. Without these trees, the people of the forests could not survive. This was the universe without which they would die.

Yet the roots of the ash strangled those of its neighbours. The smoke from burning rowan was believed to summon demons. Willow had long been associated with the dark side of the moon.

Light and dark.

Good and evil.

The sacred and eternal balance.

Claudia glanced at the cliff, thinking of the slave village that lay hidden by trees on the hill. For all the silver birch's ability to self-propagate, this remained the one thing the Hundred-Handed could not do. For their line to continue they needed men. Men like Gabali, who were healthy, handsome, strong and intelligent, but who also possessed other qualities – a deep capacity for love, for instance. His treasured Andalus was one example, not to mention a daughter he'd been forbidden from seeing but which didn't stop him from wanting to protect her. In denying Gabali what came naturally to him, hot (but forbidden) love had mutated into cold (but remunerated) justice.

What of the other men who lived locked inside that palisade? How might their anger and suppression find an outlet?

Gabali wasn't unique. Like it or not, prime specimens had been sold into slavery since the dawn of time, but there had always been an order to their subjection. They'd married, raised kids, and even though those children had been born into slavery, family order had still been maintained. Stability was part of the deal. Admittedly, from time to time stories surfaced of sadists who beat their servants and sold them like cattle, but these, thank Jupiter, were the minority. An isolated few, who made the news for all the wrong reasons and simply because of their wrongdoings.

Brushing against banks of wild mint as she strolled by the river, Claudia's hems released clouds of its invigorating fragrance. The Hundred-Handed weren't cruel to their male captives in the physical sense – indeed, Beth would be outraged at the very suggestion. But their behaviour flew in the face of every convention as these 'prime specimens' were kept not only locked up, but under the control of women who used them for work and sex and then, when they'd outlived their usefulness in the eyes of the priestesses, sold them on like redundant cookpots. If that wasn't cruelty, Claudia didn't know what was, the only surprise was that more hadn't snapped. The question was, would that rage extend to taking it out on a twelve-year-old child?

Maybe this magnificent, chained and powerless male believed that, in killing a novice, it was the start to sparing future generations from becoming like him? That if the Hundred-Handed were eliminated – cut off at the root, as it were – the plant would wither and die?

If so, that put three little flaxen-haired beauties in the path of some very real danger.

'What happened to you, Clytie?' she whispered. 'Were you the victim of a sick, twisted mind who looked to an executed butcher as some kind of hero?'

Beth clearly thought so.

'Or is Dora right? Were you the tragic result of a warrior's trial run, or is my theory closer to the mark? That you were sacrificed on an altar of despairing male principles?'

Quite literally, given the shape of the rock, and maybe that in itself was important. But tempting as it was to seek logic in murder, Claudia's notion of putting an end to the sect by killing novices would only work if every priestess was beyond child-bearing age. Dora and several others certainly were, and although Beth, Fearn and Ailm were fast approaching that stage, there were still plenty of nubile Initiates on hand to do their duty. If Clytie's killer hoped to eradicate the Hundred-Handed, his object was self-defeating. The College would probably double in numbers overnight.

Watching a grass snake slither through the thyme, another theory began to take shape.

Orbilio had called the Hundred-Handed idealists, but idealists came in many forms. Suppose someone believed that by killing Clytie they were setting her little soul free? Once again, Claudia's eyes were drawn to the cave with two mouths. One for humans to pass through, decked with honeysuckle and rose. The other garlanded with yew that was reserved for the spirits, and which led straight down to the Underworld.

It's our holy obligation to learn Nature's lore and store the knowledge inside our hearts, Vanessia had said.

It's our purpose for this reincarnation.

This reincarnation, that was the point. Suggesting the Hundred-Handed were not reborn into their own cult and thus begging the question, if not back here, where did their saintly souls go? As a flock of finches swooped down to drink from the shallows, she remembered Dora remarking that, in her view, the painting and arranging of Clytie's body was a clumsy attempt to imitate the previous murders.

Until now, Claudia had assumed the killer was male, but as both Gabali and the Oak Priestess had taken pains to point out, no sexual assault had taken place and was that what the Hundred-Handed were hiding? That they knew — or suspected — she'd been killed by a woman? One, in fact, of their own . . .?

I know, the note by her bedside had read and despite the heat of midsummer, Claudia shivered.

She couldn't see them. She couldn't hear them. But around the dark side of the cave, spirits hovered like bees.

Waiting to lead another soul down to be judged.

Nine

To be shunned was to be voted invisible, and once invisible the outcast was forbidden to speak, wash, even worship within his own community.

The length of expulsion was determined by a number of factors, though obviously it was influenced by the proportion of black pebbles over white in the voting jar. As a rule, the higher the number, the longer the exile and though a unanimous vote could result in a lifetime ban, such cases were rare. Shunning was intended as a deterrent. A hope that, by being forced to live on the edge of society for anything from a few weeks to a couple of years, with the penitent obliged to fend for himself and unable to communicate with friends and family – even drink water upstream from them for fear of polluting them with his guilt – he (and it was always a he) would return home humble, contrite, but most of all an example to others that rules were laid down for a reason.

Murder and rape were capital crimes, but there was no room in society for the likes of assault, theft or the sabotage of another man's crops, nor would extortion, slander, cowardice or arson be tolerated, either. For moving his neighbour's boundary stones, a farmer might expect to be shunned for three years, since he had callously planned to enrich his own life at the expense of another's and used deceit under the guise of friendship. However, falsely accusing one's sister-in-law of adultery might result in a couple of months, while stealing livestock or grain fell somewhere in between.

No one ever expected small communities to live in close proximity without flare-ups of temper and temperament, the Whisperer reflected. It was a question of weighing the damage.

If accusations of adultery went ignored, what level of

70

malicious lies might then follow? If one man moved his boundary by five yards and wasn't punished, why not claim fifteen yards? Fifty? In the eyes of the tribes, shunning was simply a piece of legal machinery. When your harvester starts bending the corn instead of cutting it, don't you dismantle the box and sharpen the metal teeth back to points? It was the same with recalcitrant tribe members. Unscrew them from the community, clean them up and then, once they're in a fit state to resume their original purpose, connect them back up to the machine.

The young patriot barely heard the chatter of jays in the branches or the distant thwack of an axe. He heard only the words of the Chieftains inside his head, declaring him guilty of treason against his own tribe and sentencing him to a lifetime of shunning. Even now, he wondered they could face themselves, hypocritical bastards that they were.

'It's you who've sold the people out, not me!'

They were the ones who advocated a laying down of arms before the Roman advance. They were the ones who insisted the tribes kowtowed to Roman rules and paid Roman bloody taxes. *Taxes?* Lenus almighty, we work our own soil, grow our own grain, cut our own timber, raise our own beasts and then have to pay ten per cent for the privilege?

'What right do these oppressors have, tramping in here, riding roughshod over good, honest people then telling them how to live their own lives?' he'd demanded. 'Are they gods? Superheroes? Tell me, are they monsters? Demons? Supernatural beings who cannot be slain?'

He'd challenged the Chieftains to deny it, but all he got back was the usual crap about how the Roman militia protected the Nation far better than they'd defended themselves, how ten per cent tax was a trifle compared to the profits Aquitania was reaping thanks to the new trade links and how the tribes were stronger, healthier, better educated under the eagle. Surely, they asked, he could see this?

'Fuck, no! All I see are cowards who cover themselves in metal and tell you it's glory. Bullies who oppress you and tell you it's freedom. What I see,' he'd told them, 'are jackals who feed off your flesh while telling you they're cuddly puppies, and by Lenus, you cretins believe them.'

'Do not talk to us of bullying,' the Chieftains had countered. 'We have seen for ourselves the weals you left on your wife.'

Women again, and which one of those bitches in the village had been telling tales this time? he wondered. Cooking up mischief, when they should have been cooking a decent meal for their family. Spreading rumours, when they should have been spreading their legs for their husbands. Too much time on their hands, that's the trouble.

'Nothing she didn't deserve,' he'd told the Chieftains.

Bloody Romans, this was. Putting ideas in his wife's head that women could answer back.

'And your children? Did they deserve their beatings, too?'

'Discipline's breaking down under these bastards and you're castigating *me* for enforcing it in my own home?' He couldn't believe what he was hearing. 'You ask whether I'm blind to progress, but it's you who can't see that Rome's cut off your balls under the pretext of friendship.'

His loyalty was to his bloodline, he thundered. Where was theirs?

'I won't stand by while the tribes are annihilated through your self-centred apathy. You say trade benefits our people? I say they're selling their souls. You say peace is a good thing? I say it's man's duty to fight, not only to defend what is his, but to take from his neighbour if his neighbour is weak, for weakness cannot be tolerated in any society, least of all ours!'

The Chieftains had glanced at each other, but more in pity, he'd thought, than discomfort.

'You are still a young man,' they said. 'You have a wife, who will be married off to another should you be cast out, and whose husband will raise your children as his own. Think carefully. You are denying yourself, as well as them, the chance to speak to or hug them again, and you might wish to consider those consequences before we cast our votes.'

'Men are born to be warriors and though my sons might be forbidden from speaking to me, you cannot strip away their respect!'

As they grew up, they'd see it was their father who led

Aquitania to freedom and drove the oppressors from Gaul. Standing in that circle of longhouses, surrounded by brow-beaten weaklings, the Whisperer's heart had swelled as he pictured his sons growing into warriors in his own image. Tearing up law courts, pulling down temples, putting an end to the trade that brought foreign ways into the region. What use were aqueducts anyway, when women were perfectly capable of fetching water from the river in buckets? Thanks to him, there would be a return to the old ways, when life was simple, the only tongue heard was their own and men went to war, as they should do. A return, moreover, to a morality in which children obeyed their fathers and wives didn't dare question how their husbands spent the household income.

He snorted. Stupid bitch couldn't understand that men drank to relieve the pressures of raising a family, that it was *them* who went out to work, *them* who deserved a treat for their slaving. Ach, the man who took on that lazy cow, good luck to him, that's what he said. Let some other poor bugger listen to her whining on about having no money for food because he'd drunk it away. Let some other poor bastard find out what it's like, coming home late at night and wanting his woman, then having to fight for what's his because she objected to being bent over the bloody table or was cramped up with a toothache. Who the hell wanted to look at her fucking face anyway? Good riddance to that selfish bitch.

'If you cowards won't back me,' the Whisperer had shouted to all the tribespeople who'd gathered to vote, 'there are enough Aquitani who aren't happy shouldering this foreign yoke. Who needs you?'

It was them who'd need him, watch and see. Them who'd bloody need him. Because who had united the Nations, eh? All right, some of these hotheads were bitter for all the wrong reasons, but who was it who'd stirred up passion among the dispassionate? Who'd inspired the disenchanted? Who'd roused the anger that had lain dormant for a whole genera-tion? Through him – through his carefully executed crimes and his extensive contacts – an arsenal of weapons and supplies had been amassed, traps set, pits dug, nets sewn that would spring down from the trees, and when the battle cry rose up, the Oppressors wouldn't know what bloody hit them.

And if the Chieftains thought shunning would teach him a lesson, they were right. Instead of standing on the steps of the basilica and railing against his people's indifference, the Whisperer had adopted patience and stealth in his quest to rid Gaul of these pigs. Changing his name, changing his identity and being all things to all men, he moved from daylight into the shadows, conducting his business in secret and discussing rebellion in whispers. Oh, but soon. He smiled. Soon he'd be free to emerge from the darkness and lift his face to the sun. No more shadows. No more whispers. Only screams.

The screams of Roman women as his sword ripped their throats and hacked the heads of their children clean off their shoulders. The screams of Roman babies, the screams of filthy half-breeds, but most especially the screams of the Hundred-Handed, who'd done so much to suck the power from men, even to preaching that all life in the universe stemmed from a woman. Well, let's see how swiftly this earth mother rides to their rescue when their eyes are being gouged out and their precious gesticulating hands are chopped off. By the axe of the Thunder God, he'd leave so much carnage in his wake that the beehive of Rome would buzz wild with anger. And once grief and outrage had blinded it to all reason, that's when the Whisperer would slough off his disguise and lead the charge for freedom.

No armour. Not for him. He'd ride down on them shirtless to prove he had nothing to fear, and it wouldn't only be Rome who paid the price. The Chiefs would pay dearly for not backing him. Them, and that bitch of a wife.

He thought back to this morning, to the slave block in Santonum, and spat. He didn't hold with these Roman-style auctions. Slaves should be captured in combat and brought back as trophies. Let the bastards understand every day for the rest of their lives who was boss. But what he wouldn't have given right then to put the cow that he'd married on that auction block and see her sold into bondage.

That was another lesson he'd learned since that voting jug was upended with not a single white pebble in sight. Just how many different ways there were to hurt women. How many methods by which he could inflict pain.

Well, let's see the bitch answer back now. See who calls him a drunk and a loser, then.

As the gong summoned the new male slaves to assemble, the Whisperer counted the hours until he set the beehive buzzing.

And could finally step out of the shadows.

Ten

'Souls?'

Given that her role was devoted entirely to death, Ailm seemed the obvious person to ask, and it was no sacrifice on Claudia's part that the questioning took place in what the Hundred-Handed termed the Hall of Purification – and everyone else called a bathhouse.

'It's not often a Roman enquires what happens to a Gaul's soul,' Ailm added drily, 'but since you ask, its future is determined by Avita the Mother, who lives deep in the earth and breathes life into all living things.'

Unlike the bathhouses Claudia was accustomed to, this was no stone-built complex of steam rooms, promenades and gymnasia. No works of art hung on its walls, no statues lined its entrance, no attendants wafted round with wine and sweetmeats. Indeed, there was little to differentiate the Hall from the rest of the rectangular, windowless, single-roomed buildings within the sacred precinct apart from the hyssop that decked the lintel for purification. Lit by candles tinted with green dye and scented with fragrant oils, and with its interior walls insulated with colourful woven withies, the Hall oozed peace and serenity. Begging the question, how stressful could watching trees be?

'Souls have three paths,' Ailm said. 'First, those that are judged to be honest and pure Avita ensures are reborn into a better life.'

While she explained the system, a young girl with a cap of blonde, almost white, hair helped Claudia to undress, then escorted her to a wooden table which was warm to the touch and on which Claudia was invited to lie face down. Carefully positioning her arms and brushing her hair free of her neck, the girl then placed a row of heated stones down the length of Claudia's spine. It was not a therapy she had encountered before and she wondered who'd first thought of laying hot stones on a backbone. And why it took them so long.

'Those whose deeds encompassed wickedness and sin she returns to a life of misery,' Ailm explained, 'that they might make amends and find redemption.'

Her voice made no distinction between those who'd been good and those who'd been bad, but that didn't surprise Claudia in the slightest. Remembering how the Death Priestess had distanced herself from Claudia and the others last night, keeping her hands folded neatly in front of her, she'd sensed a woman who preferred observation to partic-ipation, and the repressed rarely voice their opinions. And yet was Ailm repressed? Her black robe had the sharpest pleats she'd ever seen, and did you see the filigree on those bracelets and rings? There were whorls and serpents and figures-of-eight that must have sent the silversmith blind as he squinted, while the embosswork on her belt of linked gold chains smacked of a woman who took immense pride in her appearance. Were women like that repressed? Claudia did not believe so.

'Finally,' Ailm said, 'those souls that are found to contain nothing but evil are thrown to the three-headed dragon that stalks the Underworld.'

'Who feeds off the heads of his enemies and slakes his thirst with the blood of the wicked,' the fair-haired girl added cheerfully.

'Thank you, Elusa.'

Ailm didn't sound like she meant it, but the blonde didn't seem to notice the edge in her voice.

'Don't forget the exception to the paths of incarnation, O Lady of the Yew,' she said, replacing the rocks on Ailm's back with fresh ones.

'I had not forgotten, Elusa. Now massage my head, if you will.'

As pale skin plunged into the rich swirl of peat-coloured hair, Claudia noticed that the dye was so artful that not a single silver strand was showing through, not even at the roots, and Ailm was the only woman she'd known who wore cosmetics in the bathhouse. They'd surely cake to a crisp in this steam.

'The exception Elusa is referring to is that every priestess who qualifies for the fifty elite is reborn as a raven.' The Death Priestess smiled contentedly. 'Ravens mate for life, did you know that?'

The stones on Claudia's back suddenly cooled. For binding themselves in servitude to the earth, the Hundred-Handed's sole reward was for their souls to be given freedom to fly? That was *it*? What they'd been forced to forsake in this world would be theirs in the next? And maybe it wasn't so much that the priestesses didn't care about Clytie. Maybe they'd never been taught how . . .

'No,' she said, as Elusa helped her back into her robe. 'No, I didn't know that.'

'The penalty for slaying a raven is severe,' Ailm said, turning her head to face the wall. 'The perpetrator is cast into the Pit of Reflection, as are runaway slaves and, of course, any man found inside the walls of our precinct.'

At the door, the blonde girl glanced nervously over her shoulder to check that Ailm wasn't looking, then whispered in Claudia's ear.

'So are any women who try to escape,' she said. 'They're thrown into the Pit of Reflection, too.'

There were tears in Elusa's eyes as she turned away. Not of sorrow, though. Tears of pain.

Late rooks cawed from the treetops and the last vestige of sunlight leached from the sky as Claudia slipped away from dinner pleading a headache. In stark contrast to the dormitories, the kitchens and the rest of the buildings that made up the College, the dining complex consisted of a series of large and small rooms arranged round three sides of a courtyard, and it was here that the priestesses and initiates, novices and workers broke their fast, took their midday meal and celebrated the close of another day with their dinner. Claudia had never seen anything like this complex, indeed had never heard of people eating like this, and yet its very oddness rang a bell. Three sides of a courtyard . . . Three sides of a courtyard . . .

Architecture wasn't the only thing that niggled at the edge of her brain, either. Looking at Sallie, the Willow Priestess, dressed in catkin green and seated, appropriately enough, between Fearn and Dora, Claudia was reminded of the ancient proverb.

When tempests blow, the oak might fall but the willow just bends in the wind.

Willow wasn't merely supple and easy to transplant, thus symbolizing a capacity to adapt and adjust. Willow was one of nature's true survivors, and taking in the blonde's slender figure and long slim fingers, she realized that the girl Pod met by the cave, the girl in the pink robe called Sarra, was the spitting image. The Willow priestess was her mother.

But with so many women crammed into a relatively tight space, all of them clucking like hens in a coop, it was impossible to sustain an intelligent conversation for more than two minutes. Perhaps that was the designer's intention? But from casually chatting to Beth about how long she'd been in the job, an interesting detail was thrown up.

'I took office almost to the day that Rome took up official occupation in this province,' she'd told Claudia with a laugh. 'And whilst it's not for me to say whether that was propitious or not, I do feel fate had a strong input in the matter.'

Fate? Claudia wondered. Or a more secular hand at work?

Promotion in their society was accorded by age rather than merit. Now if the previous Birch Priestess had been anti-Roman, for instance, while an ambitious initiate held opposing views, how easy would it have been to nudge the ailing (or even not so ailing) incumbent towards divine ravenhood and fill the gap that was left before another priestess died and she was allocated that role instead?

Studying once more Beth's youthful figure and chestnut-brown hair, the Head of the Hundred-Handed didn't look like a murderess.

But then again, few of us do . . .

At the tip of the arrowhead of rock, the first bats of the evening flittered and an owl swooped low over the treetops. It was too late to investigate this mysterious Pit of Reflection, but she resolved to search out Swarbric at first light, because if anyone could tell her about the punishment that brought anguish to a pretty girl's face, it was the man in charge of College security.

Hedgehogs snorted mating calls in the undergrowth, mice and voles searched for beetles among the crispy leaf litter, but night hadn't cloaked the landscape completely. And in the midsummer twilight, Claudia could just about make out a curvaceous figure hurrying home to the College. In the fading light, haste was understandable, and even in the dusk, she saw that Mavor was flushed and dishevelled. Yet she wasn't scurrying home down the hill from the village where the male slaves were kept, and, judging from her expression, her untidiness did not stem from passion. Alarm, Claudia thought, was too strong a word. But that was certainly concern on the redhead's face, and if she could 'just happen' to meet her at the gate and engineer a conversation—

'Oof!'

Something grunted as it collided with her bosom when she turned round.

'Jupiter, Juno and Mars, the last thing I expected in the sacred precinct at dusk was to find myself tripping over something short, green and exceedingly solid.'

'Then next time watch where you're going!' the object retorted, rubbing its nose.

Claudia grabbed him by the arm and dragged him against the wall. 'Gurdo, what the bloody hell do you think you're playing at?' she hissed. 'If Beth finds you up here—'

'Ah, don't get your knicker cloth in such a twizzle. I've got the run of this place, or didn't they tell you?'

'No, they didn't tell me,' she snapped. 'But it explains why you go skulking around in the dark in search of cheap thrills.'

'Can I help it if you're not flat-chested?'

'I hope you broke your bloody nose, you little green pervert.'

From the corner of her eye, she noticed Mavor straighten her robe, push back her hair and saunter into the Dining Hall with her normal composure. Damn.

'Why does the Guardian of the Sacred Spring have access where other men don't?' she asked.

80

'Lady, in the eyes of the Gauls, dwarves aren't real men,' Gurdo said and in the moonlight she saw mischief dancing in his eye. 'But like my dear old mother used to say, if life's intent on throwing eggs at you, make sure you catch 'em then whisk up an omelette, coz that way you'll never go hungry.'

'Have you become a good fielder or just a good cook?'

'Me, Lofty Legs,' he tapped his chest with his finger, 'I'm both, and before you accuse me of being vain and fanciful, which *also* happens to be true, let me tell you, life might not have dealt me the fairest of dice, but I'm a free man and *that* counts for a lot.'

'Guardian of one of Aquitania's most important religious sites, freedom of the College, Pod, food, shelter—' Claudia reckoned up the tally on her fingers.

'No persecution, no being made to turn tricks.' He twisted up one half of his face. 'See? The dice of life don't fall too badly for Gurdo.'

She thought about the dwarves given mock swords and forced to clown around in the arena. Until now, she'd laughed with the rest of the crowd . . .

'What about women?'

Gurdo let out the dirtiest laugh she'd ever heard. 'You'd be surprised how many local lasses have been healed by that water then insist on showing their gratitude! But if you're asking, do I want a woman fluffing round me day and night, making my bed, washing my shirts, sweeping my floors, then I've got 'em coming out of my ears. The College girls do all that, since these caves run deep under their sacred ground, so I lack for nothing, Lofty Legs, trust me.'

'I'd rather trust a nest of spitting cobras,' she told him truthfully. 'But how come Pod's still free?'

'That lad was knee-high to a crab when I found him wandering the reed beds, naked as the day that he was born. Three, four weeks passed and still no one came forward to claim him, so I took him on. Raised him as my own from that day on, and I told Beth straight. The boy remains free-born or else I'm off. And,' he glowered, 'since the Hundred-Handed *do* believe us little folk have inbuilt healing powers, she didn't want the spring to lose its lucky charm.'

'Although I'm sure you pointed out how attractive the alternatives were for a dwarf under Roman occupation?'

'Is it my fault these women aren't streetwise?'

Claudia wasn't sure that was entirely the case.

'What happens to male babies?' she asked.

Gurdo sniffed. 'Stand here in the daylight and to every horizon on the clearest day, that's College land you'll be looking at. Most of it's forest, giving them timber and fuel and yielding fruit trees and nuts, but there's fields of grain to be cared for, livestock to tend, vegetable gardens that require back-breaking work.'

'You're saying the boys grow up as slaves, as opposed to those girls who don't qualify for the fifty elite and merely provide a free labour source?'

'You want to be careful, that tongue of yours'll rip your cheeks to shreds, but no, that's not what I'm saying.'

He folded his arms over his chest.

'Have you any idea how many mouths there are to feed between this College and the men? These vast lands allow the Hundred-Handed to be self-sufficient and in a good year they might sell a few hams, but because it's mostly forest, like the rest of Aqui-bloody-tania, they don't have anything that other Gauls in the region want.'

Something flipped over in Claudia's stomach. 'Except babies.'

'Who are you to judge, huh?' This time the finger prodded her breastbone. 'We all trade something we're not proud of, lady.'

She thought of her marriage vows to Gaius Seferius. Of trading her beauty, her wit, her youth, her vitality for a man who was three times her age, three times her girth and whose wine business earned him a fortune.

'You have all the qualities for being reborn as a wasp,' she told Gurdo.

'Skip the flattery, it only goes to my head, and when you're my size, Lofty Legs, that's not a long journey.'

He disappeared into the blackness, whistling happily, while high overhead Hercules strode through the heavens, the Swan spread her wings and the Pole Star twinkled like torchlight. Twisting her head up to the blackness, Claudia could see why the lovely Sarra was worried. Like the dark half of the cave, Pod was out of bounds, too, because chirpy and virile though he was, the elf was a free man, not a slave. And free men want a say when it comes to raising their children. They really don't *like* their sons being sold on.

Once again, though, their clandestine courting emphasized that, whilst advocating peace through the worship of nature, the Hundred-Handed operated rules which brooked no disobedience. Claudia understood how such guidelines might reinforce their sense of identity and lend weight to their gentle authority, but what lengths would they go to protect their mysteries? What price would the dwarf's son and the Willow Priestess's daughter have to pay for their forbidden love?

Yet for all Pod's intensity, it was impossible to forget the granite in his eyes after Sarra had left, still trailing her spray of battered white roses. Or the fact that he'd picked up sign language from watching her.

It was only much later, as she made her way to bed, that Claudia remembered that it was Pod who'd found Clytie's body.

This time there was no arched-back, spitting, cross-eyed demon to impede the search. Deft hands rifled through soft linen underwear and smooth cotton robes, holding up pendants set with amber, earrings shaped like leaves and bracelets inlaid with mother-of-pearl. They flipped open a fan of peacock feathers and wafted the air for a while. They held up finely dyed sandals and examined the tooling. They eased the stopper off an alabaster phial and dabbed rich Judaean perfume on their own wrists.

Then they lifted the mattress, searched through the satchel, poked under pillows and sheets. They checked under the couch, behind the cushions, searched for secret compartments in the jewel chest.

Eventually, they reached for the wax tablet beside the bed and flipped open the hinge. Picking up the metal stylus, they began to write.

In the centre of the world, between earth, sky and sea, at the point where the realms of the universe meet, Rumour gathered her friends all around her. Envy, Confusion, Malice, Resentment, Flippancy, Folly and Pride. Huddling close together for warmth, for Rumour's house has no doors and the windows no shutters, their murmurings echoed through the brass chambers like the sound of the sea's waves heard at a distance, or the last rumbles of Jupiter's thunder.

But in the heat of their embrace, Sorrow was smothered, Truth became suffocated and Remorse died in the womb.

Falsehood poured another glass of poison and toasted her own success.

Eleven

Swarbric was engaged in conversation with a youth with a fuzz of dark curls when Claudia approached his hut shortly after breakfast. Actually, she thought, conversation might be too strong a word. What Swarbric was actually engaged in was grabbing the youth by the fabric of his collar, pressing the boy's back against the wall and snarling into his face. Which, when you looked closely, was quite a handsome young face. But then she'd never seen so many hunks to the square mile before.

Having taken a stroll round the perimeter of the village on the way to his hut, from glimpses through the palisade she'd noticed that the workforce was universally young, universally strapping, universally unblemished and universally intelligent. Perfect sires for the priestessly foals, and yet not one of them over the age of forty. What must it feel like? she wondered. What must it feel like to be valued for your physical attributes and your core characteristics, but never, not once, for yourself?

She hid behind a holly bush and watched the exchange. Overhead, low clouds began to cover the sky.

'It doesn't matter whether you like it or not,' Swarbric was growling. 'You bloody well do your job.'

'Never,' the boy hissed back. 'I'm not some sodding bear that can be forced to dance or be beaten to within an inch of its life.'

'Wrong, Connal, that's exactly what you are. See these?' Swarbric indicated his own tight linen pants. 'See this?' He ruffled his shirt whose drawstring hung open halfway to his waist, revealing the sort of chest armourers used when fashioning models for breastplates. 'This is the livery of a performing bear, Connal, and you either get used to it—'

85

'Not all of us are like you,' the boy spat, 'and maybe when you fall in love, you'll know how it feels.'

'Love! Do you think any of these women cares a copper quadran for you? They don't know the meaning of the bloody word.'

'That's where you're wrong! Elusa loves me, I love Elusa, and somehow we're going to get out of – ow!'

The youth's face twisted in pain as Swarbric tightened his grip on his collar, choking Connal with his own shirt.

'Listen to me, you stupid bastard, there'll be no talk of running away, do you hear?'

'The hell I—'

'Do you know what they'll do to Elusa, if they find out what you're planning?' he rasped. 'Because they will, son. They *always* find out. These trees have ears, they have eyes, trust me, the Hundred-Handed know everything. They pool secrets the same way they pool their knowledge of nature, the same bloody way they pool us, and what the trees don't give away, pillow talk does. Now for gods' sakes, Connal, grow up.'

He released his grip and his anger drained with it.

'Meet with Elusa, love with Elusa, but you damn well do what you have to do, son, and you do it with good grace or believe me, they'll sell you faster than you can say knife, then you'll never see Elusa again.'

'I know you mean well – ' Connal wiped his nose with the back of his hand – 'but times are changing, Swarbric, just look at us. You're German, I'm a Briton, the world's opening up, even for the Hundred-Handed. With Santonum having trade links all over the world, thanks to sailors' tales, to merchants, from the Gauls travelling themselves, people don't accept blind authority any more.'

'If you mean Elusa—'

'Not only her. Lots of the younger ones have minds of their own.'

'We all have minds of our own, son. It's our bodies that are in thrall, that's the trouble, and the Hundred-Handed are slaves to their system every bit as much as we are.'

'But—'

'But nothing. Don't you imagine Beth was as passionate

when she was Elusa's age? Don't you imagine Dora or Fearn or Ailm had the same fire in their bellies as you have? As the younger ones have today?'

The youth shrugged one surly shoulder. 'They might have, I suppose.'

'Then no more talk of escape, right? You've only been here a year, son, you're still learning. Now go on with you.' He gave him an affectionate shove back to the village. 'And trust me, Connal. You'll get used to it.'

Would he, though? Claudia wondered, as the boy slouched miserably off up the hill. Would he ever get used to the concept of never being able to marry, never being able to settle down, never raising kids of his own? Croesus almighty, if the men were bitter and resentful in youth, what on earth were they like in middle age? How poisoned would they be in their dotage?

Her mind pictured the young girl with blonde, almost white hair, laying hot stones on her back, and the pain that had filled the girl's eyes. Swarbric was wrong. Elusa *did* care for Connal, but was it hot, searing puppy love, something deep and eternal or a novelty which would pass once duty superseded it? At the moment, though, the definition of Elusa's feelings was irrelevant. All that mattered was that the girl believed herself deeply in love and was prepared to sacrifice everything to be with him. Yet another forbidden fruit.

Claudia looked round the valley, at the willows, the iris, the dragonflies and the bees. She looked at the water gushing out of the rock. At the stream that danced its way through the meadow.

And saw not paradise.

But Hell.

Where all manner of dark creatures slithered. Including fear . . .

The night before, when she'd returned to her bedroom – one of several small private chambers sectioned off in the longhouse that served as the guest quarters – the note was the first thing she'd noticed. As, indeed, she'd been meant to, since a candle had been lit adjacent to the writing tablet and the stylus laid elegantly across it.

I know, it had read. But now seven new words had been added. *I just cannot decide who to tell.*

Since she was the only guest at the moment, that narrowed the list.

To approximately five hundred women.

Of whom one was also a murderess.

'The Pit of Reflection?' Swarbric seemed surprised by her question. 'Yes, of course I can take you there.' He tipped his prematurely grey head to one side and raised one eyebrow suggestively. 'I can assure you, the Lady Claudia won't lack for privacy up there.'

'Sorry to disappoint you, but it's only the Pit that the Lady Claudia's interested in.'

'We'll see,' he said cheerfully. 'But I have to warn you, it's quite a hike.'

He wasn't kidding, though quite how the seams of his pants stood the strain of the climb, she wasn't entirely sure. 'And it's up here?' she wheezed.

'Nope.' He gave his short sword an airy jab towards the opposite hill. 'It's up there.'

Maybe it was the sweat in her eyes, but – 'Wouldn't it have been easier to have walked *round* the arrowhead to reach that second hill?'

'Much easier and a damn sight faster, as well.' He helped her down a slope that would have given the average mountain goat palpitations. 'But that way I wouldn't get to hold your hand or have you lean against me, now would I?'

The old joke sprang to mind: If I said you had a beautiful body, would you hold it against me?

'I'll say one thing, Swarbric. You don't lack for confidence.'

'No, ma'am, that I don't.'

But for all his cockiness – or maybe because of it – she imagined there would be many among the Hundred-Handed who went to sleep at night dreaming of that wide, disarming grin.

'Do all novices go through the tomboy phase like Clytie and the other three?' she wheezed, leaning forward to catch her breath.

'Clytie wasn't a tomboy,' he said, resting his foot on a rock and letting his shirt billow in the breeze. 'In fact, she wasn't a bit like Vanessia and the others.'

Claudia had got her wind back, but pretended she hadn't. 'How so?'

'Put it this way,' he said. 'Our Clytie was never caned or put into detention. Our Clytie would mend the tears in Aridella's smock and clear up the honey Lin spilled, and she'd re-make their beds and re-wash their underclothes, and every morning our Clytie went out spotless and tidy, and at night came home exactly the same.'

'Was she clever?'

'No idea, I can't follow the signing, but that child was certainly conscientious, if that's what you mean.'

'The class swot?'

'Like I said.' His mouth twisted up. 'Conscientious.'

And that was clearly the end of that conversation.

Halfway up the second hill, Swarbric offered to carry the Lady Claudia the rest of the way. Three-quarters of the way, the Lady Claudia wished that she had let him. Overhead, magpies chattered in the oak trees. She had a feeling that they were laughing. But at the top, the woods opened out to a wide, grassy clearing in which limestone outcrops were dotted with poppies, where lizards basked in the warmth of the sun and where birds deafened the eardrums with their warbling. Chaffinches, goldfinches and blackcaps.

'This is beautiful,' she puffed, sinking down onto one of the rocks and sending a family of lizards diving for cover. 'Absolutely—' She jumped up and covered her nose with her hand. 'Oh dear god, what *is* that?'

'The putrefying remains of wild animals,' Swarbric laughed, steering her downwind of the smell. 'Young ones, usually, who hadn't learned prudence by the time they fell in and discovered it was too late to learn it afterwards.'

Still shielding her face, Claudia peered into the diamond-shaped fissure from which the stench was emanating. 'Curiosity killed the cat, eh?'

'And the lynx and the wolf and once, even, a bear.'

It looked innocuous enough, that hole in the rock. Why

'reflection', she wondered. And why 'pit'? To her surprise, the hand that clamped round her arm and jerked her back was neither gentle nor seductive.

'I don't advise standing too close.'

Searching round for a loose stone, the German tossed it into the aperture. Claudia counted four before she heard the dull thud.

'That is deep.'

'That is very deep,' he corrected. 'The opening's narrow, but don't be fooled. Like a pear, the chamber inside gets bigger the further it goes down and the rockface, like the rest of the region, is sheer. Once a penitent is thrown in, it's impossible to climb out.'

The Pit of Reflection, shaped not like a pear, but a teardrop, she decided. With plenty of time to reflect on one's sins, stuck inside a dank, dark hole with just a crack of daylight above to mark the passage of time and with only old bones for companionship.

'What's the average sentence?' she asked, tossing in a rock of her own and waiting for it to land.

'You don't know, do you?' The grin dropped from his face. Every trace of the cavalier had vanished. 'When I said it's impossible to climb out, I mean *impossible*.' Swarbric drew a deep breath. 'They don't use it often and never, thank the Fire God, willingly, but this is how the College deals with execution.'

Something primordial slithered inside.

'By distancing themselves from the act and thus ensuring none of those dainty little hundred hands gets dirty?'

It was arguably the nastiest form of punishment she had ever encountered, certainly the slowest and the most painful. Forgetting the possibility of breaking a bone or three in the fall, the prisoner was doomed to die of thirst and starvation in a pit filled with rotted remains. Reflection, my arse, she thought bitterly. This is murder by any other name. Murder, moreover, through the slowest torture known to man.

The penalty for slaying a raven is severe. Ailm's voice floated back, but Claudia remembered how the Death Priestess had turned her head to the wall when she spoke.

The perpetrator is cast into the Pit of Reflection, as are runaway slaves and, of course, any man found inside the walls of our precinct.

Small wonder Elusa was terrified.

So are any women who try to escape, she had said. *They're thrown into the Pit of Reflection, too.*

'I've seen enough,' she said, turning away.

This land was beautiful, the women ditto, they were graceful, elegant, rotten to the core.

'Maybe I can show you some other less unpleasant but equally clandestine sites?' As he offered his arm, his shirt contrived to fall open even further. 'There's a little waterfall not far from here that is mossy and shady, as pretty as you are, or I could take you to a glade in the forest where—'

'You enjoy your job, don't you?'

The young German had 'choose me, choose me' written all over him. Like willow, he, too, was one of nature's survivors.

'Let's say I've become skilled at it,' he said, throwing in a winning, lopsided grin for good measure.

'What about the other side of the work?' she asked, as they retraced their steps back to the College. 'Doesn't it bother you, playing policemen to your fellow slaves?'

'My task is to stop people from getting into the grounds, not getting out.'

This time they followed the track below the arrowhead of rock, lined by sweet chestnuts and where peacock butterflies flitted and a dove cooed out its sleepy call.

'That's a job for the local Gauls,' Swarbric said. 'They volunteer to take turns to guard the men in the village.'

That explained why was it so hard for them to escape. Dedicated followers of College philosophy would prove more effective than the fiercest mastiff.

'How come you can take time off to show me the sights?' Claudia asked.

'Because there's only one road down to the gorge and therefore only one way in. Guards posted at points on the hills warn us of impending visitors by blowing a horn.'

She'd heard the blasts. Simply taken no notice.

'Do all the men get the same amount of free time as you?'

Swarbric leaned close and grinned. 'Teacher's pet,' he confided in a whisper. 'I get special dispensation.'

Special duties. Independent living. Teacher's pet indeed. But which teacher? she wondered. Surely only the pentagram priestesses had the authority to give that kind of permission.

'The job carries an awful lot of trust,' she pointed out. 'What did you do to earn it? Throw people screaming into pits?'

'Not me.' He leapt up to pluck an early apple from an overhead bough and tossed it to her. 'Sharp, but surprisingly tasty.'

After seeing the pit, Claudia had no appetite. She tossed it back. 'So if you don't throw them in, then who does?'

'Down here, I have very little contact with the men in the village,' he said, crunching, 'so I can't say who has the dubious honour these days.'

'Not the locals, though?'

'The Pit of Reflection is the Hundred-Handed's last resort, but it is also their ultimate deterrent.' He tossed the core into the undergrowth. 'As I've been singled out as Guardian of the Sacred Gate, so others are selected as Guardians of the Sacred Trust.'

'A noble title for an ignoble task, but if you expect me to believe that you don't know the name of the man who's been elected as the College executioner, you must think I'm stupid.'

Swarbric spun round on his heel and stepped in front of her. 'I find persistence a heady quality in a woman,' he said huskily, 'and as much as I'd like to be pressed further' – his grin was pure wolf – 'I honestly don't know who's taken over from the Spaniard, and maybe that's because I'm much happier not knowing whose killer eyes I look into.'

Claudia looked up so quickly that she tripped. 'Did you say Spaniard?'

'Odd character.' He caught her, even though she was in no danger of falling, and seemed in no great hurry to let her go. 'Didn't much mix with the rest of the men and didn't much enjoy his work with the ladies.'

She wriggled free, yet could still feel where the German's hands had held her firm at the shoulders.

'I suppose that's the reason they sold him,' he added, with a rueful cluck of the tongue. 'A man needs to be content in his work, even a slave.'

Happiness wasn't her concern. 'This Spaniard. I don't suppose you can remember his name?'

'Ribolo, why?'

'Ribolo!'

Mistaking her sigh for something other than relief, Swarbric hooked a ringlet that had come astray and tucked it back under its ivory hairpin.

'*Ri* – ' he let his fingertip slide on down her cheek – '*bo* – ' under her chin '*lo*.'

As it began to trace a line down her throat, Claudia moved away. 'Good heavens, is that the time? If I don't hurry, I'll be late for Mavor.'

Swarbric glanced up at the sky, where clouds obscured the sun that kept track of the hours. 'Mavor is good,' he said, and his eyes were dancing. 'In fact, our Bird Priestess is better than good.'

Now *that* was where she'd seen the redhead coming home from last night. From the direction of Swarbric's hut.

'Though a man's hands are stronger and can massage far better than a woman's, but don't take my word for it. Ask Mavor.'

'I'm sure she'll give you a glowing report.' In fact, she was sure they all would.

'If you need me at any time, Lady Claudia, you know where to find me.' He performed a theatrical bow in farewell. 'And I was wrong about it being Ribolo, you know. He was the Guardian of the Trust before last, and anyway, he came from Rhodes, now I think about it.'

The first spot of rain started to fall. Claudia did not feel it.

'And the last Guardian?' she asked. But why bother, when she already knew?

'Oh, he was a Spaniard, I got that part right,' Swarbric said, as he strode back up the path. 'But that executioner went by the name of Gabali.'

In the Governor's Palace, intelligence was coming in thick and fast – and from every direction.

The Aquitani were going to attack! They were going to attack tomorrow, at midsummer, Rome had better be ready!

The Druids were dissenting! They were angry, because witchcraft was rife among the Hundred-Handed, Rome had better do something!

Those three assassins were mercenaries! They'd been hired by one of the Governor's own generals, Rome was under attack from within!

Orbilio's staff processed the informants' claims with weary formality and paid the rumours no heed. Every two weeks, it seemed, stories would surface about the Aquitani's latest plans for insurrection, invariably giving dates, locations, numbers of rebels, their methods of attack – and every time it amounted to nothing. This was all part of the Scorpion's plan, of course. Spreading rumours then watching Rome dance to his jig, knowing they'd be wasting their time, money and most importantly precious manpower while they chased after shadows, but, equally, knowing that they could not afford to dismiss any of this out of hand.

Convinced that this latest intelligence was the same bull-shit, and seriously doubting that that pathetic raggle-taggle band of self-styled warriors could inflict more than a pin-prick, much less free Gaul in the three short months that remained of the campaigning season, the Security Police were still taking no chances. There was no room for complacency within the Roman administration. Wild-goose chases went with the territory. So with painstaking patience, Orbilio's staff logged the details of this impending midsummer attack and passed them on to the army.

As for the Druids, that was a political issue. Claims of witchery would certainly need close investigation, and if found to be true the sentence was punishable by death. But the Druids were crafty old buggers, not above spreading lies if it suited their purpose, and since Rome backed the peace-loving priestesses over their sectarian bigotry, large pinches of salt were required when it came to information purporting to come from them. But if the Druids resented the loss of political, religious and secular control over their fellow Gauls, they only had themselves to blame. Rome was quite happy for them to continue acting as judges and philosophers, intermediaries and priests providing they stopped incinerating their own people inside wicker effigies while the poor sods were still alive. Except the Druids refused, claiming human sacrifice was their right and their gods needed the blood, leaving Rome no choice other than to impose its own laws outlawing such practices. Was it any surprise the Gauls then flocked to the side of those who protected them?

And where those rumours sprang from that the three men who'd tried to kill the Governor were part of a coup, the Security Police had no idea! Very little by way of torture had been required before the would-be assassins were singing like thrushes. The Scorpion put them up to it, they said even before the second iron was drawn from the fire. None other than his second-in-command, a man called Ptian, had given them their orders in person, and they'd been proud to sacrifice their lives for the greater good of Gaul, etc., etc., etc. No one bothered to point out how fast their enthusiasm had waned at the first sight of the bone screws and pincers. The point was, their testimony wasn't in doubt.

So whilst Orbilio's staff went through the motions of chronicling this sudden upsurge in intelligence and cursing the long hours spent over their desks, their real interest lay in their boss.

Where was he? Why leave so suddenly? Why only the briefest of explanations? Had Orbilio really taken a furlough to reconcile with his ex-wife? They'd like to know more, because that Claudia was an absolute stunner, though what a dark horse he'd turned out to be! Why, only this morning, a second wife had appeared on the scene, eager to speak with her ex, and what a shame. One had trekked all the way from Rome to be with him, the other had travelled from Lusitania, and the bastard didn't deserve either.

Ambition goes hand in hand with ruthlessness, they concluded, agreeing that they'd bloody well need to watch their step when he was around, and promising to look out for one another, because patricians were renowned for their back-stabbing qualities. Only twenty-eight years old, yet already Orbilio was head of the Security Police in Aquitania having left two broken hearts (at least) in his wake.

God knew, that was exactly the sort of bastard that would hang his staff out to dry if he cocked up himself.

They made sure their notations were meticulous in every degree.

Satisfied that he'd left the running of his office to a team whose judgement he could trust unreservedly, Marcus Cornelius Orbilio emerged from the wash house with a different worry on his mind. Tugging at his pants, he vaguely remembered that Cappadocian tribesmen sheathed their swords in leather belts that were held in place by a strap that passed under their crotch. But then the Cappadocians divided their time between arid salt deserts and volcanic mountains, where the wind whistled with unrelenting chill. Up there, discomfort was probably a basic criterion for tribal acceptance. Thus preoccupied with the twin issues of nipping stitches and biting seams, he descended the steps and found himself tripping over one of the slaves who'd also been sold on the auction block yesterday. The chap's name, he recalled, was listed as Manion.

'Sorry.' Manion pulled an apologetic face as Orbilio grabbed the stair rail to steady himself. 'Having trouble adjusting?' he asked, with a wry arch of his eyebrow.

Orbilio gave another tug at his crotch. 'I don't know how the Hundred-Handed expect a man to walk, much less father a bloody child.'

Manion laughed. 'You'll get used to it.'

'Which? Walking bow-legged or a lack of circulation to the essentials?'

'Don't worry. By the time the bruises on your face have faded, you'll be walking normally again, and until then, Pretty Boy, no priestess in her right mind is going to pick you over the others. Not unless she wants to wake up with nightmares.'

'Thanks, but speaking of right minds, do you have a rational explanation for scrabbling around in the grass on your hands and knees in the rain?'

'I dropped my ring while we were being herded in for – what did they have the cheek to call it?' He grinned. 'The Purification Bath? Besides, this is only light drizzle.'

Pitching into the search, Orbilio found nothing remarkable to note about Manion's appearance. Average height, average build, eyes neither green nor blue. The sort of looks no one remembers, he thought absently. From the distance there came a rumble of thunder.

'Ah,' he said, fumbling beneath the wooden steps. 'Think I might've found something. Here.'

He rubbed the silver band on his shirt then tossed it across. But not before he'd noticed the engraving of an exquisitely worked scorpion. Complete with stinger, ready to strike.

'Thanks, Pretty Boy.' Manion slipped the ring on his finger and clapped Marcus on the back. 'I owe you one.'

He was laughing to himself as he sauntered off.

Orbilio forgot about the problems of tight pants.

Twelve

The rain had eased by the time Mavor's expert fingers began massaging Claudia's neck and shoulders with oils of fennel, thyme, cypress and marjoram, but thunder still growled round distant valleys. Clouds rolled in lower, and heavy. Typical midsummer storms, Claudia mused. But unlike Roman storms that trapped the heat and intensified the humidity, the temperature in this part of Gaul remained pleasantly temperate. Its proximity to the sea, she supposed.

Closing her eyes as Mavor kneaded and squeezed, her mind travelled away from these rolling, wooded hills fed by thousands of streams to the ocean that encircled the world. Bedevilled by whirlpools and demons, giant fishes and monsters, this watery universe was ruled by Oceanus the Titan, but what was this old man's parentage?

From the Darkness sprang Chaos, and from the union between them, Day and Air were created. From Day and Air, Mother Earth and the Sea were then born, and from Mother Earth and Air came forth the Titans. But so, too, did Anger, Strife, Vengeance and Fear, but always, yes always, it came back to Mother Earth. To the priestesses who preached peace through the worship of nature. But her grandchild – Oceanus's daughter – was none other than Nemesis, and Oceanus's own granddaughter was Venus herself. Venus, that oh-so-beautiful goddess of love, who rose from the ocean's foam surrounded by sparrows and doves, while the Hundred-Handed were universally beautiful and Mavor was the Priestess of the Birds—

'I'm sorry, my dear, did I wake you?'

'No, no,' Claudia lied. 'Just drifting.'

Mavor took a step back and tapped her lip with her finger.

'I can't feel any change in you,' she said thoughtfully. 'Maybe I'll try a different treatment.'

'It's only been three days,' Claudia reminded her.

'Yes, but you should be showing some signs of improvement by now.'

'That pain in the neck seems to be under control.'

If Clytie's killer was among the male slaves, Orbilio would soon root him out.

'Possibly,' Mavor said, 'but my fingers aren't sensing a difference, suggesting your relief is merely psychological.'

When she reached up to pluck a bunch of downy wormwood hanging from a hook in the ceiling, the action accentuated the generous curve of her breasts. She laid the leaves on the hot stove with a sensuality she was probably unaware of.

'I think we should try moxibustion.'

'Does that have any connection with the word *com*bustion?' Claudia asked warily.

'It does.'

'Then I think maybe we shouldn't try that.'

Because inventing a medical condition was one thing. Having it treated with burns was another.

'Nonsense.' A surprisingly firm hand pinned Claudia to the table. 'This will do your poor neck the world of good.'

'A noose would be quicker.'

And a damn sight more pleasant. No wonder wormwood deterred lice and beetles!

Mavor laughed. 'Don't tell me you'd rather suffer a painful spine than endure a tiny little unpleasant whiff! Now lie still, please. I want the heat to penetrate into your bones.'

Bones? It was penetrating the bloody table.

'Your boyfriend has a very high opinion of you,' Claudia said. 'Although not quite as high as the one he has of himself – are you all right?'

'The, er, oils on my fingers. Made the pot slip.' As she bent down to pick up the shards of the broken jar, there was a look of alarm – even panic – on Mavor's face, which she concealed, but not quickly enough. 'What did he say?' She tried to make the question sound casual.

'Basically that you were good in bed.'

'H-he said that?' Alarm was replaced by confusion.

'Not very gentlemanly conduct, I agree, but he also insisted that a man's hands are better suited to massage than a woman's, and suggested I speak to you for confirmation.'

Mavor let out the breath she hadn't realized she'd been holding. 'Oh, you mean Swarbric.'

Claudia recognized that sigh. She had let out a similar one, when he'd told her it was Ribolo . . .

'You may think it's because he wants to rub his hands over naked ladies, but actually he does have a point. I wouldn't disagree that men make better masseurs.' Mavor lifted the wormwood and replaced it with a new batch of heated leaves. 'And he blooming well ought to speak highly of me. I fixed his shoulder when it dislocated earlier this year, though between you and me, he yelped like a girl.'

The usual consequence of adding two and two together in a hurry, Claudia thought. Swarbric had been amused, because she'd used time as an excuse to leave, when the sun was patently obscured by the clouds. And when he said Mavor was good, he meant she was good – in her professional capacity.

Damn.

'Such an injury must need regular treatment,' she pointed out.

'Not at all.' Mavor pressed down lightly on the warm leaves. 'Luckily, I was able to treat the joint within minutes of the accident occurring and could keep him swaddled like a baby until the risk of ligament damage passed. That prevented any recurrence. Swarbric's as fit as a flea.'

Then why were you sneaking down to his hut? Why the alarm when I mention the word boyfriend? Why the relief when you know it's only Swarbric?

I know, the note on Claudia's table had read. *I just cannot decide who to tell.*

Outside, the thunder rumbled that little bit closer.

'How well did you know Clytie?' she asked.

This time the reaction was no less pronounced. Except the emotion was cold rather than hot.

'Hardly at all,' Mavor said stiffly. 'She was still learning plant lore, which, on account of its complex medicinal aspect, takes a long time to master.'

'The birds and the bees come along later, then?'

The joke wasn't enough to soften the pinch to her sensuous lips. 'You will have to excuse me,' she said briskly. 'It's the solstice tomorrow and much preparation needs to be done for the ceremonies, but I need you to remain perfectly still to allow the after-effects of my manipulation to settle.' She notched a mark on a candle. 'Then I'd like you back here at dusk, please, so I can assess whether there's any change.'

There was change. Claudia's neck had never felt so stiff or uncomfortable.

'Before you go,' she said, 'as the Bird Priestess, does your protection extend to ravens as well?'

When Mavor opened the door, the flames on the candles angled forty-five degrees. 'My dear, I am responsible for all mother nature's feathered creatures.'

'Including the souls of your ancestors?'

Mavor's shoulders lost their stiffness. Her whole body slumped. 'Especially the souls of my ancestors,' she said hoarsely.

With the candles flickering, it was hard to tell. But Claudia could have sworn she was crying.

With the advent of rain, the birdlife of the forest burst into action. There was no need to shelter from the fierce rays of the sun now, or fear the shadow of predators. They were free to feast on the abundance of insects that were only yesterday flying too high to catch. Nestlings could start feeding themselves.

Watching this activity with his back to a birch beneath the palisade on the hill, a young man ran his finger down the spine of his arrow then trailed his nail over the cock feather. Thanks to his industrious agents, rumours were bubbling among the Druids faster than brews in a witch's cauldron and the mix was increasing in potency with every hour that passed. Again, thanks to his labours, tales were coming to their ears of men being reduced to blubbering simpletons after drinking the waters of the Hundred-Handed's sacred spring. Of virility being sapped, travellers disappearing, of clouds being conjured to cover the moon. *See for yourselves, O Holy Ones. Cows, pigs, even horses are sickening without reason, as the Hundred-Handed cast their evil spells.* Drunkards were being brought in from outside the area and thrown at the Druids' feet as evidence. The case was building nicely.

The Whisperer notched an arrow into his bow. A quail fluttered once then lay still.

'Bitch.'

A wood pigeon took off. He aimed at that. Another substitute priestess.

'Bitch.'

A jay next.

'Bitch.'

Then a crow.

'Bitch, bitch, bitch.'

But as his resentment grew, so his aim became weak. He laid down his bow. He must take care not to lose control, because leaders are strong, leaders are powerful, leaders are dedicated to their cause. He must not allow hatred to overshadow his judgement. This was war.

Glancing back towards the palisade, he thought of the tribes who embraced the Oppressors as allies and were genuinely indebted to the foreign troops who patrolled their borders. They kept our roads and our waterways free of bandits, they claimed, and if there were skirmishes to be fought, better their sons be mourned than our own. Really? How short their memories, the Whisperer thought. Don't they remember how their grandfathers had resisted Rome with a ferocity that had caught the invaders off guard? Their whole bloody army had proved no match for the Aquitani. A whole legion was cut down like rats in a run, while the soldiers Caesar sent to avenge them were also decisively routed.

What happened? he wondered. What had turned proud warriors into self-serving cowards?

What acid had rotted the heart of the Nation that was, until so very recently, a force to be feared?

What female poison made eunuchs of men?

The Whisperer adjusted the bandana round his neck and

straightened the ring on his finger. So the Chieftains had allowed themselves to be seduced by profit and greed and then sold that concept to their own people! Who cared? Thank Lenus, there were enough patriots left who were willing to stand up for what they believed in.

Freedom.

Freedom to choose what wars they fought, choose who they died for, even who they paid their bloody taxes to, as well as the freedom to discipline women and children in their own home – and to hell with this bollocks about nature and peace, the Hundred-Handed had it coming.

'Power-sucking bloody bitches.'

The woodpecker flew on with its beakload of grubs, unaware of the arrow that thudded harmlessly into the trunk of an oak. The Whisperer swore, but lunch break was over. It was time to return to College business – paste on a smile – make all the right gestures – but not for much longer, thank Lenus! Replacing his bow beneath the overhang of rock, he wrapped his wrist grip in his bandana, tucked them both inside his quiver then concealed the lot with leaf litter and branches.

Damned bitches – he brushed the dirt off his hands – deserved everything they bloody well got, and closing his eyes, he pictured the flames of their thatches lighting the night sky. Imagined their screams carrying into the forest. Carrying, but where nobody heard . . . He would show them. He'd show them what women were really for. One after the other, after the other.

It was time to put an end to their power-sucking strategies.

It was time to give men their balls back.

'Can I tempt you with a honeycomb, my lady, now that the sun's pushed the clouds out of the way?'

A young man with a voice as smooth as the sweetmeat he was offering bridged the stream in one agile leap.

'Providing you join me,' Claudia said.

She recognized him immediately from the auction block yesterday, though for the life of her she couldn't say why. There was nothing about him that was particularly memorable. Average height, average build, even his eyes were neither green nor blue but some point in between, and, like the sea, always changing. But with his dark hair cropped short and the spring in his step, there was something compelling about this young man and it was easy to see why the Hundred-Handed had picked him. But not why he'd picked Claudia out—

'With pleasure, milady.'

Perhaps it was a prerequisite of male slaves, but this one also wore pantaloons tighter than skin. Except whereas Swarbric had chosen fabric, these were cut from pale yellow deerskin. Soft, supple and smooth.

'Manion,' he said by way of introduction and, as he stretched out on the rock, she detected a faint smell of nutmeg. Being limestone, the rock was already dry from the midsummer sun and an earwig scuttled between the grass in the fissures. Maybe the storm was passing, after all. 'The new beekeeper,' he said with a chuckle.

'What happened to the last one?'

One indolent shoulder shrugged. 'Who knows?'

As he broke the honeycomb in half, she noticed a band of pale skin round his seal finger, as though it was missing a ring.

'Doesn't it worry you, being stung?'

He cast her a sharp glance from the corner of his eye. 'Perhaps they know I sting back.'

Claudia didn't doubt it. For all his oozing of charm and consideration, there was a predatory aura about Manion. As well as something teasingly familiar— Maybe she'd run into him last year in Santonum? Maybe it was his voice that sounded familiar? Maybe he just reminded her of somebody else?

But barely had he taken a second bite than he was springing to his feet.

'Leaving already?'

Seascape eyes darkened as he leaned over her.

'Only dead men do nothing,' he whispered.

With the edge of his thumb, he scooped a drizzle of honey from the side of her mouth and unhurriedly licked it off.

Watching him lope back up the hill, Claudia wondered

why, if she didn't recognize him, she couldn't rid herself of the feeling that she'd met him before. And what slave ever had use for a seal? Not so much bees, she reflected, more a hornet's nest he was stirring up.

She'd never eat honeycombs again without thinking of him.

'What was that about?' Orbilio asked, striding down the path with a bundle of hay perched on his shoulders. Yet for all his jauntiness, the narrowing of his eyes and a strongly clamped jaw suggested he'd seen everything. And hadn't liked what he saw.

'Oh, just a slave bringing me something to eat.' She handed him Manion's half. 'Want some?'

He grunted, but she didn't think it was in everlasting and grateful thanks.

'He didn't say anything, then? Manion?'

'If you must know, we enjoyed a riveting chat about bees.'

'Bees.'

'You know the things, Marcus. Fluffy buzzy creatures. One sees them all the time flittering round flowers.'

Marcus tore his gaze from the trees into which Manion had disappeared and stared at her. 'Are you referring to those fluffy buzzy male drones that do all the work, while the queen watches from the centre of the hive?'

Perhaps they know I sting back, a little voice echoed inside her head. Rubbish, she told it. Not everything has a subtext, sod off. *Only dead men do nothing*, the little voice wheedled . . .

'Have the Hundred-Handed branded you yet?' she asked cheerfully.

Orbilio wiped his sticky hands on the grass and when he looked up, the hardness in his expression was gone. 'They couldn't find an unbruised patch of skin, and with luck I'll be gone before they can.'

'Tut, tut, Marcus. The Governor is absolutely *delighted* that you and your ex-wife are about to become reconciled. He said take as much time to recuperate as you need, I quote his very words.'

'Yes. Well. As much as I find slave labour an excellent

aid to marital counselling, there is the little matter of an uprising that ideally I'd like to prevent.'

Claudia popped the last corner of honeycomb into her mouth, confident that the Head of the Security Police wouldn't be playing Masters & Slaves if the whole of Aquitania was poised to explode. But why *had* he agreed to come here with her? Why so quickly, and with only a token protest? The smell of rat had slammed into her nostrils the instant he'd said yes. Rat, with a large helping of weasel.

'Then the quicker we solve Clytie's murder the better,' she breezed. 'Now then. Apart from the fact that tight pants are a bitch, what else have you discovered?'

Marcus hefted the bale onto the opposite shoulder. '(A) women are to be avoided, they're deadly and dangerous, (B) men have no brains or we'd steer clear of them and (C) that working with livestock,' he patted the bale, 'leaves indelible stains on a chap's kit.'

'It took you twenty-eight years to work that out?'

'I'm a slow starter.' His expression became serious again. 'You know, for three centuries, the Hundred-Handed have provided spiritual guidance for small, isolated communities in the surrounding countryside who rely on this forest for their very survival. In leading by example, the priestesses set high moral standards—'

'I hope that was a joke.'

'Far from it.' He spiked his fringe out of his eyes. 'Have you stopped to think what they give up?'

'Apart from their male babies at birth?'

'Including their male babies at birth. Claudia, I know you don't approve of their ways, but this is a far from easy life for these women.'

'Thus speaks the wisdom of a sex slave, Orbilio. I just knew you'd feel right at home here.'

'Mock all you want,' he said, 'because yes, I suppose every man does dream of being a sex slave – until that dream becomes a reality. But I'm serious. Times are changing, Claudia, Rome's seen to that. And thanks to us, the world has got smaller for the Gauls, and *this* world,' he indicated the College with a nod of his head, 'has to adapt. If it doesn't, quite frankly, it dies.'

'Are you saying the Hundred-Handed are under threat? Because if so, I really don't give a damn.'

He set down the bale then lay flat on the rock, resting his feet on the flat of the bale. 'Peace is a funny thing. You and I, we're part of the new generation who aren't content to sit back and put our trust in our elders and betters. We demand a say in our future and don't obey laws without satisfying ourselves first that those laws are fair.'

'That's the second time I've heard those arguments today.'

'Because independence is a hot topic in these parts at the moment,' he said, folding his arms behind his head and crossing his feet at the ankles. 'Hence my point about insurrection.'

This is not a good time to be a Roman.

'Nonsense. Those rumours have been rumbling for months.'

If the Scorpion intended to stage an uprising, he'd have started before midsummer, and no matter how well organized the rebel forces, they couldn't achieve much in the remaining three months of the campaigning season. The smell of rat doubled in strength.

'This business of challenging authority, questioning orders and not accepting what we're told without corroboration,' Marcus said, 'that's called democracy. And while you and I take it for granted, for the people of Aquitania, it's a whole new concept.'

'Then the quicker it comes the better.'

'Not necessarily.' He propped himself up on one elbow to face her. 'If change comes too fast, it's liable to have the opposite effect of what it's intended to do. It can destroy rather than build.' He paused. 'Why don't you give a damn?'

'Goddammit, Orbilio, if you'd been doing just a *fraction* of your job, you wouldn't be asking that question! It's monstrous! Barbaric! Utterly obscene—'

'What is?' he asked calmly.

'The Pit, Marcus! They throw the condemned down there alive, so they can reflect on their sins while they die slowly and painfully over a couple of weeks, and dear god, you say these women want peace, but I've never heard of anything so diabolical in my life!'

'I have.' His voice was still calm as he shifted position to sit on the hay bale, resting his chin in his hands. 'It was how the Spartans used to execute criminals. Only for the direst of offences, mind you. The punishment was intended as a deterrent.'

'Spartans?' Something about that rang a bell.

'The Greeks and the Gauls share an interesting history,' he said. 'The Greeks came to Gaul, the Gauls went to Greece, and not necessarily for the purpose of cultural exchange. However!' He grinned. 'Not all their legacies involved funerals, blood and smouldering ruins. You know what nereids are?'

'Sea nymphs who serve Neptune.'

The grin deepened. 'The Greeks believed these nymphs served the sea goddess, Thetis, and they founded colleges of priestesses in their honour. Fifty of them, to be precise. Moon priestesses, dedicated to a gentle goddess who could nevertheless assume, guess what? A hundred different shapes.'

Of course. The Dining Hall. Claudia had never visited Greece, but the structure of three sides round a courtyard was typical for mass catering at sanctuary sites.

'And we all know who the son of Thetis was,' Marcus murmured.

Achilles.

'If you're saying the Pit of Reflection is their Achilles heel, I still don't care about these bloody women.'

'In Sparta, the prisoner would be dragged in chains through the streets, where he'd be whipped and humiliated by a line of his peers. Shamed,' he said, 'anguished,' he paused, 'and degraded.'

'And if the moral of that tale is that the Hundred-Handed have evolved with a soft spot, you're still wasting your breath.'

'Strange how often this becomes the case when I'm talking to you.'

'Whoa, there! I *paid* my back taxes.'

That was the reason she was in this wretched mess, and damn those greedy bastards for taking advantage of a poor grieving widow struggling with a mountain of debts.

'So . . .' He scratched his chin. 'No outstanding frauds, then? An end to the forgeries? No more—'

'You were talking about the Pit,' she snapped.

'Indeed I was,' he said turning away, and from this angle, it looked like his shoulders were shaking. 'And I'm saying that the way the priestesses distance themselves from the physical act of execution suggests cowardice.'

'The word, Marcus, is callousness.'

He leaned across, plucked a blade of grass and chewed on the juicy end. 'Cruelty isn't quite so cruel if you don't witness it personally.'

'Closing eyes and closing minds. Yes, I'm starting to see how they're really nice people.'

'I didn't say I agreed with it, but the fact that Beth believes Clytie's killer is a copycat, Dora thinks it's an experiment and that only the souls of the truly evil are thrown to the three-headed dragon suggests a certain amount of optimism to me. That the Hundred-Handed always think the best of people and need to be convinced beyond doubt of their dark side.'

So he had been doing more than just a fraction of his job, then.

'Beth took over at the same time as Rome officially took office,' she told him.

'Is that important?'

'You tell me.'

'Actually, I was rather hoping there was something you might want to tell me.'

'Such as?'

'Well, let's start with the reason you came back to Gaul. The reason, in fact, why you're here.'

The Security Spider luring the fly into his sticky little web? Honestly, Marcus! Does it look like I have wings?

'Providing you tell me why you're here,' she said sweetly.

'Because you asked me.'

'If I asked you to jump in the river, would you do that as well?'

He looked at the stream.

'My ankles would get awfully wet, but I suppose I might make the sacrifice.'

The twinkle died in his eye.

'Claudia.'

He leaned so close that she could smell his sandalwood unguent even over the smell of livestock and hay. And, she thought, maybe a faint hint of rosemary.

'For someone who flies in the face of male chauvinism herself,' he said, 'you're surprisingly antagonistic towards these priestesses and alarmingly passionate about solving this child's murder. Don't get me wrong, I find it admirable, but at the same time I can't help wondering – what does Clytie mean to you?'

There it was again. Thirteen long years ago, climbing the stairs . . . opening the door . . .

Dammit, no matter how many times that memory flashed, it never changed and never softened. Not even in her dreams – in her nightmares – had Claudia walked into that room to find her mother laughing and happy, arms outstretched in welcome, sober and delighted to see her. The memory had stayed true in every respect. Her mother remained limp. Waxy. Somebody else.

And there was never a note beside the body.

Suddenly, the stench of congealed blood overwhelmed the scent of sandalwood and now all she could hear was the buzz, not of bees, but of blowflies. Bluebottles, gorging themselves on her mother's spent life—

She looked at Marcus with eyes that were as dead as her mother. As dead as the life she'd left behind.

'Nothing,' she said coldly. 'Clytie means nothing at all.'

From deep in the undergrowth, a pair of eyes that were neither green nor blue but somewhere in between followed the exchange with interest. Too far away to catch the exchange, enough words drifted across to convey the gist. That bit about insurrection was particularly interesting. As was the part about the pit.

Hidden by the thicket, his crouching figure went unnoticed by the girl as she went striding past, and half a minute maybe more passed before Pretty Boy eventually stood up, hefted the bale on to his shoulder and marched off down the path, whistling under his breath.

The eyes in the bushes might not be either truly green or truly blue.

But truly they were smiling.

The Scorpion slipped his ring back on his finger.

The hinge of the writing tablet flipped quietly open. With painstaking care, the stylus scored deep into the wax.

No secret can ever be safe.

The pen hesitated. Should it, or shouldn't it, add anything else? It tapped against the lip of the writer while it weighed up the consequences. Then, without bothering to etch another syllable, it positioned itself diagonally across the open wooden tablet.

The author took another long look round Claudia's room and, nodding in satisfaction, withdrew on silent feet.

Thirteen

In the Hall of the Pentagram, the flickering candles turned the robes of the priestesses iridescent as they took their seats round the star-shaped table. Sparkling silver next to flashing yellow. Shimmering brown beside flaming red. Sinuous black merging with silver again. But this tableau of elegance and sophistication was betrayed by the rapid amount of finger flicking, hand tossing, signing and gesticulating that passed between the five women. An infusion of lime blossom and lavender simmered softly in the corner. It did nothing to calm the mood of the meeting.

'I don't understand why this Claudia creature is so interested in Clytie,' Fearn flashed furiously.

'Is she?' Dora countered. '*So* interested, I mean, rather than *simply* interested? After all, a twelve-year-old girl was murdered, one of our novices, then her body moved, painted and artfully arranged. Wouldn't that fire anyone's curiosity?'

'That woman doesn't strike me as the type to engage in morbid curiosity for its own sake,' Luisa signed, with an agitated fluff of her rowan-red gown.

'Typical.' Dora rolled her eyes in disgust. 'Decline has barely spoken to the girl, yet once again she's treating us with the benefit of her expert opinion.'

'My judgement's based on instinct and observation the same as yours,' Luisa retorted hotly, 'so don't you dare presume to question it.'

'It might be based on the same criteria, my dear, but it doesn't follow that it's sound.'

'The point is,' Fearn cut in, 'someone needs to tell that meddling bitch to keep her nose out of our affairs!'

'Curiosity killed the cat,' Luisa signed, looking at no one in particular.

'People come to the Hundred-Handed for guidance and healing.' Beth stood up and began to pace the room. 'They're bound to be curious about what this College stands for, its beliefs, its customs, its laws. But on this occasion I do find myself agreeing with Growth.'

Fearn gave a told-you-so toss of her raven black hair in Dora's direction. Luisa wrinkled her nose in support.

'Claudia's curiosity does bother me,' Beth added.

'She's questioned Vanessia, Aridella and Lin,' Fearn pointed out. 'She's talked to Gurdo.'

'And Mavor and Swarbric,' the Rowan Priestess listed helpfully. 'And they're just the ones that we know of.'

Beth circled the table twice then sat down, smoothing her silver gown flat.

'What convinces me that Claudia's questioning goes beyond straightforward prying is that she enquired about souls, isn't that right, Ailm?'

The Death Priestess threw her hands in the air.

'You slated me for not getting involved in the witchcraft vote, yet it's midsummer tomorrow, the second most important date in the calendar after the New Year, yet the best you can talk about is some stupid Roman who'll be gone from here in two days.'

She stood up and marched to the door, her black robes billowing behind her.

'I'll be casting the death runes if anyone wants me.'

'Ailm is right, of course,' Beth signed, as the door reverberated on its hinges, extinguishing half a dozen or more candles. 'I don't underestimate how unsettling it is for – well, *all* of us to have a stranger stirring up this unfortunate tragedy, but we do need to maintain perspective.'

She glanced at Dora, who stared impassively back.

'If, after two days, you wish to call another Pentagram, Fearn, should the problem still persist, then you may do so. Until then, though, and since my vote is worth three and Ailm's opinion we know, I declare this assembly null and void, and since it never took place, we will not speak of it again.'

'*Now* can I go and get my lunch?' Dora asked aloud, and though it was to Fearn and Luisa that her words were addressed, it was to the Head of the College that her fingers signalled once behind her back. The message that the priestess flashed was simple.

'Thank you.'

Fourteen

With the approach of midsummer, preparations for the solstice were in full swing. Alternating between the force of her personality and her stentorian tones, Dora had conscripted a large percentage of the priestesses to help organize the festival that was dedicated to the mighty oak and everything it stood for. Leading her troops down the cliff and over the bridge towards the Field of Celebration, maturity, strength, courage and endurance would be the theme for a range of activities that would last a full twenty-four hours, commencing at sunset with the one event universal to all religious beliefs. The bonfire.

Here, in a wide open pasture edged with poplar and alder, the sheep that cropped the grass and kept the College in tasty lamb and mutton had been corralled into makeshift pens, while what appeared to be the entire male labour force had been put to work erecting daises for the priestesses and rigging up canopies to shield the crowd from the ferocious noonday sun. Dressed in his customary green shirt and pantaloons, Gurdo scribbled chalk marks on the grass as indicators for siting casks of healing spring water, while under the watchful eye of their plump, brown-robed general, novices in headdresses made from gilded acorns practised their routines. The older girls glided back and forth with graceful precision. The plates in the hands of the younger ones wobbled with nerves.

'No, no, no, Aridella.'

Dora's voice boomed out even over the sawing of timbers, the knocking of nails and initiates rehearsing the Oak Song.

'Good heavens, child, the flames you're supposed to be carrying will either have blown right out or set the whole congregation alight. Like *this*, dear.'

For her size, she was remarkably nimble and, as she balanced the dish high on splayed fingertips, Claudia caught a glimpse of the stunning sylph Dora once was.

'Try again, Aridella.' She handed the bowl back and watched the little novice imitate her actions. 'Excellent, absolutely perfect,' she said, even though there was little discernible difference. 'Now you try, Vanessia. Good girl!'

On the far side of the meadow, Claudia could see Orbilio and Manion, wordlessly engaged in the business of bonfire construction, aided by the youth she'd seen with Swarbric earlier. Though the sky was still mostly covered by cloud, the temperature had started to soar and all three had removed their shirts to cope with the heat, their bodies glistening with sweat. Connal's face was dark with something more than concentration on his task, though, and she wondered whether, like Pod and Sarra, he and Elusa were also planning to use these preparations as a cover for their illicit activities. How far would they get? she wondered dully. Connal was a foreigner and Elusa had never left the College grounds. Neither had a clue what lay beyond the vista they could see and frankly Claudia doubted they'd cover five miles before the guards tracked them down. Watching Connal's scowl deepen with every branch he threw on, she knew that either way the lovers were heading for tragedy.

But Pod's tryst had given her an idea and she, too, had decided to exploit this surge of activity by taking a peep inside the other cave – and in any case relief from this heat would be bliss. With the advent of cloud cover, the breeze had dropped, trapping the heat and generating humidity, and despite changing her robe for a fresh lilac one, the cotton was already sticking like skin to her back.

'Sarra, isn't it?'

The Willow Priestess's daughter was sitting on Clytie's stone, her knees drawn up to her chin, and from the red rims round her eyes and the puffiness to her cheeks it was clear she had been crying.

'Do you want to talk about it?' Claudia asked softly.

Sarra wrinkled her nose. 'Thank you, but I'm fine.'

'You look it.'

The girl smiled, and though she made no effort to respond, she didn't get up and walk away either. Encouraged, Claudia settled herself on the flat rock while swallows shrieked low over the meadow in search of flies.

'I suppose it must be a terrible blow, not to be admitted to the fifty elite?' she began.

Sarra blew her nose. 'It's not that,' she said, as indeed Claudia knew fine well. 'Beth called me in five years ago and told me I wouldn't qualify for Initiatehood. I don't have the necessary dedication to be a priestess, she said, but told me I'd make a wonderful supervisor for the middle novices, and do you know, she was right. I love it!'

'I've met three of your charges. Aridella, Vanessia and Lin. Spirited little fillies, wouldn't you say?'

Sarra pushed her long silky hair back from her face. 'Sometimes you'd think they were boys, the way they carry on, but don't be fooled by that rough-and-tumble. Those games stimulate their sharp little brains and believe me, they're clever, those girls. Vanessia's already qualified for Initiatehood, and without any shadow of doubt, the others will follow.' She sighed. 'Those three have the dedication and determination I never had, that's for sure.'

Dedication to duty and determination to succeed were not necessarily virtuous traits, Claudia mused, studying the girl who didn't meet the criteria yet was totally fulfilled in her work. But then again, *only* in her work. She looked at her, blonde and ethereal, the fairy in love with the elf. Come to think of it, didn't the Gauls call the elder the Elf King, believing that to wear clothes dyed from the juice of the tree would invoke the protection of the benevolent spirits that lived in the forests? Interestingly, it was the very dye Gurdo clad himself in—

'So if it's not your career,' she said, carefully mirroring Sarra's pose, 'it must be love that's making you miserable.'

Without mentioning the pregnant Aquitani girl, she confessed to having been behind a boulder when Sarra met Pod the day before and to overhearing their conversation. Far from being indignant, though, the fairy seemed more relieved that she was at last free to talk about her dilemma and with someone objective who came from outside the

117

College, instead of keeping her feelings bottled inside. Thus for the next twenty minutes Claudia was treated to a comprehensive list of Pod's breathtaking features, his fine upstanding character and let's not forget all his other wonderful attributes. Dear me, if she hadn't already met the boy, she would have hated that young man on sight!

'I gather you don't find him physically unattractive, either,' she murmured. 'Though you might want to wash those grass stains off the back of your pretty pink robe before you go back.'

Sarra squealed in alarm, at least sparing Claudia further nauseous Pod-praising since the next twenty minutes were dedicated to the removal of stains which, though stubborn, were no match for four determined hands.

'These marks,' Claudia puffed, pummelling the pink robe against a boulder in the stream, 'and the fact that a girl who went out with the express intention of collecting mallow returned with only two dog-eared stems suggest to me that you two lovebirds didn't spend your afternoon quarrelling. So why were you crying?'

Sarra's face crumpled as she reached for a stick. 'It's this, don't you see?'

'Um. Actually, Sarra, I don't.'

A stick is a stick is a stick. And unless it pokes you in the eye, Claudia couldn't see how it was remotely likely to make someone's eyes water.

'Look at these,' Sarra said, and suddenly the stick was no longer a stick, it was a document. Notches had been carved along the length. 'The College uses sign language as a sort of shorthand to communicate and for when we're conducting rituals and ceremonies, but since we have no written language, records are kept by the scoring of twigs.'

Similar, Claudia realized, to the memory aids employed by the Druids. 'So this is . . . what? The equivalent of a page that's been removed from a file?'

'It's a message.' One slim finger traced the notches. '*Ill seed begets ill reed*, it says, and it's not the only one I've found on my pillow.'

Claudia thought of the writing tablet laid open beside her bed. It was the first thing she saw when she opened her door (well, all right not the first, that was the headless corpse of a baby robin, a thank-you-for-bringing-me-back-to-Gaul present from Drusilla). But, having disposed of mangled remains, she noticed the message, especially the stylus laid elegantly across the tablet, almost like a signature.

No secret can ever be safe. That's what it said. *No secret can ever be safe.*

'Someone knows I'm meeting Pod,' Sarra was saying, as tears began to flow again. 'Oh, Claudia, if Beth finds out, the Hundred-Handed'll vote him invisible, I'll never see him again, and then I'll be punished by being put to work in the kitchens instead of being responsible for the middle novices like I am now, and I'll be forbidden from even setting foot beyond the precinct.'

Claudia wrung out the robe as though it was Beth's neck. 'This note's nasty but, Sarra, if the author knew about Pod, she would say so.'

And it had to be a 'she', who else knew the language of sticks?

The fairy wasn't convinced. 'Ill *reed*, Claudia! It specifically says *reeds* and that's where Gurdo found Pod. Wandering by the reed beds. The message couldn't be clearer.'

Maybe. Maybe not. But there was no consoling the girl.

'They'll vote him invisible and ban him from setting foot on College land and I—' Her shoulders heaved with the sobs. 'I'll need to decide, won't I? Never see my darling Poddi again or risk both our futures . . . and . . . and I don't know that I'm strong enough to make that decision.'

There was no weakness in being unable to decide between love and duty. The flaw lay in its invidious choice.

'Why don't you talk this over with your mother?' Claudia suggested gently, throwing the dripping robe over the branch of a willow to drive the point home.

'Sallie?' Sarra shook her head. 'The Willow Priestess gave birth to me,' she snivelled, 'and naturally I resemble her in appearance, but just because we deliver a baby, it doesn't follow that we bond differently with that child than we do from any other.'

'You make it sound like a cat having a litter of kittens.'

'And you make it sound like there's something wrong with

that arrangement, when it's simply that our family structure is alien to you.' She splashed her swollen face with cold water. 'Admittedly we don't have mothers or fathers as such, but' – her smile was as weak as it was wry – 'we have a hell of a lot of sisters!'

Claudia examined the twig into which those sinister notches had been carved.

'That can't always be easy.'

Jealousies and resentment would be rife in such an isolated and blinkered environment, propelling emotions that would normally have a million mundane outlets to spiral in upon themselves and take on unnatural – and indeed artificial – proportions.

'It's not,' Sarra agreed. 'We may be brought up as equals, but, like all families, some of us rub along better than others.'

This was Claudia's chance and she seized it. 'You ought to know,' she said, fanning herself cool with the neck of her robe. 'Those novices must prove quite a challenge at times.'

Children have an inbuilt instinct to create pecking orders and so, in a society where hierarchy is determined by rigid rules, the girls would need to find other ways to establish their identity. With Vanessia, Aridella and Lin, this came in the form of tomboy rebellion. But what about the fourth member of the quartet? Of course, she could easily have broached the subject of Clytie at the beginning, when Sarra talked about the other three's qualification to Initiatehood and her own role as supervisor of novices. Only that wouldn't have evoked Sarra's confidence . . .

'I expect Clytie was a handful as well, wasn't she?' She took care not to look at Sarra as she nonchalantly kept the heat at bay.

'More so, in a way.'

In her undershift and with her silky hair hanging down over her shoulders, the fairy looked fifteen years old.

'Because she didn't share her friends' desire to climb rocks, swing from ropes or go poking around in caves and things, she'd come to me ostensibly to get thread to sew up a tear in Aridella's robe or a new ribbon because Lin had lost hers, but basically Clytie was lonely and wanted someone to talk

120

to. And whilst I felt for the child, it . . . well, it put me in an awfully difficult position.'

She heaved a sad sigh.

'I didn't want to snub her, but at some point in the conversation it would slip out *why* she wanted these things – and once that happened, I was duty bound to put the girls on report.' Sarra rubbed her upper arms. 'It was such a shame. At the Disciplinary, Clytie would rush forward and speak up for her friends, apologizing for landing them in it, but the trouble was, the damage was already done and Beth was left with no choice. She had to punish the girls.'

Pretending to watch the tiddlers darting in and out of the shallows, Claudia tried to make sense of the mixed messages she was receiving.

On the one side of the scales, there was a society that was self-absorbed and self-contained in which duty overrode personal feelings to the extent that only those who could remain aloof qualified as priestesses. Heaped up alongside, keeping the balance weighed down, was their view that men were on the same level as draught beasts and that even their own babies were simply commodities to be parcelled up and classified according to the rulebook.

Yet – look at their enormously strong sense of loyalty, sisterhood and belief in their convictions; plus Elusa and Sarra were proof that the capacity for love and affection on a personal level hadn't been bred out of the women over the course of three hundred years. Among five hundred women, these could not be the only two who'd suffered heartbreak at having to choose between lover and family. At any given time, there'd probably be a score of women living in a similar state of anxiety, facing guaranteed separation from one of the two things they loved most in the world.

Now if it was simply ingrained responsibility that drove Sarra, then she'd be sitting here sad, but not wracked. Miserable but certainly not fearful. No, no, Claudia thought. Emotional attachments had to have been made time and again, it was basic human nature pulling the strings. The question was, how strong were they allowed to be formed? Was that why the men were forced to leave when they reached forty? To prevent too deep an attachment forming between College member and lover? Who knew, but the point was, very few women, no matter *how* deep the indoctrination, could simply hand their baby into communal care without watching or following or worrying about them. Dammit, someone in this College had to be grieving for the daughter who had been butchered!

'Sarra, who was Clytie's mother?'

The pink robe wasn't quite dry, but Sarra unhooked it from the willow branch anyway. 'Fearn,' she said, frowning. 'Why do you ask?'

'*Why?*' Was this girl kidding? 'For heaven's sake, Fearn's the Growth Priestess responsible for the spring equinox,' she said angrily, and it beggared belief that no one, not even Gabali, had seen fit to mention this fact. 'Didn't it occur to anyone that there might be a connection here?'

'Beth had reservations initially.' Sarra pulled the gown over her head. 'In fact, under her guidance the pentagram priestesses investigated that angle very thoroughly.' Her voice became muffled through the linen. 'But what you have to remember is that the Hundred-Handed only mix with local people on the first day of the month, when each tree priestess assumes responsibility for that month's protection, on the four quarter days—'

'You mean the two solstices and the two equinoxes?'

Sarra nodded as she wriggled into her robe. 'That's only sixteen days a year, plus of course when somebody dies and we administer the funeral rites. Otherwise we have no contact with outsiders, so it's hardly surprising that Clytie's killer picked one of those days. He didn't have any other choice.'

Claudia watched her go, light and ethereal as though nothing touched her, even though the girl's heart was as heavy as lead. Or was it? Were the children perhaps raised from the start to manage their own emotions? To 'work it out of their system' as it were? Again, Claudia thought of Connal and Elusa, of the tragedy they would face if they tried to elope.

And for some reason saw Manion's measureless blue-green eyes and the white band on his finger where a ring should have been . . .

At her feet lay the stick that had been left on Sarra's pillow.

She picked it up and twizzled it round in her hand. The notches were cut sideways in ones up to fives, and occasionally these marks had diagonal scorelines running through them, north-west to south-east. Again these were in lines one to five, but if there had been any doubt that the writer of the note in Claudia's room had been a male slave who'd somehow slipped in and out of the precinct unseen, the angle of the stylus put paid to the theory. It had been left at exactly the same angle as these diagonal scorelines.

I know, the first note had read.

I know. I just cannot decide who to tell, said the second.

And now: *No secret can ever be safe.*

At first she'd thought the note was left by someone who knew about Clytie and was tortured inside by that knowledge. Someone who, in their second message, was wondering if it was safe to confide in Claudia, a stranger, a foreigner and a Roman. That suspicion had been reinforced by the fact that someone had been through her belongings. A slipper out of place here, a gem out of place there, and the stopper on her perfume phial had been pressed down too hard. Little things that gave the searcher away.

And even when she'd found that third note, it seemed that the author was worried. Not so much that the secret about Clytie would have to come out. More the way it would be exposed. But now, reading this – *Ill seed begets ill reed* – and knowing it wasn't the first twig Sarra had found on her pillow, Claudia was reminded of an incident that took place the day she arrived. A mile or so outside Santonum, the gig had passed a Gaulish funeral which was so unlike anything she was used to – I mean why enclose the dead inside a moated cemetery? Were they worried they'd try to get out? And what was this ridiculous preoccupation with burying the deceased with all their belongings? If they believed in an afterlife, she could understand it, but they didn't. They believed in the reincarnation of souls. Captivated by their obscure rites and shadowy customs, and curious why the Aquitani denounced gravestones to mark their dead in fear of malevolent spirits rooting them out, Claudia had asked Junius to pull over.

At first she'd imagined it to be another part of the ritual

when a young urchin thrust a note into the distraught widow's hand – until the poor woman collapsed. Someone, her brother judging from the resemblance, snatched at the note and read it aloud, prompting every mourner in the group into a frenzy of anger, outrage and/or indignation. Intrigued, Claudia asked Junius to translate and it appeared that the widow had just received a note to the effect: *Are you sure it was the sea that claimed your husband, not the wine?*

Even when that young mother-to-be had been brought to the edge of reason with that malicious note, Claudia had paid it little attention. *While you let your horse starve, someone else is bringing him oats.* Babies can engender a tremendous amount of spite and resentment. A spurned lover, a barren neighbour, even a jealous mother-in-law can be vicious when her nose is put out of joint. But put those notes together, add in Claudia's missives and the notched twigs on Sarra's pillow and this was no longer coincidence.

Whoever left those messages for Claudia hadn't been owning up to knowing about Clytie. The author was out to make mischief. The question was, how many others had received those invidious notes? And how much damage had that poison inflicted?

Fifteen

'Anything?'

The figure that stepped out from the alder grove startled her, and her first thought was, It's Orbilio playing the fool. But since when had the Security Police taken to practical jokes? Since when had his baritone carried an Andalusian accent, no matter how faint? *Since when had he ever deliberately set out to scare her?*

'G-Gabali.'

Claudia's nerves were still jangling, her voice still ragged as she took in this lean, unadorned, unassuming assassin. For a man who earned his living killing people, she thought, he seemed exceptionally composed and she realized that the only thing that separated him from a bookbinder, say, or a banker were those penetrating brown eyes. Despite the oppressive heat, goose pimples rose on her arm.

'What are you doing out here? Checking up on your investment?'

The Spaniard bowed. 'It would be foolish not to, don't you agree?'

She didn't imagine she and Gabali would agree on anything, frankly, but this wasn't the time, much less the place, to say so.

'It's foolish to trespass on College soil,' she replied instead. 'The penalty if you're caught is the Pit of Reflection – although, silly me, you're already familiar with that sweet little hidey-hole.'

A muscle contracted in his cheek. She wasn't convinced its cause was humour.

'*Si*. I am acquainted with the Pit, but as repugnant as you obviously believe the practice to be, Merchant Seferius, I assure you I would have no qualms about despatching

125

my daughter's killer to its protracted embrace.'

Once again, she was struck by his thin pointed face and hair which, dammit, she could still only describe as longer than a Roman's but shorter than a Gaul's, and with a shine you could kohl your eyes in. Claudia glanced at the rock she was still standing on. The place where Clytie had died.

'Since I'm a wine merchant,' she said, 'a trade in which the solving of murders is not normally part of the remit, I'm sure you'll sympathize' – wrong word, but too late – 'when I tell you that I have absolutely no idea whether I'm making progress in this investigation or not, and that I'm still no closer to giving you her killer's name.'

Spaniard cracked his knuckles. 'It's early days yet.'

'Suppose I never discover the culprit's identity?'

It was a distinct possibility.

'Let's not involve ourselves in negatives or start playing the "what if" game,' he murmured, and the goose pimples crept up to her shoulders. 'Why don't you tell me what you *have* discovered instead.'

'Very well, but I should warn you, it's precious little.' Claudia's gaze fixed on the ominous stains in the rock. 'Although it appears the killer knew where Clytie used to come with her friends, suggesting' – she held back from using the word 'she' – 'it's somebody local.'

He steepled his fingers against his lip and studied her through hooded eyelids the same way he had in her garden. 'It is as I thought,' he said, nodding. 'What else?'

She debated whether to tell him or not, then decided she owed this cold-hearted son-of-a-bitch nothing.

'Your daughter was a conscientious and well-meaning young lady,' she said, drawing a deep breath. 'But equally she was a lonely child, which made her extremely garrulous, suggesting her killer might have wanted to ensure she didn't repeat something she had overheard, and, if you're interested, she died on this very rock.'

For several minutes Gabali said nothing, and his face said even less. With anyone else she'd have wondered whether he'd even heard her, because he certainly didn't dip his gaze to the stone, which was the reaction she'd have expected from a bereaved father.

'Anything else?' he asked eventually.

'The Hundred-Handed are hiding something. Do you know what it is?'

His mouth twisted sideways. 'They're a secretive society, guarding their mysteries in the way all cults and sects do.'

Wrong. There was something else, something deeper, that the College was desperate to keep a lid on.

'They're frightened,' she said. 'No one has admitted it and there's no solid evidence, but stop, look and listen. Fear floats around this place like a cloud.'

He ran his tongue round the inside of his lip. 'That'll be the threat of the Druids,' he said. 'Rumours have been circulating to the effect that they're witches. That the Hundred-Handed – what was it? – "suck clean the minds of men" and various other nonsense.'

'If it's nonsense, why should they be scared?'

'Just because a mirror is a two-dimensional surface doesn't mean the reflection is make-believe as well. What else have you found out during your stay?'

His expectations were high, but then in fairness, so were results.

'There's a spate of poison-pen letters going around which might or might not be connected,' she said. 'But the very fact that they're prolific indicates that there's one member of this College who makes a point of knowing everyone else's business and is endangering their own life in the process.'

Gabali shrugged it off. 'Who cares?'

'I rather thought you might, given that that person could well be the only one who knows the truth about Clytie.'

The Spaniard's eyes narrowed into slits of hostility. 'Or silenced my daughter because she'd stumbled upon their little perversion.'

That fitted too, Claudia thought. With her friends merrily swinging off ropes and poking in caves, and with Clytie blacklisted because of what she kept letting slip – *providing they don't catch us in the act – and no one reports us – and as long as we still learn our lessons – then nobody minds* – she had ample time on her hands to wander from longhouse to longhouse in search of someone to talk to. And finding instead one of the College dipping her quill in neat poison.

'You think the anonymous letter writer killed her, then covered it up by making it look like the previous murders?'

'Why not?' Gabali said. 'If it's true, then their method is certainly proving effective.'

'In which case, it might take months before I crack this particular nut.'

A flicker of amusement kindled in his eyes. 'That is a possibility, *si*. But as Mavor will tell you, necks can take a long time to heal. The Hundred-Handed will have no suspicions.'

'My dear Gabali, you cannot imagine what a comfort it is, knowing I'm stuck in a hen house without an end in sight, especially when my bodyguard tells me there's an uprising looming and it's a bad time to be a Roman.'

'There we go again. Rumours.' Olive hands were held up with their palms facing outwards in a gesture of reassurance. 'You must not allow empty words to alarm you.'

'Then perhaps I ought to be alarmed by the prospect of the Scorpion, now that he is not plotting imminent rebellion, having time to notice wine merchants double-crossing him right under his nose.'

The Spaniard clucked his tongue. 'You worry too much,' he said dismissively. 'I have reported your death to my master and the Scorpion is satisfied. Trust me, he's forgotten all about you.'

'Are you sure?'

'I may be many things, Merchant Seferius, but I am not a liar.'

Claudia felt something lift from under her ribcage. She thought it might have been a burden. Either way, she felt a hundred times better.

'Talking of being many things, Gabali, it appears that you forgot to mention that you were the Hundred-Handed's executioner.'

His jaw clenched. 'It is not a factor in this investigation.'

'You also failed to tell me that Fearn was Clytie's mother.'

The jaw tightened further. 'You've seen how this place works,' he rasped. 'That is not a factor either.'

128

'Really?' Claudia rubbed her temple. 'Not a factor, either of them? Well, let's take those two one at a time, shall we, starting with the Pit of Reflection. Now we both know how slow and nasty that death sentence is, so what if someone decided to take their revenge on you, Gabali, Guardian of the Sacred Trust, for tossing their loved one into that hell-hole? Can you imagine how sweet it would be, killing your daughter then arranging her body in a way that would ensure it would be gawped at and talked about for months without end?'

For the first time, something flickered in those unfathomable brown eyes. It could, she thought, have been pain.

'No, you didn't, did you. Any more than you thought about the consequence of your relationship with the girl's mother.'

That something disappeared as quickly as it had come.

'There was no relationship.' He practically spat the denial at her. 'Fearn sent for me whenever she wanted . . . I don't know . . . companionship? Release? I have no idea what went on in that woman's head, but I do know there was no laughter, no conversation, no exchange of confidences that might make what you call a "relationship".'

Claudia pictured the Growth Priestess, her raven-black hair shining with health against a backdrop of bright yellow cotton. Strong, intelligent, dedicated – but also objective to the point of dispassionate.

'You're saying it was sex pure and simple?'

'It wasn't pure and it certainly wasn't simple,' Gabali rasped. 'She was stiff, cold, it was as difficult as hell, and I honestly don't know what she got out of it.'

'Apart from a baby?'

'She didn't want that, either,' he snapped. 'The Hundred-Handed have potions for unwanted pregnancies, but unfortunately for Fearn none of them worked. Once it was born, she couldn't hand what she referred to as "the brat" over fast enough.'

The painting was amateurish in the extreme, Fearn had said in a voice that she might have used to discuss a barn wall rather than her own murdered daughter. And on the very day of the spring equinox, in the same month protected by her sacred gorse, there was no clue that this sacrilege affected her personally.

Just because we deliver a baby, it doesn't follow that we bond differently with that child than we do with any other, Sarra had said, which was probably true – except bond was the operative word.

Claudia hadn't realized she'd been bunching her robe until she let go of the linen. 'Did she continue to send for you afterwards?'

A soft snort escaped from his nostrils. 'It was as though nothing had happened,' he said. 'Business as bloody usual.'

Business for him. But for Fearn—

'You might have lived among five hundred of them, but you know sod all about women, Gabali.'

'I have never pretended to.'

'Maybe that was your mistake, because that was indeed a relationship Fearn had with you, my friend. The problem was, you didn't know it.'

Was he blind, blinkered, callous or simply conditioned? she wondered. Dammit, Fearn was one of the decision-makers in the College, surely he must have realized that powerful women aren't normally stiff and tongue-tied round their male slaves, particularly not in a society which is uninhibited on the issue of sex. There was only one explanation for her awkwardness around Gabali.

'I hate to be the one who breaks the bad news, but I think you'll find Fearn was in love with you.'

'*What?*'

'The trouble is the Hundred-Handed are such egalitarian creatures, they will believe in this concept of sharing, so let me ask you another question, Gabali. Did you form any other, shall we say more tender attachments while you here?'

A tight expression came over his face. He pushed his long hair back from his face. 'I – may have done.'

'May have done isn't good enough,' she told him. 'Because the thought that's running through my head right now is that old chestnut about hell having no fury quite like a woman scorned.'

'If you must know, then *si*. I . . . I fell in love with one of the Hundred-Handed, and it is not immodest to say that she cared something for me in return— Oh, no!' He bunched one fist and slammed it into the palm of his other

130

hand. 'No woman in her right mind butchers her own child!'

'Medea didn't just kill hers, the nice lady boiled them up in a cauldron and served the stew to their father.'

'Yes, but – Fearn killing Clytie to get back at me, just because I fell in love with somebody else?'

'I sincerely hope not, but like you said yourself, it's early days yet, though it's a point you'll need to bear in mind.' Claudia paused. 'Because at some stage, Gabali, if she *is* guilty, you'll have to decide whether you're actually prepared to execute the mother of your beloved daughter, even though she may have killed her own child.'

And if he was, then that three-headed dragon that stalked the Underworld would have his soul for sure.

Sixteen

After the stifling heat, the cool of the cave was sheer heaven.

In the dark, though, it was sheer hell.

The flames of the torch cast flickering shadows that combined with the uneven surface to trip Claudia up, snag her robe on the cave wall and stub her toes against the stone. If this is the Cave of Resurrection, she thought, rubbing her shin, this wasn't the exit or new souls would come out deformed. But gradually, her eyes acclimatized to the gloom and, following the channel in the rock that diverted the spring water, she progressed deeper and lower into the hillside.

Very quickly the cave became a corridor, narrowing in places so that she needed to turn sideways to pass through the gap or duck under the rock. But always, always, the corridor twisted. Always, always, she was aware of descent.

The air grew cold. Echoes sighed and moaned the length of the tunnel. This must be what Hades was like. Full of whispers and murmurings as loss and regret mingled with sorrow and apathy, and perhaps this was what the spring water was for? To replenish the Pool of Forgetfulness that the dead drank of when they arrived in the Hall of Shades, that their grief at leaving loved ones behind would be erased.

Morbid thoughts were banished by something white near her feet. Bending, she realized it was a scrap of paper. A corner, torn round the edges. Peering closer, it seemed to be from a note about millstones. She turned it over, but that was all. Something about millstones grinding, which must have somehow blown in and got caught. The Gauls exported millstones, she remembered, and there was a quarry near

132

here, where redundant male slaves were often sold on to. It had no connection at all to the poison-pen letters and as it fluttered to the ground like a white butterfly, her mind turned to the death spirits that hovered in this cave like invisible bees. Waiting to guide the souls of the dead—

Claudia pulled up sharp. To her surprise, the tunnel opened into a chamber of stone lit by flickering candles, whose walls danced with handprints and animals. She recognized lynx, antelope and panther exquisitely painted in black and red, while bones and clay offerings lay beside of a cairn of white rocks. Seven skulls that could have been bear faced outwards from the cairn in a semicircle, but the channel of water didn't end. In fact, it seemed to take great pains to skirt the edge of the chamber. She glanced back, but she'd come too far now to give up. With a purse of her lips, she followed the channel, entering deeper and deeper into the mountain. Now water dripped from places she couldn't see. The walls and the floor were wet to her touch. A rope had been attached to the rock with metal hooks, and the rope was smooth from centuries of soft female hands. The knowledge brought comfort in a comfortless place, where strange icicles formed even stranger shapes on the cavern ceiling while others rose upwards from the cavern floor.

What surprised her was that the icicles were formed in rings of differing colours. Black, purple, lilac and blue. A bizarre underworld rainbow.

The death spirits pass the time weaving shrouds on looms made of stone.

These, then, were the looms . . .

Further into the mountain, there came the sound of rushing water until finally, turning a bend, Claudia was confronted by a stream surging through the mountain, white and frothy, and it was into this that the water from the Cave of Miracles emptied. The balance of nature, she realized, as water was returned to water, and its discovery left her decidedly cheated. This was the place where souls were supposed to be judged, yet it was nothing. Just water pouring back into water, no clues – not a thing – to suggest the source of the Hundred-Handed's secret fears. Nothing to shed light on Clytie's murder.

Retreating along the rope handrail towards the painted chamber, her thoughts turned to the people who'd beautified this rock with their art. Who were they? How long ago had they lived here? And were those bear skulls part of some ancient religion, or simply a hunter's proud trophies? Approaching the white cairn, she noticed something else white behind it and bent to investigate. Another stone?

'*Janus bloody Croesus!*'

'I apologize if I startled you, my dear.' Beth stood up from where she'd been sitting and straightened the creases from her silver robe. 'I watched you go past, but decided against calling out in case I scared you.'

Liar. You could hear footsteps in this underground echo chamber a bloody mile off. The Head of the College had hidden on purpose.

'I'm surprised you take an interloper's presence so lightly,' Claudia said. 'Considering the cave is out of bounds for people like me.'

'It is indeed.' Beth sighed, and it was that, she realized, that had echoed round the tunnel. 'But there are so many things happening at the moment, so many changes afoot, that one tiny transgression doesn't seem worth getting angry over.'

Times are changing, Claudia, Rome's seen to that. Orbilio's words floated back. *Thanks to us, the world has got smaller for the Gauls and* this *world*, she remembered how he'd nodded towards the Hundred-Handed, *has to adapt. If it doesn't, quite frankly, it dies.*

'You choose what you get passionate about?' Claudia asked, wishing she could read the expression on the older woman's face.

'When several fires burn simultaneously,' Beth said with a sad smile, 'it's unwise to attempt to extinguish them all at once lest, instead of a few trees alight, one ends up with a forest fire raging out of control.'

If change comes too fast, it's liable to have the opposite effect of what it's intended to do. Orbilio might as well have been in the damned cavern with them. *It can destroy rather than build.*

'I suppose you're concentrating on the Druids?'

'Then you suppose wrong.' Beth ran her hands over her

chestnut-brown hair. Even in the torchlight it shone. 'Somehow, yes, we do need to get across to the Wise Fathers that we are neither sorceresses nor witches and I won't deny that isn't a problem. However.' She traced one elegant finger round the rim of the top stone of the cairn. 'It is the College that requires my full concentration.'

Claudia waited and for once, patience was rewarded.

'It is not the Conquest itself that has divided us,' Beth said quietly. 'Rather the philosophies it has brought.'

'Women in Roman society aren't equal,' Claudia pointed out. 'Far from it.'

'No, but whereas before Rome took administrative control of this region our status as priestesses was sacrosanct, now there are those within our community who would like to rewrite the rules.' There it was again, that sad, distant smile. 'Modernize is the word they use.'

'Keeping men for stud and breeding your own workforce sounds pretty progressive to me.'

'For a liberated female, I find your hostility surprising, but that is your prerogative, my dear. It is our policy not to judge,' Beth said, in what was clearly a calculated choice of non-passion. 'We believe everyone is entitled to her own opinion and, as pentagram priestesses, it is our role to listen to those opinions and then make decisions based on the views of everyone in the College. The trouble arises when opinions spread discord and that discord breeds division—'

'Which it does at the moment?'

'Seething is not too strong a word, since some of us are bitterly opposed to the change mooted, while others among us wish to embrace it with open arms.'

'And you?'

'Me?' Another long sigh. 'We need to move forward, one always must, but not by changing our teachings, my dear. What needs to change is the way that life is perceived here.'

'I'm sensing that we're not talking about how outsiders see you?'

'If only it was that simple,' Beth said. 'Unfortunately, there is a strong movement within the College that is pushing for priestesses to marry – and not just priestesses. Initiates, supervisors, they believe every one of us has the right to what they consider to be a "normal" life.'

'Which you feel will dilute your status as a religious body and lower your standing in the community?'

'I am not against love, how could I be? Love is the pivot upon which the world turns and it is the reason we expel our menfolk at the age of forty, while they are still young enough to raise families of their own – I see that surprises you.'

Claudia shifted her torch to the other hand while her eyebrows returned to their customary level. 'Actually, yes.'

'Did you honestly think we wouldn't want people we cared for to be happy?' Beth asked. 'Of course we want them to have wives, children, grandchildren and all the other things they deserve but which we cannot give them.'

'And which you yourselves are denied?'

'Our system is far from ideal, I agree, but I am prepared to lay down my life to preserve it, flaws and all, in order to retain the respect of the tribes.' In the torchlight, she looked older than her forty-six years. 'These people,' she said wearily, 'look *to* us for spiritual guidance and healing, and in doing so, they look *up* to us as well. We cannot teach them that nature is constant if the very College that serves it keeps changing.'

Claudia stared at the ancient handprints daubed on the walls. At the bears, which, she realized now, had undoubtedly been sacrificed to long-forgotten gods.

'What happens to those who rebel?' she asked dully.

And how could such a hideous death chamber be sited in so beautiful a location?

'Ah.' Beth clucked her tongue. 'You know about the Pit, then.'

For several long minutes, both women remained locked in their own silence. It was the Head of the College who finally broke it.

'Fearn argues that by changing our way of life to incorporate marriage, it will eliminate the necessity for the Pit, and such a philosophy is bound to gather momentum.'

'Especially among the younger girls,' Claudia said, picturing Elusa's blonde, almost white, hair.

'Who cannot imagine old bags like me ever had feelings,' Beth replied with a soft laugh. 'But instead of bending and thus making the College weaker, I believe we must show strength by believing in ourselves and standing by our convictions.'

'Whatever the cost?'

An eternity seemed to pass before she finally answered. 'Yes,' she said at last. 'Whatever the cost.'

Maybe it was the cool of the chamber that kept Claudia bound to the place. Maybe it was the pull of ancient religions, a sense of holiness in pagan surroundings. But she couldn't have walked away if she tried.

'What happens to priestesses when they die?' she asked. Because the Gauls liked to honour their dead every bit as much as a Roman, though instead of lining their approach roads with sumptuous tombs, they opted for moated graveyards way out of town. Yet Claudia had seen nothing resembling a cemetery round these parts, even though the Hundred-Handed had been established here for three hundred years.

Beth pointed upwards, and Claudia lifted her torch. High above their heads, with access that could only be reached by a ladder, a ledge had been gouged out of the rock. On it sat a series of huge painted pots. At an educated guess, they numbered fifty, and each was as tall as a man.

'Their ashes are kept in these urns.'

Ashes? This was contrary to all Gaulish principles, where they liked to line their graves with planks of wood, preferably oak, and send their loved ones into the next life with as many personal possessions as they could cram in. Oh, and yes. Where it was crucial that the corpse remained as close to physically perfect as possible! Then she remembered Orbilio saying how the Greeks came to Gaul and the Gauls went to Greece, and how the cult of the water priestesses had somehow merged into this cult of nature priestesses. The women who talked with their hands.

And the Greeks, like the Romans, cremated their dead—

'I must go,' Beth said. 'Tomorrow is midsummer, there is much work to do, and my absence will be noticed before long.'

137

All the same, she seemed in no hurry to return to the upper world.

'This is your escape,' Claudia said.

'My dear, as head of the order, there *is* no escape,' the Birch Priestess laughed. 'But down here I am at least free to think.'

'Among the dead?'

'Among old friends,' she corrected with a smile. 'And when there is so much discord among the living, believe me, this is no bad place to reflect.'

Claudia studied the rows of pots high above her head. 'Is Clytie here?' she asked softly.

'Only those who qualify for the fifty elite may have their ashes added to their predecessors',' Beth said, and her dark eyes were sad. 'For the rest, their ashes are scattered to nature and this is one of the hardest tasks that falls upon me. Telling the novices that they will not be admitted as Initiates of Light.'

'The scattering of ashes doesn't seem to bother them.'

'It is because they know no better, but to us, to the Hundred-Handed, the preservation of remains is sacrosanct. It is a secret that we, quite literally, carry with us to our graves.'

And beyond, Claudia thought, and now she looked closely she realized that the paintings on the pots were not random. Yellow for gorse, silver for birch, black, green, purple for heather, red like Luisa's shiny bright rowans.

'What disqualifies a novice?' she asked.

'I prefer to think of it in terms of what gifts they can bring,' Beth said, smoothing her robe. 'But basically we look for balance, sound judgement, sensitivity and altruism. There is certainly no room for fluster or panic.'

Don't be fooled by that rough-and-tumble, Sarra had said, talking of Vanessia, Aridella and Lin. *Those games stimulate their sharp little brains and believe me, they're clever, those girls. Vanessia's already qualified for Initiatehood, and without any shadow of doubt, the others will follow. Those three have the dedication and determination I never had*, the fairy had added. *That's for sure.*

'Was Clytie up to the job, Beth?'

'No.'

The answer came without hesitation. Only with sadness.

'Did you tell her?' Claudia asked, biting her lip.

'No.'

The answer still came without hesitation. Except this time, it was accompanied by relief.

'No, my dear, it is my one consolation that I hadn't got round to telling the poor child.' Beth sighed. 'At least Clytie died without knowing she'd been rejected.'

As Gauls from the surrounding forests flocked to celebrate the summer solstice in revels that would last through until sunset the following day, Marcus Cornelius Orbilio tossed the last log on the bonfire. It was a giant of a pile, the biggest he'd ever seen that was for sure, although he wasn't sure the night would need additional heat. Hot and sticky, the temperature had barely dipped as the light faded and he decided he wouldn't fancy being close to this fire once it was lit. In these pants, he saw himself poaching to death.

Whereas the spring equinox, now. He brushed the dust off his hands down the length of his trousers. The spring equinox was celebrated by many religions, not purely Roman, with beacon fires to represent the sun's triumph over darkness and with gorse representing the golden rays of the sun. Glancing at the crowds pouring into the Field of Celebration, Orbilio wasn't convinced either that Clytie's killer used the festival to sate some demonic bloodlust – how could they, for a start? The meadow was fenced off with a forbidding palisade whose gates were guarded by local men armed with knives and spears.

And the murder seemed a lot more complicated than mere logistics, too. Clytie had been lured, undoubtedly by prior arrangement, down to that rock by the river. Now a young woman might be tricked into such a meeting – love makes fools of us all – but no twelve-year-old child would be duped by a stranger. Especially when that child lived her life in a bubble. And if Orbilio needed a seal on that hypothesis, it was that sex wasn't the motive for Clytie's murder.

He wished he knew what the hell was.

To a slow beat of drums, the Oak Priestess mounted the dais resplendent in a brown robe embroidered with thousands of tiny gold acorns. As the choir sang sweet hymns in praise of courage and strength, the four other pentagram priestesses joined her, holding hands to form the eternal circle of life, from birth through until death. Novices of all ages came skipping forward and each was handed a bowl by a smiling Dora, who seemed totally unconcerned that the sky was full of clouds rather than stars as her finger joints repeated the same quick triple flick to each girl before they skipped off. The bowls, he'd been told, were to collect the midsummer dew. The novices would have their work cut out for them with this dawn, he thought.

Stifling a yawn as the bonfire was lit to deafening cheers, Marcus knew sleep was out of the question. Tonight he had been co-opted to turn the ox on the spit. Tomorrow he was one of the fifty men chosen to fire an arrow into the zenith of the sun (they'd be lucky as well!). But as a seasoned investigator and with his military background, he was well used to the concept of catnaps. He could catch up on sleep if he wanted.

He didn't.

All afternoon, he had been building up that bonfire with the help of a man who called himself Manion. The man who Orbilio now knew was the Scorpion.

Watching children dance round the fire as the dull grey clouds fused with the night and Gauls in bright chequered plaid and with jewellery adorning every spare inch of their body tossed back horns brimming with beer, he mulled over what Roman intelligence had been able to gather about the Scorpion's background.

His tribe was the Bituriges; it translated as 'Kings of the World', which was precisely what they were to the Gauls. Through shrewd political alliances (plus some pretty resolute defending), their influence extended over every tribe from the centre of Gaul to the Pyrenees and right up to the River Loire. Ferocious warriors with a penchant for guerrilla tactics, Julius Caesar had wisely left the Bituriges alone and even Augustus had resorted to diplomacy to win them over. Well. Diplomacy with the twin carrots of prosperity and autonomy dangled before them, but who's counting?

And since it was one of life's ironies that the Bituriges

only ever went to war to maintain peace, they were more than happy to have other men fight their wars, whilst taking ostentatious pleasure in policing the lesser tribes to ensure they abandoned their old headhunting ways and gave up their wicker-man sacrifice. In fact, revelling in their status as imperially approved overlords, the Kings of the World broadcast the fact that there was no room in this prosperous, modern, forward-thinking society for any hothead with insurgent tendencies.

So when an impatient young man pushed for war against Rome, they decided the most effective way to deal with this burr under the tribal saddle was to expel it.

Similarly, there was no room in the impatient young man's life for cowards and, styling himself the Scorpion, he turned to crime to finance his cause. Heaven knew there were enough Gauls who had not settled happily under the yoke, malcontents who didn't work and didn't want to, and thus didn't profit from the occupying force. And when you took in the sheer number of tribes that comprised the Nation as a whole, the Carnutes, the Pictones, the Vocates to name just a few, the Scorpion wasn't short of allies. Cunning, passionate and wholly dedicated to ousting Rome from Aquitania, he managed to turn small-scale theft into a large-scale, well-organized syndicate that then became a burr under the imperial saddle instead.

Luckily for Orbilio, newly promoted to this equally new branch of the Security Police, most of the crime centred around Santonum, since this was the seat of most trade and therefore the most profitable to rob. Fine. Orbilio was well used to handling gangsters and, embracing the challenge of scotching rebellion, he'd pored over the intelligence reports. And could see why the Governor was worried.

After several months of concerted investigation, everything his men knew about the Scorpion could still be written on a thumbnail with room to spare. Average height, average build, no distinguishing features: he became the garrison's nightmare. Paste on a false beard, he was an Assyrian. Comb his hair back, loop up his tunic and he was a Spaniard. He'd proved as oily as grease, the reports stated with monotonous regularity, covering his tracks more thoroughly than an

Egyptian sand tracker and ensuring that no felonies could be traced directly to him. Any that were, he swiftly dealt with, they added. Or rather employed shadowy figures to deal with on his behalf. And the reports were clear. No one crossed the Scorpion and lived to tell the tale.

Turning the giant handle on the spit, Marcus watched the juices drip off the ox and recalled one particular instance where the soldiers thought they had this self-styled sponsor of Aquitanian independence cornered. A reliable informant had passed on details of a meeting between the Scorpion and his deputy, a man called Ptian, another of society's outcasts. This was good news, since Ptian was rumoured to be as cunning and callous as his general and, surrounding the tenement, the captain in charge saw promotion writ large as two birds were felled with the same stone. Yet when his informant gave the signal that the ringleader had passed inside the building, a thorough search of all six storeys revealed no Scorpion, no Ptian and sod-all by way of evidence, either. It was only one pen-pusher's afterthought that mentioned a pair of drunks slumped in the gutter, and Orbilio raised a wry smile as he'd read it. The slippery bastards had sloughed their skins when the first shout of *Raid!* hit the rafters.

Around him, revellers feasted on roast meats, cheeses and bread while the men sang loud songs which talked of brave deeds and heroes, victories and blood feuds, while small boys waved imaginary swords and the women clustered in small knots to gossip.

'. . . dreadful . . .'

'. . . don't believe a word of it . . .'

'. . . me neither. If she was going to cuckold her husband, I'm sure it wouldn't be with his spotty apprentice.'

'The boy hotly denied it, but the miller had evidence and he threw the lad out on his ear.'

'Evidence?'

'Yes, somebody saw them, didn't you know, and sent the miller a note. *The lowest millstone grinds as well at the top.* Couldn't be plainer, could it, my dear?'

'Yes, but what about our flour, that's what I want to know. There'll be a backlog now that they're one hand short—'

Marcus Cornelius turned his attention back to the Scorpion

and the problem he had been faced with. Namely, how could he hope to achieve what his predecessors could not and trap the Scorpion and thwart his uprising? Well. For a start, he had at his disposal the Governor's foresight to form a new branch of the Security Police. And since insurrection relies on good communication and sound information, Orbilio had set this dedicated force to wreaking as much havoc as possible within the Scorpion's own intelligence network. In the same way that Rome received masses of misinformation, part of the role of his taskforce was to plant informants of their own and relay the same equally incorrect information back down the communication lines. A tactic that would cause sufficient confusion to at least delay any uprising until it was too late and the campaigning season was over. Until yesterday, Orbilio thought that tactic was working.

He wiped the sweat from his brow with the back of his hand.

That Manion had staged that business of the lost signet ring was beyond doubt, just as he'd swapped the task that he'd originally been allotted to work alongside Orbilio to build up the fire.

He needed to be careful he was not growing paranoid. It might well have been nothing more than an elaborate charade to draw another disenchanted sucker into his scorpioidal net.

But his money was on Manion knowing exactly who Pretty Boy was.

Orbilio listened to the fats sizzle as they dripped into the flames and, as slices of beef were carved off and passed round, his thoughts turned to rebellion, to blood feuds and Claudia Seferius.

And the way the Scorpion had wiped the honey away from her mouth . . .

Seventeen

'So who's your money on, Lofty Legs?'

Dawn was breaking thick, dull and sticky when Claudia felt a sharp finger prodding her in the ribs.

'Vanessia or the girl with the widow's peak?'

'Excuse me?' She frowned at the dwarf, who was rubbing his hands together in a gesture she just knew was a parody.

'Don't give me that sniffy I-don't-like-a-bet look, I know you.' Gurdo's face twisted up at one side as he examined the pendant round her neck. 'Amber makes a good stake.'

'What are you putting into the kitty?'

'Me?' His shoulders shrugged. 'Lady, I never lose, but if it keeps you happy, I suppose I could toss in a whistle-stop tour round the Cave of Resurrection.'

The malevolent glint in his eye told her that he knew damn well she'd already taken it. Like Pod said, the crafty little bugger *could* see round corners.

'Thank you, but I've lost interest in dark, murky places,' she said, unhooking the pendant and slapping it into his open palm. 'I'll let you know what I want once I've won, and do you mind telling me what we're betting on here?'

'The dew-gathering, Lofty Legs.' His green shirt was dark in the places it stuck to his body and sweat-dampened tendrils of hair clung to his forehead. 'Because just when you think you know these women, something catches you by surprise, doesn't it?'

Fruitlessly trying to fan some air to her own clammy skin, Claudia considered Beth's revelations that the men were released at forty to enable them to settle down, albeit in slavery, and her confidences regarding the discord seething within the College. It wasn't so much a case of what this little green dandy knew, she realized. More what he didn't know . . .

'See, it's not enough that they send novices to collect the dew on the quarter days, is it? There's a competition to see who brings back the most.'

'I suppose cheating is out of the question?'

Gurdo's laugh gargled in the back of his throat. 'Might have known you'd think of dirty tricks straight away, but these little lovelies are raised on a diet of kindness and honesty. Something you don't know much about, that's for sure.'

'I am *this* tempted to cut off that ponytail and feed it to you via your nostrils.'

'What are you going to cut it off with? Your tongue?' He crossed his arms over his chest as he puffed it up. 'Now about this competition. Are you backing Vanessia or the girl with the widow's peak?'

'Why *any* contest?' she asked. 'The Hundred-Handed don't strike me as the competitive type.'

'Stick around, Lofty Legs, and you'll see rivalry on every issue great, small and infinitesimal, you wouldn't *believe* what goes on inside that precinct. But this, this is to see who's learned the best lesson about how dew forms and where. An exam, if you prefer.'

'In which case, the answer's Vanessia.'

He clapped his hands and jumped up and down in another ridiculous parody. 'I *knew* you'd say that!' He planted a loud smack of a kiss on the pendant. 'You're mine, little beauty, all mine.'

'If you're lucky, I'll let you kiss it goodbye too,' Claudia told him. 'But dawn's a way off, so while we're waiting, why don't you tell me what other special dispensations you Sacred Guardians have.'

'Who says we have any?'

'Well, for one thing, you have free access to the precinct.'

'Only because I'm a dwarf and like I said, lady, we ain't real men.'

'Yet they trust you enough not to enslave you, to leave you in charge of the cave *and* give you your own private accommodation, just as Swarbric is in charge of security at the gate and has his own hut, too. Not to mention seemingly endless amounts of free time.'

'Free? Funny word considering Swarbric's a slave, but if you're talking about leisure time, then the same can be said for any of the men.' He swiped his forehead with the back of his hand. 'You can budget for time like you can budget for anything else, Lofty Legs. It just needs planning, that's all.'

'Which Swarbric is good at?'

Gurdo cast a sideways glance at the mop of grey hair and wide disarming grin busily charming two initiates and a priestess at the same time. 'What isn't that slimy bastard good at,' he snarled from the corner of his mouth. 'He could smarm Chastity into lifting her skirts, him.'

'I'm sure he speaks equally highly of you,' she chirped back. 'What's between him and Mavor?'

'Who says there's *anything* between those two?' Green eyes narrowed in suspicion.

Claudia thought of the expression on the redhead's face as she'd scurried back to the Dining Hall the evening before from the direction of Swarbric's hut. Remembered the flush on her cheeks – from anger? alarm? – and the way she'd taken pains to rectify any dishevelment before going in to join the others. No, no, something was definitely cooking in that particular kitchen, and yet there was no denying the dismissive manner in which she'd ruled Swarbric out as a lover while massaging Claudia's neck. But though Gurdo didn't deny that there was something between the Bird Priestess and the German, even if it was not of a sexual nature, she knew that Gurdo had brought the shutters down on that particular issue. To prove it, he jabbed a finger towards the dais.

'Look, the girls are back with the midsummer dew.' He tutted. 'Beyond me how they can collect anything on a muggy morning like this.'

'Just proves that studying trees for three hundred years really does pay off in the end.'

His chuckle wasn't entirely due to her quip. Rocking back and forth on his heels, he was rubbing the necklace with his thumb while the Oak Priestess solemnly measured the droplets.

'Oh and dear me, if Vanessia hasn't won the competition,'

Claudia said, and it was worth winning just to see his scowl when she hung the pendant back round her neck.

'Fluke,' he grumbled, turning round and stomping off. 'That's what it was. A damned fluke.'

As the sky changed from dark grey to light grey and Vanessia accepted the crown of oak leaves from Dora, revellers, priestesses and male slaves alike prepared to snuggle down to sleep before the next round of festivities. All, that is, except a tall, dark patrician standing beside the roasting spit, who was watching her carefully from across the field.

'Sorry to disappoint you, Gurdo.' Claudia patted the amber with affection as she matched the dwarf's stride. 'But you see, the girl with the widow's peak might be a year older than Vanessia, but what you have to remember is that a bright girl like Blondie will always want to compensate for her adventurous streak by learning her lessons twice as carefully as her peers.'

It wasn't a question of having something to prove. It was a case of having something to lose.

'What do you want?' Gurdo scowled as he clambered over a fallen log on what was obviously a shortcut back to the cave. 'Gold?'

'Information,' she said, clambering with him. 'Tell me everything you know about Clytie.'

'Bugger off.'

'With pleasure. In fact, I think I'll bugger straight off to Beth and tell her about your game with the healing springs. How you make the sick and needy cross your miser's palm with silver before you allow them the water the Hundred-Handed give out for free. How much have you got stashed away, anyway?'

'A man in my position needs to plan for his old age. Beth'll understand that.'

'You're a sore loser, Gurdo, but you still owe me.'

'All right, all right. I've got this nice little torque inlaid with coral—'

'Clytie.'

' – or a twist of gold rope that will really suit your long neck—'

'*Clytie.*'

' – or how about a bracelet engraved with panthers and bears that have been inlaid with jet? Take it or leave it, that's my stake.'

'Fine. I'll take it.' She waited until triumph lit the green of his eyes. 'I'll take it straight to Beth and explain how you exploit vulnerable women, bedding them simply because they've been cured by the sacred spring.'

'Eh, eh, not so fast.' He made a placating gesture with his hands. 'What is it you want to know?'

She told him.

'You're a nosy cow, you know that? From the minute you arrived, you've been poking that snout of yours into places that don't concern you – and trust me, lady, the dead here don't concern you.'

'That's where our opinions differ, because Clytie *is* my business, Gurdo, and if you think I'm making life miserable for you now, imagine what it will be like if you don't tell me the truth, the whole truth and no lies by omission, either.'

'I'm not surprised you've got a pain in the neck, you're bloody contagious,' he retorted, but the puff had gone out of him. And, as they crossed a glade ringed by fruit trees and nuts, where a goldfinch trilled from the top of a conifer and a family of blue tits squabbled for grubs, Gurdo described how Pod had found Clytie laid out on the grass next to the stream.

The night of the spring equinox had passed in much the same way as the night Claudia herself had just passed, he explained, pausing as he relived the memory. Gorse had decked the dais and its brilliant yellow was the colour of the novices' robes. As usual, a bonfire had been lit to celebrate the balance between darkness and light, good and evil, cold and warmth, and, just like midsummer, flames from the fire were carried in bowls by the novices for Fearn to pass over her sacred gorse to purify it.

But there was one significant difference. As King of the Forest, the oak took the shortest night of the year, and with his wood turned night into day with a massive bonfire that would burn right through until noon, when fifty blazing arrows from its dying flames would be fired into the sun's zenith. On the dawn of the spring equinox, however, the fire was extinguished, signalling the end of the revelries, and instead of sleeping in huddles round the field, the weary celebrants would be wending their way home.

'Just like Pod was,' Gurdo said grimly. 'Me, I'd hung back to take a platter of beef back – what? You want me to starve, just because I'm not as tall as you, Lofty Legs?'

'You're a hoarder and a miser, and you'll never starve, you little green monster. I'll bet those ox bones were white by the time you picked them clean.'

'Can I help it if I hate waste? The point is, by the time I reached the cave, my lad was a wreck. White, shuddering, he was in a right old state and I can't say I blame him. There was more blood on that rock than you've seen in an abattoir, and what with the kid laid out in her nightdress with kohl round her eyes and rouge on her cheeks and her skin the colour of—' Gurdo shook his head. 'I don't know what colour. I've never seen that shade before in my life – here, are you all right?'

'I'm—' Deep breath. 'Fine.' And again. Breathe. Now once more, and concentrate on the child, not your mother – 'What did you do next?'

'What any decent self-respecting person would do,' he snapped back. 'I washed the rock clean, and I tell you that wasn't easy. The gore had congealed, it stank to high heaven, look are you sure you're all right? Maybe the beef tonight was a bit off?'

Claudia clenched her fists until her nails bit deep into the palms of her hands.

'Yes,' she said. 'The beef. That was it.' She squared her shoulders and lifted her chin. 'So what did you do after you washed the' – she almost said evidence – 'blood away?'

'Sent Pod to break the bad news to Beth.' He tugged at his ponytail. 'Well, I could hardly leave him with her in the state he was in, could I? And *someone* had to stay with the poor cow.'

A hot sticky breeze began to play with the leaves, but Claudia didn't notice. 'How well did you know her?'

'Clytie?' His lip curled. 'As well as anyone knew that self-righteous little prig, I suppose.'

149

Memories of her mother's waxy corpse faded. 'You didn't like her?'

'Did anyone?' he asked, clomping through a gap in the trees.

'I don't know . . . I assumed . . . Gurdo, the girl was twelve years old, for heaven's sake! How can anyone not like a child?'

'Listen, lady, there's no law that says a person has to reach a certain age before becoming a pain in the arse.'

'Which Clytie was?'

'Here, if you want to go around bad-mouthing the dead, you go right ahead, but me, I like to show some respect— Holy Dis, what the bloody hell's that?'

Beneath the bole of an oak, a young man was clutching something bloodied and limp to his breast as he rocked back and forth on his knees.

It took a moment before Claudia realized that the young man was Pod.

And that the mangled mess in his arms was a woman.

Sarra.

Eighteen

Eyes that were normally blue had rolled upwards to white. Skin that was normally fair was now grey.

Green grass and white roses ran red with blood . . .

The pair faltered, but only for a moment. Because even as Claudia's horrified eyes met Gurdo's, the same thought passed through their minds. Pod had been first on the scene at Clytie's murder, now he was first on the scene at Sarra's. *Neither Claudia nor Gurdo believed in coincidence.*

'Take him to the cave,' she hissed. 'A preparation of hemlock should do the trick.' God knew, the stuff grew rampant enough in these parts. 'You do know the dosage?' she added sharply, remembering the trug brimming with hellebores, hedge hyssop and monkshood that she'd seen over his arm, each a deadly poison in its own right.

'If you're asking, will I make it too strong so it does a Socrates on him, save your breath,' Gurdo retorted, 'I want my boy calm, not bloody paralysed. I'll use black hellebores. They'll put him in a deep sleep.'

But the sting to his words belied the fear in his eyes. This time it was the Guardian of the Spring who was looking for miracles.

'Stay with him while I tell Beth,' he said, and Croesus almighty, it was taking every ounce of their combined strength to prise Pod off the corpse.

'I'll go,' Claudia insisted, as they finally dragged him away. 'If ever a boy needed his father, Gurdo, it's now.'

That was a lie. As savage and shocking as this murder was, Claudia was more concerned with Beth's reaction when confronted with this second tragedy.

'Just make sure the pair of you are gone by the time I get back,' she called over her shoulder.

151

Gurdo nodded grimly, gratitude showing despite the rigid jaw and blenched skin, but his gratitude was misplaced. This wasn't just about Pod's potential shunning. All right, if even one sniff of his relationship with Sarra got back to the Hundred-Handed, he'd be banished on the instant and that the girl was dead – murdered – counted for nothing. He'd breached sacred rules against which there was no appeal, but Claudia wasn't doing this for Pod or for Gurdo. She was doing this for Sarra, and Clytie before her . . .

Me mother? No more than wind at the door. Pod's words flooded back as she raced down the path to the Field of Celebration. *Seven summers old, I was, there or abouts, and what with me having no memories of me own—*

Why no memories, though, that was the worry. Ducking the overhanging willows as she ran, she recalled numerous cases where death had visited a child's life so violently that the very horror of it had wiped clean memories of the event.

That little girl they found wandering the Capitol, for example. Her entire family had been butchered by a next-door neighbour acting on the orders of Almighty Jupiter himself, who'd told him these people were fiends in human form and that only by chopping off their heads would mortal man be free of demons. Mother, father, grandmother, eight-year-old son, six-year-old daughter and baby still in its crib were all slaughtered, except for the four-year-old, who'd been playing under the bed when the monster broke in. In his axe-wielding frenzy, he'd not noticed the child and though she escaped with her life and the memory of that terror had been blissfully erased, the girl had nevertheless grown up troubled and difficult, striking out at nothing, hurting relatives and friends for no reason. In the end, and aged only sixteen, she took her own life. But then tragedy always rolls on and on.

Whether trauma of that kind had crossed Pod's path, Claudia had no idea, but by drugging him, at least his stupor would slow everything down. It would give her time to grieve for a girl she'd barely known, yet who had been butchered with a savagery she would never forget. And it would give her time to think this whole thing through, because even as she first saw Pod, face blank in grief as he clutched Sarra to his breast, darker thoughts had run through her mind.

That his grief was genuine went without saying, but that four-year-old wandering the Capitol had triggered other memories. Like the cloak-maker's daughter who strangled her cousin ('I didn't know death meant for ever'). The cobbler's son, who started with kittens before slicing up his baby brother. And especially, yes especially, the poulterer's boy. Claudia remembered the story so vividly—

His father coming in from the back yard to find the boy kneeling over his mother, her chest so badly mangled there was hardly room for his blade. He kept stabbing and stabbing, as though he was an automaton, not recognizing his father, he couldn't say his own name and later, could remember nothing about it . . .

She pictured Pod as she'd left him, ashen and trembling, with only animal sounds coming from his mouth as he clutched a mangled spray of white rosebuds to his breast. The fact that there was no knife found at either murder scene didn't mean he hadn't thrown it into the undergrowth, while the fact that he had blackouts didn't mean he hadn't killed those two girls. And the fact that he'd killed Clytie and Sarra certainly didn't mean Pod wasn't sorry—

Claudia's footsteps echoed over the footbridge.

Two young girls, two crucial dates in the Hundred-Handed's calendar, copious amounts of blood. And yet . . . And yet . . .

As she ran up the steps onto the dais to wake Beth and break the bad news, there was only one thought tumbling around in her head. Assuming Sarra's arms had been spread out at her sides – and there was nothing to suggest they had been – her cheeks hadn't been reddened with rouge, her eyes hadn't been painted with kohl.

'Sarra?' Ailm barked, her voice still rough from sleep. 'I was only talking to the girl an hour or two back!'

Her face drained from shock, Beth couldn't speak. Dora, rising beside her, blinked rapidly.

'Are you sure she's dead and not pretending?' Luisa asked. 'Some of those novices are terrible practical jokers.'

153

'I'm so sorry, but there's no mistake.'

With a voice cracked with emotion, Claudia reported the multiple stab wounds that left Sarra's pink robe shredded in an attack that was almost orgiastic in its frenzy.

'If it helps,' she added, as finger signals flashed back and forth between the five women, 'Sarra put up one hell of a fight.'

The cuts in her hands stood proof to that. Her palms had been cut to ribbons.

'We have decided,' Beth said, and the calmness of her voice belied the shaking of her limbs. 'For once it is unanimous – ' she cast a glance at both Dora and Ailm – 'but it is our opinion that nothing of this must be broadcast to the outside world. It will achieve nothing while engendering panic.'

Four heads nodded firmly in unison.

'I shall ask some of the sisterhood to take Sarra away to be prepared for the Journey, of course. But the pentagram will remain, the ceremony will continue, we will fire fifty blazing arrows into the sun's zenith as though nothing has happened.'

Like it did with Clytie, Claudia was tempted to snap, but then remembered that these women had just received a terrible shock. Arousing their animosity would gain nothing.

'You can't simply ignore it,' she pointed out calmly.

'Indeed, no,' Beth said kindly, holding up three bent fingers with the ghost of a smile. 'See? Swarbric has already been sent for.'

'So if you'll excuse us?' Ailm made no attempt to hide the hostility in her voice. 'We wish to mourn in private, if you don't mind.'

'Of course,' she replied, 'I understand perfectly,' and all things considered, was it any wonder they wanted her gone? Closing ranks was the one thing the Hundred-Handed did best. That, and covering up murder.

I suspect you meant to call me an angel, but you've just labelled me an old bat! The fairy's soft laugh rippled through the leaves in the forest. *This is the cipher for angel.*

Absently watching half a dozen tearful women slip away as Beth whispered instructions to a stony-faced Swarbric, images floated before her.

For one more moment, Sarra was still trailing her spray of white roses down the path behind her . . .

Blushing furiously, but unable to meet Pod's eyes . . .

Timing her walk so that she'd bump into the young woodsman . . .

Through the thick sticky heat, Claudia saw the shine on the girl's long, silky hair. The even longer kiss the lovers had exchanged. The grass stains she and Sarra had laughingly removed from the girl's pale pink robe. At least Sarra's last hours had been happy, she thought, and dammit there was something in her eye that was making it water, and she just could not rub the bloody thing out.

While deep within the Cave of Resurrection, the spirits that buzzed like invisible bees guided a gentle soul down to the Underworld.

Nineteen

Midsummer for the Druids was also significant. Oak priests themselves and intermediaries of the gods, the sun was the fire from which all life began and Bel was the sun god, 'the Shining One', the god of light, and it was at midsummer that 'the Horned One', Hu'Gadarn, god of the underworld, died in the fire and was reborn on the winter solstice.

Light and fire.

Light and fire, that was the point, except this year they could not make their sacrifice in the fire, and the omens they read in the sky and in the entrails of beasts were not good.

With the wicker man standing empty and silent, the Druids cast runes then passed round the Keys of Wisdom written on yew, for yew was the tree of eternity. And as the Keys passed in silence from hand to hand, the air was heavy with foreboding. Human sacrifice was vital to maintain the balance of life and continue the thread of eternity. Quite simply, it was one life, good or bad, exchanged for another. It was the symbol of redemption and peace.

Without it, the gods would not be pleased. They would punish the Gauls for this terrible slight. Their insult would not be overlooked.

In the runes, the Druids saw cattle ailing, crops failing, they saw disaster and ruin, hunger and despair – and why? Why should this be? they asked themselves.

But the answer lay there. Written on yew. The Keys of Wisdom told them the reason. Rome sacrificed humans in the arena. They sacrificed men to wild animals in the name of execution, and if possible, so would the Druids. In fact, none of the present Council could recall a single instance where a criminal had not been burned at midsummer. It had always been their favoured method of execution, and keeping the offender alive for the wicker man had always been their preferred choice. A life for a life, in Rome and in Gaul. It was the sacred and eternal balance again.

Except now—

Thanks to fifty women the cycle was broken, the thread had been cut; no wonder the gods' anger was building. The Druids did not understand how Rome, whose dominion stretched for thousands of miles, could be fooled by a handful of simpering nature priestesses to the extent that the whole structure of Gaulish religion was crumbling. How could Rome possibly not see the damage these women were causing?

Until someone in their administration had marked out a territory and named it Aquitania (which it wasn't), the Druids had been left in peace. And though Rome might have called their headhunting and wicker men barbarous, they had not outlawed the practice until recently. Shortly after Santonum was chosen as the province's capital, as it happened, and how strange that the College of the Hundred-Handed was close by!

Staring at the Keys of Wisdom, the Druids knew the reason.

Rome, no strangers to sacrifice, for they themselves pitted grazing beasts against lions in the arena, had been bewitched by the Hundred-Handed into practising double standards. The Druids hadn't wanted to believe the rumours, but now they were left with no choice. The evidence was laid bare for everyone to see. The Hundred-Handed were not nature priestesses who advocated peace. They were witches. Witches, who'd sucked the minds of the Romans clean: and there was only one cure for witchcraft.

Burning.

No other method would eradicate their insidious evil, and it was no use turning to Rome for assistance. Rome was already under their spell. No, no, the Druids must act independently in this matter – and they knew exactly who they must contact. A young warrior, who'd been shunned by his tribe for speaking out against Rome. A young warrior with an army in waiting.

Most importantly, the Druids agreed, they needed to act swiftly, before any further damage was done.

Like wasps, burning the nest was the only solution.

The whole thing must be destroyed.

High on the hill, the young warrior breathed on his ring then buffed it up on his shirt. There was no sunlight to make the silver shine, but the fact it was round his finger was enough. Engraved on it was the symbol of everything that he stood for, and he smiled.

He had whispered his poison into the Druids' ears and the Druids had drunk every drop. And now that they'd been barred from sacrificing the wicker man, it would not be long now before they called on his services. He, and the Saviours of Gaul, were prepared.

Staring out across the valley, he thought about the other whisperings he had put about.

Some were true – the Druids' dissension, for example – which would force Rome to confront the wily old priesthood on their intentions regarding the Hundred-Handed, knowing full well that the Druids would not admit weakness in the presence of their oppressors. This would lead nicely to a climate of lies and distrust, which would then swing a good many don't-knows in his own favour.

Some of the rumours were deliberately untrue, including the notion that the men who'd tried to assassinate the Governor had been hired by one of his own trusted generals. The Whisperer had no doubt that the craven little cowards would have been quick to confess that they'd been given their orders directly by the Scorpion's deputy, Ptian. That wasn't the point. A seed of doubt had been sown, and no matter how small, that seed was strong enough not to blow away. Rome already knew it had harboured informants within its own walls – why not something even worse? It wasn't a case of not believing the lies. More a case of not *wanting* to believe them. And these things mattered, if the beehive was to be set buzzing. The more emotional unrest that could be created, the better.

He watched a rabbit sniff the hot sticky air and wished he'd had his bow with him. One arrow and he'd have that coney roasting over his camp fire, slathered with hot oil and mustard. Not that he was hungry, of course. There had been enough food at the revels to feed his army for weeks, but tempted as he was to stash some away, he resisted. People would notice. *Beth* would notice. Nothing escaped that bitch's eye.

Which brought him to the other rumours he had spread. The ones that were neither true nor false, but somewhere in between. Like the Aquitani were primed to attack, for example. He'd had it put about that they were planning an uprising at the peak of midsummer, he'd leaked places, numbers, as much information as he could, knowing Rome would have to follow up but equally knowing their heart wouldn't be in it. Stretch a bowstring too tight for too long and it ceases to remain taut. In this case, the bowstring was Rome. They'd been led on so many wild-goose chases now that they really didn't believe it could happen. To them, war was something to be conducted from spring through to autumn, and already they were growing complacent. He'd seen for himself how the forces were growing thinner each time one of these rumours sent them hither and thither, and complacency suited the Saviours of Gaul. For the Aquitani, fighting for freedom and their very survival, there was no 'season for war'. Their lives at stake, their territories, their families, their whole way of life. *And Rome expects them to stick to fucking rules?* The Whisperer spat. Let them. Let them grow slack. Then when the Saviours of Gaul strike late, and at targets they won't be expecting, the bastards won't know which way to turn.

Ah, but afterwards! The warrior felt the excitement of battle run through his veins, as exciting as – no, more than – sex. He saw the Druids restored to the glory they once had. He saw them august, respected, strong and revered, and it would all be thanks to one man! Under a free Gaul – *his* Gaul – they would be exempt from tithes and would once more become the priests, judges, teachers, physicians and philosophers they were destined to be.

He would restore the wicker man, too. The wicker-man sacrifice that was designed to show power. To show strength. That would give the gods the blood they needed to grow stronger again, and the right gods, this time. Not some stupid fucking nature lore spun by some bloody priestesses. *Man's* lore. In a *man's* world. Where women knew their bloody place.

And he thought, what a sweet, sweet moment that was. Standing on the edge of that glade earlier watching the dwarf's dim-witted bastard blubbering over that wishy-washy little blonde cow. Did he think no one knew what they did in that glade, those two? He sneered, remembering how he'd seen them himself only yesterday afternoon. Her with skirts up round her waist, dirty slut, sucking the power out of another poor sod. And now she was dead. Butchered like a boar with her blood soaking the ground and did he care? Fuck no. Good riddance to bad rubbish, that's what he thought, and even better, this second murder would have the Hundred-Handed jumping at every damned shadow.

The Whisperer rubbed his hands in delight. The bitches won't feel safe anywhere in their own grounds now, and that was perfect for the Whisperer's plans – and oh yes, he had plans.

Several plans.

With another poised to spring into action right now.

Twenty

'You look sad,' a voice murmured in Claudia's ear.
She recognized it at once. As soft and smooth as his deerskin pants, Manion's tones were the only distinctive aspect about him.

'You don't,' she replied. 'You look like the cat who's found the lid's off the cream dish.' Smug wasn't the word.

'Well, you know how it is.'

He flexed his muscles with a comical gesture before leaping the stream to join her, where she'd been staring at the place where the river gushed out of rock, thinking about Sarra and Pod. Another time and the sun would have alerted her to his presence with a shadow. She wondered how long he'd been standing there. Watching.

'Strength and endurance, it's what this festival is all about, isn't it?' he asked with a wink, and now that he was standing close she could smell perfume on his shirt, and a faint hint of nutmeg beneath.

'Every man must do his duty?'

'Exactly,' he said. 'And this is the only job in the world where the mistress keeps a dog but still can't bark herself.'

'Woof, woof.'

He settled beside her, facing the waterfall, and ran his hand over his closely cropped hair. 'Why don't you tell me what troubles you, my lady. I find sadness is always best when it's shared.'

'I think everyone's sharing this sorrow, Manion. Or doesn't it touch you that a young girl has been butchered?'

'Dead?' he rumbled. 'Another one?'

And she could almost believe he hadn't heard, if it wasn't for those unfathomable eyes. Neither green nor blue, but

161

somewhere in between. Why did she have a feeling she'd seen them before?

'No wonder you're worried,' he said, breathing on the seal ring that had been noticeable by its absence yesterday. 'It's clearly not safe for a woman to be out alone.'

As he polished the silver against soft yellow deerskin, Claudia caught a glimpse of an engraving. It looked like an animal or perhaps a sideways figure-of-eight, but when he caught her looking, he twizzled it round so only the whorls on the other side of the band were on show. And she thought of the water that rushed out of the rock, and the other river that ran inside the hill. How many other rivers had made torrents through these hillsides? Eroding the soft limestone as they churned, leaving caverns and caves by the score? She thought of the people, long faded from history, whose hands left prints and art on the walls. We are *all* just memories, she thought dejectedly. And wished she could believe, like the Gauls, that one soul passed to another in time. That life was eternal and good.

'I'm used to being on my own,' she told Manion. It was the truth. 'I actually prefer it that way.'

'Do you?' Either the wind had sprung up or he was leaning so close that her hair moved with his breath. 'Do you really prefer being on your own?' he whispered. 'Or are you just frightened of letting a man in?'

'Frightened?' she laughed. 'My dear Manion, I eat men between slabs of bread with my supper. The male of the species doesn't scare me at all.'

'Men, no, but a man? One man? The right man, perhaps?'

Something flipped over inside.

'I don't need anyone.'

'Your scars run deep, then, my lady.'

His voice was husky with something she did not recognize. It might have been desire. Then again, it might have been laughter. Or pain.

'You fear abandonment, which is why you will not – perhaps cannot – trust a man enough to let him into your heart. Am I right?'

'Does it matter?' she retorted. 'The fact that you think you know me seems enough for your ego. Colossal isn't the word.'

'Now you're getting prickly, because I'm close to the mark. Too close for your comfort, it seems. But I'm right, am I not? My lady,' he added. 'That to win Claudia Seferius, a man must first win her trust?'

'Define trust,' she snapped. 'It's just an empty word meaning all things to all men, and I really have no time for the stuff.'

'Who abandoned you, I wonder? Your father? Your mother—?'

'None of your business!'

'Oh, dear me. Both.'

He leaned forward and dabbled his fingers in the cascade, then held the drips to Claudia's lips. She spat them away.

'Because your parents left you, and I'm guessing through death when you were still very young, you carry within you a morbid fear of being abandoned by someone else that you love.' He licked the water off his own fingers. 'That's dangerous.'

She wanted to respond. She wanted to hit him, kick him, punch him on the nose, but the problem was, he was right.

'It's dangerous, because you end up pushing those people who care for you so very hard that it eventually drives them away—'

'Show me your ring.'

Whatever he was expecting, that wasn't it. His eyebrows arched in surprise. 'Now that's *my* little secret.' He sprang to his feet and the expression in his aquamarine eyes was serious. 'Tomorrow, perhaps. Tomorrow when we share other confidences, but now I fear I must leave you. Death or not, the revels have to go on.'

'And even a sex slave must play his part.'

'I didn't ask for the job,' he said evenly.

Oh, but you did, Manion, I think you did. He'd adapted too quickly, just like Orbilio had. The question is, why would someone deliberately plant himself in the slave auction for the Hundred-Handed to buy? *What was it inside this wretched College that Manion needed so badly?*

No birds moved in this hot, sticky morning, only the butterflies over the flower-filled meadows and the soothing rasp of the crickets. And for a man who had work to do, he seemed in no hurry to leave. Once again, she wondered why he'd sought her out.

'But to answer your question,' he murmured, 'trust is when the same man is always behind you, to catch no matter how often you fall.' He grinned. 'Just thought you might like to know.'

And with that he loped off up the hill, leaving Claudia's thoughts churning like a river bed after the storm, and her heart as heavy as lead.

It was only after he'd gone that she realized that the scent on his shirt was white roses. The same type that Sarra liked to collect.

Around the Field of Celebration, revellers rose, stretched and broke their fast. Glancing at the sky, their disappointment at cloud cover on such an important occasion was understandable, yet it was a different emotion entirely that consumed the congregation. Confusion. Try as she might to contain the panic among both priestesses and initiates from this second violent death, she was powerless to prevent the shock and horror registering on their faces.

'Pass the word,' she signalled to the other four on the dais. 'There will be no show of public emotion.'

'Agreed,' Dora signed back. 'We cannot allow the contagion to spread.'

Beth looked round at the tears, the clenched jaws, bloodless cheeks and tightly wrung hands that were the universal symptoms of grief. It would not be easy, Sarra was a delightful and popular girl, but duty was duty. Nature was constant, the Hundred-Handed was constant. They stood firm in calm and in storm.

'Sarra would still be alive if you hadn't insisted on not moving with the times.' Fearn rounded on the Head of the College. 'This is your fault and you know it.'

'And how might that be?' Dora's face darkened with anger.

'If you didn't forbid us to marry, prevent us from leading normal lives, people wouldn't be pushed into abnormal situations and I tell you, Sarra would still be alive.'

'Rubbish!' The Oak Priestess was one step away from

164

slapping her face. 'Her murder has nothing to do with adherence to tradition—'

'Ladies!' Beth fought for control. 'Ladies, we are all distraught, but whatever our personal feelings right now, it is Sarra who should be uppermost in our thoughts.'

'Quite right,' Luisa signed, sniffing back tears. 'Poor girl, no one deserves to die in such a terrible way.'

'Best not to dwell on that side of things, dear.' A plump arm encircled the Rowan Priestess's shoulders. 'I'm sure Sarra would not have suffered.'

Ailm snorted. 'Of course she suffered. Terrified and alone, she died in agony, let's at least be clear on that point.'

'Your bluntness isn't helping,' Beth told Ailm firmly. 'Now once again, ladies, must I remind you that our private emotions are not for public display? This is midsummer, and if there is ever a time when we need to stand shoulder to shoulder and exude the strength, courage, stability and endurance that we preach in its name, then that moment is now.'

For a beat of three, emotions wrestled with duty. As always, duty won.

But as the five pentagram priestesses linked hands to form the circle of life, chanting the Midsummer Paean with a cheerfulness that belied what lay in their hearts, Beth knew it was only a question of time before news of Sarra's murder leaked out.

This time the Druids would not wait.

Twenty-One

'What was that about?' Marcus asked, stepping out from behind an elder, and now who was spying on whom? Another one, Claudia thought, who'd been watching, hiding, sneaking around undercover! She folded the pleats in her gown between her fingers and thought, The question was, who had he been watching . . .?

'How sad, Orbilio, that that is your only opening gambit. One would have thought, you being a patrician and all, that your well-educated aristocratic brain could at least come up with a different question to ask. Such as the recipe for stuffed dormice or something.'

'Do you know it?' he asked, tilting his head on one side.

'Of course not,' she snapped. 'What do you take me for, a common cook?'

'No, I take you for someone who's trying to distract the long arm of the law from executing its duties, so perhaps I should rephrase the question in a way that brooks no misconstruction. Do you mind telling me what you and Manion were discussing just now?'

'Yes.'

'Claudia—'

'Now what! You asked me a question that brooked no misconstruction. Did I mind, you said, and the answer is yes, and anyway, how come a girl goes to all this trouble to get a bit of peace and quiet, as far removed from humanity as possible, yet within seconds the place is overrun with Security Police?'

'Hm.' For someone who'd just been told he wasn't welcome, Orbilio found a strange way of showing it as he hitched his pantaloons and sat down. 'You know, if I didn't know better, I'd say you were deliberately provoking me in the hope that I'd go away.'

Something lurched under her ribcage. 'Small hope,' she said. *Surely* he couldn't have heard? 'Isn't the leech your family emblem?'

'No, that's the weasel,' he laughed, stretching his legs out and crossing them at the ankle.

And were his eyes always that dark, she wondered, and had his baritone always been that rich?

It was the shock of finding Sarra that was responsible, of course. Sudden death has this horrible habit of bringing details into sharp relief, making them stronger, more distinctive, more precious— Wait. Did she just say *precious*? Claudia cupped her hands in the pool and splashed her face with the water. It was cold and clear. Qualities she really must learn to adopt! High overhead, jays chattered across the branches, a dunnock trilled in the willows and from the woods to their left came the sound of female chanting, their voices kept reverently low. Ridiculous, she thought, especially considering that Sarra, of all people, would never hear them. In fact, Sarra would never hear anything again. Not the song of the skylark, the hoot of an owl, nor the soft words of love from her sweetheart . . .

'Here.'

A spotless white kerchief was thrust under her nose.

'Don't need it,' she said, blowing into the linen. 'Though I'm surprised you had anywhere to keep it in those pants.'

'We men are such braggarts,' he quipped. 'And I've brought us some breakfast. You must eat.' He leaned out to fetch a knotted cloth from behind a boulder and laid it next to the spring.

'Not hungry.'

'Cheese, sausage, bread, ham and fruit.' He rattled off the list as he peeled back the cloth. 'I even squeezed in a couple of quail, but no beef, I'm afraid. I'm sick of the sight of that ox.'

'Not half as much as it's sick of you, I suspect.'

Marcus sank his teeth into a warm herby bun. 'Oh, please. I get so *embarrassed* when you flatter me. What did Manion want?'

'You don't give up, do you?'

'Persistence is my middle name.'

'Was it shortened to Sissy?'

'All the time, which is why I changed it to Tenacious. You were saying?'

She gave another hard blow and then sighed. 'Very well, if you must know Manion seemed to think I have some ludicrous fear of commitment, which is nonsense, because I was married to Gaius for seven wonderful years—'

'*Excuse me?*'

'Please don't splutter breadcrumbs, you'll bring the sparrows down, and you can scoff all you like but it was just as I told Manion. I can have any man that I please.'

'True,' he said, with a cluck of apology. 'But the problem is, you don't please any. Ouch!' He rubbed his shin where she'd kicked him. 'So . . . that was it?' he asked, and suddenly the twinkle in his eyes was extinguished. 'That was all you two discussed?'

All? she thought. The man whose eyes were neither green nor blue but some point in between had somehow managed to crawl inside her skin, rake over the most painful wounds possible then jumble her emotions – and Orbilio says *Was that all?*

'No,' she said levelly.

They'd talked about love and abandonment, which were clearly not connected, at least not in her case, Manion obviously didn't know his arse from his elbow.

'We talked about other things, too.'

What was love, anyway? I love blue, I love harp music, I love sunshine, I love honey cakes, I love dice. What has that to do with human emotions?

'For instance, we talked about trust—'

Trust is when the same man is always behind you, to catch no matter how often you fall.

'And do you?' Marcus asked through a mouthful of sausage. 'Do you trust the man who calls himself Manion?'

'As it happens, I don't,' she said, breaking off a piece of cheese. It was yellow and nutty, with a flavour that lingered on the palate. 'For one thing, he told me he didn't know about Sarra being dead, but I don't believe that for a minute.'

'You think he killed her?'

'Process of elimination,' she said, reaching for another

168

chunk. 'It couldn't have been any of the pentagram priest-esses, they remained in public view on the dais—'

'Who says?'

The cheese turned to ash in her mouth. 'Weren't they?'

Orbilio leaned back and absorbed his weight on his elbows. 'What is it you ladies like to call it?' he said, looking up at the clouds. 'Comfort breaks? Well, all five took at least one, I assure you.'

Claudia pictured the ox on the spit. Not close to the dais – Dora wouldn't want her celebrations smothered in thick greasy smoke – but close enough for Orbilio to observe their comings and goings.

'I'm guessing our fragrant five weren't tempted by the makeshift latrines rigged up at the back of the field?' she asked slowly.

'Judging by the amount of time they were gone, I'm not sure they didn't use the facilities down in Santonum,' he laughed. 'But surely you can't suspect one of *them* of butchering Sarra?'

Claudia pulled a chive bun into tiny pieces and floated them downstream on the bob. Blood wouldn't show on Luisa's red dress, while Fearn was already a strong candi-date for her own daughter's murder. Revenge on the lover who spurned her. And since Gabali was still hanging around the neighbourhood, it wasn't beyond the realms of possi-bility that Fearn had seen him and, in her obsession, mistak-enly concluded that Sarra was meeting him.

'Clytie's murder was the result of calm and calculated planning,' she said.

Someone took the trouble to lure a twelve-year-old girl out of her dormitory, making sure the visit was kept secret from even her friends. They had also taken the trouble to bring with them a tray of cosmetics—

'Whereas Sarra's was angry and vicious, the product of rage and what looks like unspeakable fury.'

And hell hath no fury like a pentagram priestess scorned.

'Yes, but both murders occurred on days central to the College's calendar,' he pointed out. 'First the spring equinox and now midsummer – and surely the oak where Sarra was killed isn't coincidence? By the way, who moved the body?'

169

His voice hadn't skipped so much as a beat.

'Clytie's?' she asked, and wished there had been a tad more conviction in the question.

'Sarra's.' His sandalwood pulsed through the sticky heat. 'Swarbric said that by the time he reached her, she was slumped about fifty yards from the oak tree where she was killed, with a long trail of blood from where she'd been dragged.'

It wasn't Sarra who'd been dragged, she wanted to say. It was Pod, who'd hung on to the girl—

'Maybe the killer was moving the body the way he moved Clytie's and was disturbed in the act?' she suggested. And dammit, the conviction in her voice was even thinner.

'Yes, of course. I'm sure that's the explanation.' Orbilio looked for all the world as though he was suppressing a grin as he sat up and cradled his knees. 'Not that it matters,' he tossed out lightly. 'I get to the bottom of every dirty deed in the end.'

He knows something, the slimy bastard, she thought, watching him spike his fringe out of his eyes. Or if he didn't know, he sensed some kind of cover-up. The question was, was it murder he was referring to, the Hundred-Handed's secret, or her own role in the destruction of evidence? Somehow she had a feeling he meant all three.

'You know the stumbling block to every investigation?' he asked cheerfully. 'Apart from you, that is.'

'Very amusing.'

'I thought so.'

He did know, then, but how? Despite the sticky heat, Claudia shivered. Who could have told him she'd helped prise Pod away from Sarra? *Who had been watching them?*

'Motive,' he said, and she couldn't help noticing that his eyes had narrowed in suspicion. 'Motive is the key to any crime, and do you know what I think?'

'Do men think?'

'I think this whole killing thing stems from rejection.'

He polished off the last of the sausage, seemingly oblivious that she hadn't so much as taken one slice. And had turned as white as a sheet.

'Take Clytie's death,' he continued evenly. 'We know for

170

a fact that the bastard who stalked Santonum raped and strangled his victims, probably at the same time, then painted
their faces to make them resemble cheap whores.'

He plucked a blade of grass and began to chew.

'Suggesting that not only decent women had rejected him,
but that prostitutes wouldn't have anything to do with him
either. Santonum's stalker made them pay for that rejection.'

Claudia's nails were biting deep into her palms. She
pretended she hadn't noticed.

'He arranged their bodies in a certain position, then left
his victims in a place where they were bound to be discovered, because that was his signature, if you like, and he was
proud of his work.'

'No great loss to society, then,' on the grounds that she
had to say something.

'None whatsoever, but what I'm driving at is, men like
that don't kill and leave clues because they secretly hope to
be caught and punished for their wickedness. They kill and
kill and go on killing, in the firm belief they will *not* be
caught, because they're too clever.'

'Sarra's murder was nothing like Clytie's.'

'Indeed it was not.' He grimaced. 'You said yourself it was
the product of rage, but rage is a classic outlet for rejection.'

'Goddammit, is there a point to this?' she snapped, and
there were red weals in her palms from her nails.

'Yes there is, because do you hear that fluttering sound,
Claudia?'

'No,' she said, straining her ears.

'You should, because that's the flutter of wings of an
avenging angel,' he said. 'So why don't you just tell me the
reason you're here.'

Claudia had been called many names in her life. Strangely,
angel had never numbered among them.

'Orbilio, I'm a woman. I flutter eyelashes, not wings.'

'How true. You normally keep them well folded as you
hang upside down in your cave at night.'

'Is that another crack that's supposed to be funny?'

'Guilty as charged, though a good lawyer should get me
off with a fine.' He picked a sprig of wild chamomile and

crushed it between his fingers. 'The point is, I've sensed a distinct change in your wing colour lately.' When he swivelled his head round to face her, his fringe flopped forward over his forehead. 'Why *did* you come to Gaul, Claudia? What made you come back?'

She took a deep breath and considered what she could tell him without it actually being a lie, while the scent of chamomile mingled with his sandalwood. Chamomile. For many cultures, this herb was sacred to the sun, though mostly these were eastern traditions. The Sons of Ammon, for instance, who placed boiled meats on an altar below a sandstone outcrop in whose cliffs the sun was believed to reside. The Persians, of course, some of whom sacrificed to the sun from chamomile on the mountain tops and who considered leprosy to be punishment for offending the sun. These peoples didn't cremate their dead like the Romans, since fire was part of their godhead, and this was what was needling away at the back of her mind. Fire and sun, sun and fire, to many peoples they were the same thing. Including certain Teutonic tribes . . .

Forget spring and midsummer. Both Clytie and Sarra had been killed at a time when sun and fire united, and she thought back to the rock where the life had leached out from a twelve-year-old child. From the outset, its flat shape had been reminiscent of an altar, and, with the exception of the Hundred-Handed, every culture Claudia knew had made sacrifice at some point in their history with blood. And a picture formed of a young German with prematurely grey hair and tight pants. Handsome, dashing, confident, funny—

The wings of the avenging angel fluttered behind her. Claudia re-folded them quickly.

'My dear Orbilio, if it wasn't for business, nothing on *earth* would bring me back to this dreary, depressing little backwater of the Empire. Unfortunately, last autumn I sold a consignment of wine to a merchant in Santonum and such was the profit, it was necessary to make a return visit in order to agree personal terms for annual shipments.'

'Ah.' He nodded in understanding. 'So you decided to investigate Clytie's murder at the College while you were passing.'

172

Dammit, that was the problem with fibs. You forget what you tell people, yet even though they were lying stark naked in the bathhouse at the time, they can still remember every word – and then have the cheek to dredge it up in your face. *I'm staying there to investigate the murder of a twelve-year-old novice* was what she believed she had told him, now that she racked her brains, and Claudia made a mental note to take more horseradish with her food. It was supposed to improve memory, and goddammit, Orbilio must wolf a whole root every morning for breakfast.

'In a manner of speaking,' she said calmly. 'The journey from Rome played havoc with my back and since the Hundred-Handed have an excellent reputation as healers, I decided to give them a try. Which is how I came to hear about Clytie.'

One lazy eyebrow tweaked upwards. 'In a silent order?'

'Kitchens carry gossip the whole world over, Orbilio, the College is no exception.' She had no intention of telling him they spoke aloud most of the time. 'And given that the murder remained unsolved since the spring equinox, I thought it was high time you started earning that preposterous salary of yours, instead of sitting around on your base end all day.'

There was a long pause, which Claudia put down to Orbilio's acceptance, until she realized he had simply been laying into the cheese.

'Nothing personal, then?' he asked, swallowing.

The feathers on the angel's wings fluttered again. This time she sat on them. Firmly.

'Does deafness run in your family, Marcus? If so, there's a place in the Forum that sells top-quality ear trumpets.'

He grinned as he rose to his feet. 'I'll bear that in mind, thanks, but just to recap. You stumbled upon Clytie's murder by accident. There's no personal crusade. You're not in trouble. You're not hiding anything from the Security Police, such as the reason Sarra's body was dragged from the oak, for instance. And naturally you're not holding anything back from me.'

When he stretched, the muscles bulged out his linen shirt and pulled the tendons tight in his neck.

'Correct on all points. No wonder you were promoted.'

173

Something twitched at the side of his mouth. Jupiter willing, it was indigestion.

'I'd best get back to the Field before they miss me.' He rolled his eyes upwards and sighed. 'Lucky me, being tasked with passing round food, offering goatskins of wine, listening to the most god-awful gossip . . . *If she was going to cuckold her husband, it wouldn't be with his spotty apprentice.*'

Despite her concerns, his comic imitation made Claudia smile.

'*The boy denied it, of course,*' this was someone else's voice he was mimicking, '*but somebody saw them and sent the miller a note. "The lowest millstone grinds as well at the top". Couldn't be plainer, my dear.*'

Marcus Cornelius blew out his cheeks and shook his head sadly.

'Fine for you to laugh,' he tutted. 'You wait till you're re-incarnated as a sex slave. It's no fun for a man, I assure you.'

'I have every confidence that you'll keep your end up, Orbilio.'

'That's what worries me,' he retorted. 'If I don't solve these murders before my bruises fade, there's no telling what will become of this poor boy so far from home.'

He was laughing, making light of the matter, but this was a man who took his job seriously and in whose eyes no job was more serious than murder. The taking of life by force and by violence. He would lay his own down before he gave up the cause.

And in her mind, she saw a twelve-year-old girl who'd had her face badly painted, and the bloodied remains of a fairy with an ethereal smile . . .

'Don't worry your pretty little head about it, Orbilio.' Claudia took care to keep her own voice carefree as she glanced at the sky where the sun ought to be. 'Another hour and you can loose your arrow into the zenith, after which you're free to go back to play in the pigsty.'

'How can I ever thank you for embroiling me in this case?' he replied with a low, sweeping bow.

'You'll cherish your office chair more because of it,' she called after him, and suddenly the valley seemed bigger, emptier, lonelier now that she was alone. Violent death again, she supposed, hugging her arms. In the same way it brought definition to details, making them sharper and more pronounced, it made a person feel unaccountably vulnerable. Why else would she feel empty once he had gone?

As swallows dived low in their search for flies, Claudia slipped off her sandals and dangled her toes in the pool. Deliciously cool from where it had run its course through the rock, the surge of the water acted as a massage and she could see why the Hundred-Handed's reputation had grown. *And* why their gentle philosophies had taken hold. For people who relied on the forest for survival, nature was something they could put their trust in, for nature was everlasting. They had no need to fear her whims and vagaries, for there was a College of Priestesses to guide them through good times and bad, and three hundred years of observation had not let them down. To the Gauls, the Hundred-Handed had proved themselves honest and steadfast, and at a time when their world was changing almost beyond recognition now that it was under Rome's administration, it made sense that they would be drawn closer to those who provided the most comfort and support.

Yet the very qualities that they looked to from the priestesses were tearing the College apart. Modernizing, Beth had called it, with a large faction pressing for normality through marriage, little realizing, idealists that they were, the great paradox of that. Namely, that marriage was itself a blight on normality. Sitting on the stone and wriggling her toes in the water, Claudia recalled her first encounter with Beth and how relieved the Head of the College had been to see her. Dora had been equally happy and that, she'd concluded, was because from the minute she'd arrived no one here had swallowed that cock-and-bull tale about a pain in the neck, Mavor's professional hands least of all. From the pentagram priestesses downwards, she'd suspected the College had had her pegged as an agent of Rome and for that reason had welcomed her with open arms. That was why Beth's top priority hadn't been concerned with the Druids. These priests might be a threat to the Hundred-Handed's existence, but the Druids needed the backing of Rome and so when Rome sent an agent in the form of Claudia Seferius, this was their chance to convince the administration that they weren't witches.

And yet . . .

Despite the pressures put upon the College by the Druids, by modernization, by a potential uprising, there was a deeper tension hanging over the place. The Hundred-Handed were hiding something – and Claudia still had no idea what it was. She wished she could confide in Marcus Cornelius, but to unburden her fears about Fearn, about Swarbric, about the poison-pen letters, would mean owning up about Gabali and the Scorpion. She would rather roll naked in nettles.

She cupped water in her hands and drank.

That the Scorpion was slippery went without saying, but even so, the authorities would know all about him. But Claudia knew how the mind of the Security Police worked, and however charming and urbane he might appear on the surface, Marcus Cornelius had his sights on the Senate. It was true, she reflected. You can take a man out of the Security Police, but you can never take the Security Police out of the man . . .

By confessing that she'd double-crossed the Scorpion, Orbilio would cheerfully overlook fraud if capturing him took him several strides closer towards the donning of the broad purple stripe, and parading the self-styled liberator of Gaul round the streets of Santonum would certainly ensure that. But equally Orbilio would expect Claudia to be the bait in his trap, since it was virtually impossible to trace the Scorpion's crimes back to their source otherwise. She was the only link. So far, so good, she thought. She could cut a deal with him there. The trouble was, Orbilio wasn't remotely concerned with her desire for longevity, and that's where things became a little tricky. Even in chains the Scorpion could still give out orders and for double-crossing him over the wine then ensuring his execution, Claudia would be dead before the first manacle snapped round his wrist.

As always, she thought, she was alone. Had she ever known anything else?

Who abandoned you, I wonder? Your father? Your mother—?

What does Clytie mean to you?

Do you hear that fluttering sound, Claudia? That's the wings of an avenging angel.

Ever since Gabali stepped out of the shadows, she'd been unable to rid herself of her nightmare. Of her father's whiskery cheek pressed against hers, as he marched off to war but never marched home. Of walking in and finding her mother, the blood drained in a lake from her wrists. While neither could be bothered to leave a note of farewell . . .

Clytie deserved more. Claudia had never seen her, didn't know her and by the sounds of things she wasn't that nice a child, but the little novice had been lonely and lost, a misfit like herself, and she'd bled to death before her life had begun.

'So what if I need to find that poor little cow's killer?' Claudia sobbed to the wind. 'What's it to you, Marcus Cornelius? All you want is accolades and promotion, and you don't give a damn who you tread on to get them.'

And if she hadn't confided in him, then so what? All right, she'd asked him to help, because at the time she'd been concerned with finding the killer in order to get Gabali off her back and knew that Orbilio's sense of justice wouldn't refuse her. (That, and the fact that he never turned down the chance to catch her in the act of fraud, forgery or tax evasion, either!) But that was then, before cold reason set in and she saw the Security Policeman for what he really was. Detached, ruthless, efficient and professional. He was certainly not the friend he purported to be, which left vengeance as something to be sorted out privately. Privately and alone . . .

As a result, there was nothing to be gained in disclosing the conspiracy that existed inside the College. It had nothing to do with poison-pen letters, Druids or even the mutiny from within.

Devious bitches, she thought. They deliberately set out to manipulate Rome through its agent, and by opening themselves up to discussions about Clytie, they intended to put the matter officially behind them by 'solving' the case with the agent's help. By fielding two opposing theories – Beth's copycat and Dora's experiment – it cleared the College of any charge that they knew what really took place on the spring equinox, which Claudia was convinced was what lay at the heart of their secret. She was sure the Hundred-Handed, or at the very least the pentagram priestesses, knew who killed Clytie and were covering it up, but how did that tie with Sarra's murder?

One possibility came to her colder even than the water round her feet, and something primordial heaved in her stomach.

Suppose Sarra's death wasn't connected to Clytie's?

Nonsense, she argued, it had to be. Look at the similarities. Huge amounts of blood spilled at both murders. Both killed with a knife, and the places where their bodies had been found were not accidental, either. The altar block for Clytie, the oak for Sarra. They had to be the same hand.

Not necessarily, a small voice argued back. Yes, blood was a common denominator both times, but Clytie was lured to her death, she didn't put up a fight (why not? had she been drugged?) and her wrists were slashed in a manner that could almost be described as peaceful.

Whereas Sarra was stabbed at least twenty times in a frenzied attack where she fought back until her very last breath, suggesting passion, rage, but maybe also desperation, and leaving Fearn as the number one suspect.

But!

Suppose Sarra was simply in the wrong place at the wrong time?

Clytie's killer sees her standing under the oak tree and knows that she's waiting for Pod. Inspiration strikes. Oak tree? Midsummer? In the grey light of dawn there's the flash of a knife blade. A struggle ensues. Blood gushes out. But surprise is the killer's best weapon. In less time than it takes to boil a hen's egg, a girl lies dead at the edge of the glade . . .

The notion was nauseating, abhorrent, sickening and obscene, but suppose Sarra's murder was a callous, *but quite deliberate*, distraction engineered purely to throw the investigation off the scent?

Claudia tasted bile in the back of her throat. This was no

178

ordinary enemy she was dealing with now, for what twisted mind would treat life so cheaply?

How cold must the killer's heart be?

Cold or not, twisted or not, Sarra's killer drew great satisfaction from a job well done.

Twenty-Two

'Have you seen Sarra?' a little voice asked. 'We need to report in—'

'– only we haven't seen her for hours—'

'– and if she finds out we've been watching otters instead of taking our nap, she'll skin us alive—'

'– and hang our pigtails up on her wall,' Aridella finished with a poorly masked giggle.

Claudia looked down. Three unrepentant faces. Three bobbing blonde heads. Three small lives about to be shattered.

Again.

'We couldn't sleep,' Lin said, her cheeks dimpling with pride. 'Not with Vanessia winning the contest—'

'– and the otter pups are *so* cuddly—'

'– though you have to know where to look—'

'– but if we don't report in to Sarra soon, Dora might find out—'

'– and then we'll get our hides spanked for *sure.*'

'I'll give you spanked hides myself, if you lot don't clear out of here,' a deeper voice laughed with a lilting Teutonic accent.

The girls spun round in unison.

'Oh, Swarbric, you won't tell on us, will you?' Vanessia pleaded.

'No, please don't.'

The young German scowled down at them, folded his arms over his chest and rocked back and forth on his heels.

'That depends on whether you reach the Field of Celebration before I do,' he said, pretending to consider. 'Suppose we say on three. One, two and—'

At the clap of his hands, the novices set off at a squealing run, their ceremonial skirts billowing behind them, their

180

acorn headdresses skew-whiff, as they pelted back down the path. The instant they'd gone, the easy grin dropped from his face.

'Best that one of their own breaks the bad news,' he said. 'That way they'll know who to turn to for comfort.' His shock of grey hair shook from side to side. 'Poor little cows,' he added under his breath.

Looking at him, his handsome face twisted in a picture of empathy and compassion, one could be tempted to take him at face value. Except that Claudia had overheard him in conversation with Connal the morning before, outside his hut . . .

It doesn't matter whether you like it or not, he'd told him, shoving him against the wall. *You bloody well do your job.*

I'm not some sodding bear that can be forced to dance or be beaten to within an inch of its life, Connal had retorted, but Swarbric had contradicted him fiercely.

See these? He'd jabbed at his tight linen pants and the shirt that revealed most of his bared chest. *This is the livery of a performing bear*, he had growled, insisting the lad would get used to it in time.

And then later that morning – *You enjoy your job, don't you?* Claudia had asked on their way back from the Pit of Reflection.

Let's say I've become skilled at it, he'd replied, which was not the same thing. Not at all. *We all have minds of our own, son*, he had told Connal. *It's our bodies that are in thrall.*

How often must a slave also be an actor? Claudia wondered. And what role was Swarbric playing now?

That he was embittered went without saying. *Love! Do you think any of these women cares a copper quadran for you? They don't know the meaning of the bloody word*, he had growled, and what happens to a caged tiger when it's had its teeth and claws pulled? Does it become less aggressive? The hell it does. It uses its massive paws like a club instead. The instinct to kill or be killed never dies . . .

She picked a sprig of chamomile and held it to her nose. 'Don't your people worship the sun?' she asked.

'Fire, the sun and the moon, aye.'

181

All three of which played a crucial role during the two equinoxes and both summer and winter solstices, she mused grimly. And all of which required sacrifice.

'Nothing you can't practise here, then?' she breezed.

A lopsided grin twisted his face. 'Assuming I wanted to, there'd be nothing to stop me, of course not. But let me tell you something else my tribe hold great store by among men. Chastity. Even their most powerful warriors believe carnal knowledge diminishes a man's muscles and makes him feeble in combat.' He flexed his with comic ostentation. 'What's your opinion on that, Lady Claudia?'

'I don't believe the preachings of men who swill beer from their boots, wear horns on their helmets and knot their hair over one ear can be taken seriously, either,' she said. 'How are your investigations going?'

He frowned. 'What investigations?'

'Beth told me she'd sent for you,' Claudia said. 'I assumed it was to enquire into the manner of Sarra's death.'

'Can't imagine why,' he said, shrugging. 'My job as Guardian of the Sacred Gate is to ensure that no one breaches the College boundaries, and on that matter I was able to reassure her. It is for others to investigate the circumstances, not me.'

'Because you're not qualified?'

'Because I'm not a woman,' he corrected. 'The Hundred-Handed conduct their own investigations and, my dear Lady Claudia, no man is privy to *that*.'

'Unless he can read their sign language.'

'Possibly, though I don't know of any who can.'

I do, she thought. Pod. And the law of averages said he couldn't be the only man curious enough to want to decipher their silent code. Gurdo, for instance, was an obvious candidate. No man could have had the run of the place, and for so long, without picking up at least the basic signals.

Oh, Pod, if they ever find out you can cipher—

Sarra's reaction had been one of sheer horror, when she discovered Pod could read hands, which meant Swarbric was either covering up for his fellow slaves or the slaves weren't owning up. Either way, Claudia decided, ignorance did not wash.

182

'So if you weren't investigating Sarra's murder,' she said, 'why were you bent over the body?'

'Hardly bent,' he said. (Well, it was worth a try.) 'But having assured the pentagram that security had not been breached by outsiders, I – I went searching . . .' He scratched his thick mop. 'Look, you haven't seen Connal by any chance, have you? Young lad, this tall,' he indicated with the flat of his hand a point just below the bridge of his nose, 'with fuzzy dark hair, only I sent him out on an errand around midnight last night and . . . well, he hasn't returned.'

Several seconds passed, in which she studied the change in his customary wolfishness which had given way to a thoughtfulness that was entirely new. A thoughtfulness that some people, she thought, might interpret as cunning—

'You suspect *Connal* of killing Sarra?' she asked slowly.

Swarbric rubbed his hands over his face. 'Quite honestly, I don't know what to think,' he said at length. 'A girl's dead, he's missing, and so is the small canoe Gurdo keeps on the river for fishing.'

Claudia smoothed her robe and straightened her girdle. 'When was the last time you saw Elusa?' she asked.

'*Foggoth Hillgund!*' He slapped his forehead with the palm of his hand. '*Foggoth* bloody *Hillgund*, those two idiots have used the festival to elope, haven't they?'

'You'll need to check on Elusa's whereabouts first, but yes, I agree. It's more than possible.'

Another stream of Teutonic swear words spilled out as he slammed his fist into his hand. 'Fools! They won't get five *miles* before somebody spots them,' he raged, 'then it's the Pit of Reflection for them both.' He spiked his hair with his hands. 'Shit, shit, shit, Connal. What the bloody hell have you done?'

He ground his teeth and swore at the heavens, then spun on his heel back to face her.

'I have no right to ask this,' Swarbric said, and his voice was now calm, his manner composed, as though he had taken a decision on which there was no going back, 'no right at all,' he stressed quietly, 'but you've seen the Pit, you know how unforgiving it is, and if you care anything at all for those stupid, *stupid* children, I beg you not to tell anyone.'

He drew a deep breath. 'I need to find them, Claudia. They'll need help to escape, because if the Gauls pick them up and report back to Beth, you know what will happen. Once any matter has become official, there's no going back.'

'But—' Claudia blinked. 'If you leave the grounds, what happens to you? Suppose the Gauls capture *you*?'

'You really think it matters what happens to me? I'm a slave, did you forget? There is no one in this place to grieve over my passing.'

'Oh, for gods' sake!' Claudia grabbed a fist of his shirt. 'You can't risk everything for two lovesick fatheads!'

Connal was passionate, impulsive, earnest and sincere, Elusa was genuine in her affection for him. But alone in the forest, living on berries and wits, whilst constantly having to glance over their shoulder, how long would love last?

'I give it a month, if they're lucky.'

'Better one month out there than twenty years stifled,' he growled, shaking himself free.

'Don't be a fool,' Claudia hissed. 'Out there, it's a case of two children playing grown-ups in the big wide world, and we both know they don't stand a chance. While in here, they're doomed the instant their first child is either swallowed up in the system or sold into slavery. For heaven's sakes, Swarbric, this is not a love that's going to stand the test of time.'

But he was already ducking the branches of alder and willow as his stride ate up the river bank.

'Just promise me,' he yelled over his shoulder, his reflection clear in the rippling stream. 'Promise you won't tell a soul about this. With luck I'll be back before the Hundred-Handed notice I've gone.'

Claudia stared up at the sheer grey rockface, where valerian danced in the sticky breeze and jackdaws made roosts on the ledge, and felt the shadow of fear crawl over her skin.

Do you know what they'll do to Elusa, if they find out what you're planning?

The rest of his conversation with Connal flooded back.

Because they will, son. They always find out. These trees have ears, they have eyes, trust me, the Hundred-Handed know everything. They pool secrets the same way they pool

*their knowledge of nature, the same bloody way they pool
us, and what the trees don't give away, pillow talk does. Now
for gods' sakes, Connal, grow up.*

And now here he was, a young man with the world at his
feet, risking his privileges, his freedom, indeed his very life
to save a couple of teenagers whose future was doomed from
the start. Claudia rubbed her face with the palms of her
hands, and perhaps it was memories of Swarbric's dashing
theatricals, maybe it was his well-honed disarming smile or
the charm he'd worked so hard to perfect, but as she watched
the seams of his pants (the ultimate livery of the performing
bear) stretch to their limits as he bridged the stream with
one bound, she found herself cupping her hands round her
mouth.

'I promise,' she called, though he was running too fast
and she knew that only the forest had heard.

While the shadow of fear grew heavier still.

Deep in the shade of a lightning-split yew, eyes followed
Claudia Seferius as she made her way back down the path
towards the Field of Celebration. When the battle cry rose
to unite Gaul in its freedom and the cobblestones ran red
with blood, how sweet would it be to make that one his
whore, the eyes wondered.

She, who marches along with her chin held high and her
shoulders squared back, as though she owns the bloody place?

What would it be like to take her, he wondered, have her
beg for mercy at the point of his knife, simpering, whim-
pering, not so high and mighty then, he'd be willing to bet,
and where would that famous Roman pride be then, eh?
Grovelling in the dust of her own bloody arrogance, that's
how fast her self-importance would fall. She'd be begging
and pleading, praying to gods who didn't exist, and he saw
her licking his boots with the length of her tongue, and then
let's see how sharp it was, that wit of hers, with the dust of
Gaul in her mouth!

He'd have her do it naked on the end of a chain.

See how it feels to be enslaved to another. Do this, do
that, can't do this, don't do that. Now you'll dance to *my*
tune, you bitch. I will have Rome writhing at my feet, washing

185

them clean with its tears of self-pity, and pity you didn't think of anyone else except your own self-serving ends. Pity you didn't think of us before now.

Because you come marching in here, you seize our people, our soil, our traditions, our gods, ah, but you can't take our spirit, you bastards. Gaul is our homeland, Aquitani's our blood, and as we drive you out as we did once before, you will rue the day you set foot in this country.

And you, my pretty flashing-eyed Roman girl. What will *you* rue as I cut off your pretty Roman-style ringlets and hold a knife to your long Roman throat? Once your jewels and your clothes, your hair and your pride have been stripped bare at my feet, who will *you* call out to, I wonder?

Scorpion. Whisperer. What was a name?

But as I take you and take you and make you my whore, be sure of one thing, you bitch.

You *will* call me 'my lord'.

Twenty-Three

Claudia stopped in the path. Turned. And shivered. It was as though someone was watching, she thought. Boring eyes into the back of her head.

Ridiculous.

It's Sarra. Her murder was vicious and brutal, nerves were bound to be jangling, and besides fear is a normal reaction after death. Self-preservation always becomes more pronounced. With a toss of her head, and heedless of the hairpin that sprang loose from its moorings, Claudia marched down the woodland path and tried not to look at the trees that seemed to close in, or the shrubs that were suddenly pressing too close. In the aftermath of murder, it was too easy to get swept up in dark thoughts and see the ash as the tree that strangles its neighbours, rather than a good source of charcoal. Or forget about rowan's rich healing properties, and remember only its power to conjure up demons. It was too much, she thought. First this talk of spirits buzzing like bees, then this oppressive, gummy heat, and with death stalking the shadows, emotions that she might ordinarily have shrugged off were suddenly swirling on an eddy of grief.

Manion, probing her painful childhood rejections with a scalpel that pared to the bone.

Orbilio dangling friendship as the bait for his trap.

There was the trauma of finding Sarra, before Claudia had had time to come to terms with Clytie's death, so horribly reminiscent of her own mother's suicide.

And now Swarbric, risking everything for a pair of selfish lovers who would not thank him for his intervention.

Combined, these things were bound to induce suspicion, mistrust, a feeling of being watched, but let's keep this in

187

perspective, she thought. Simply because one girl has been butchered this morning doesn't mean there's a maniac stalking the woods. Sarra, like Clytie, had been killed for a reason . . . even if Claudia didn't know what it was. Orbilio claimed motive was the key to solving a murder but if, as she feared, Sarra's death was nothing but a callous diversion, motive might well be the last thing she figured out.

Fearn certainly had a motive, as well as the means and the opportunity, though proving her guilt would be difficult, if not impossible. Even so, she mustn't allow single-mindedness to blind her to what, in the end, might be false speculation. Lives were at stake, young lives at that, and she couldn't afford to overlook clues in her quest to prove Fearn a murderess, only to find she was wrong. Claudia slapped a mosquito that alighted on her wrist. For one thing, she hadn't ruled out Pod as a suspect, though it was unlikely the Hundred-Handed would be prepared to conceal his role in a murder. However much they valued a dwarf's healing powers, there was a limit to how far that loyalty extended – especially when the victim was one of their own! No, no, the more Claudia thought about it, the more she was convinced that Clytie's killer was close to the College's heart – of which the pentagram was its pivot.

All roads lead to Fearn . . .

At the point in the woods where the track opened out, she could hear the singing and revelry from the Field of Celebration, as the people who relied on this forest for survival rejoiced in its ripeness and wisdom. There would be games for the children (she could hear them squealing), revolving around the dependable oak. There would be demonstrations of how to prevent weevils from making blotches and displays of the woodcarvers' skills. Dora, ably flanked by the Priestesses of Buckthorn and Broom, whose trees also favoured oakwoods, would be mingling among bargain-hunters at the Midsummer Fair, while her brown-clad novices danced an intricate jig round a board shaped like an acorn. But it was not to the festivities that Claudia's feet took her. Turning to the left, she was at Swarbric's hut within less than a minute and, staring up at its thatch, scenes unfolded like acts in a theatre.

188

It's early in the year. The trees are without leaf. An accident occurs, which results in Swarbric dislocating his shoulder blade. Mavor is summoned at once.

Despite the double tragedy that hung in the air, Claudia smiled to herself.

Between you and me, he yelped like a girl.

It was always the same, she reflected wryly. Heartbreak and comedy walk hand in hand. One rarely exists without a glimpse of its opposite . . .

The actors on the stage moved again. Now Mavor is calming his pain with soft words and a potion. She manipulates the joint, clicks it back into place. Swarbric sweats with the pain, his face is waxy and grey, but now he is being bandaged tightly for his own good. Cold compresses cool him. A soft hand stokes his forehead. Breasts that another time would pulse sensual splendour have become a bosom of comfort and care. Long-forgotten memories surface as he lies helpless on his own bed. He is a child again, three years old, and this is his mother. His mother loved him, he remembers, he loved her in return, and now Swarbric is cocooned not in bandages, but in worship, and the more Mavor returns to tend to his shoulder, the deeper the young man reveres her. Through her tender ministrations, she has cured his pain and averted deformity, and in a way that prevents any recurrence of ligament damage. In his eyes, she is deified, and of course there was no affair. It would be an insult, an affront, to the woman he adores. Swarbric will do anything for her . . .

Claudia sighed. Dammit, if he was sentimental enough to charge off in the hope of saving two infatuated lovers from the Pit of Reflection, Jupiter knows what cause the empty-headed fool might champion for a redheaded beauty!

'. . . what a mess, what a mess, don't you understand, we can't hide it—'

Mavor's voice inside the hut was full of anguish, but it was calmed by a male voice that was too low for Claudia to hear who she was talking to.

'Of course we can't hide it here, how could we? You're asking too much of Swarbric and too much of me—'

The man cut in again. His tone oozed sympathy, reassurance, sorrow and doggedness, but above all, his voice remained calm and no matter how hard Claudia strained to listen, only an indistinct murmur came back. If the hut had had windows, perhaps she might have caught a few words. But nothing penetrated the walls or the thatch.

'You don't *understand*,' Mavor cried, and Claudia could almost sense her pulling away from the man as he attempted to calm her. 'Look, I know how hard this is for you, truly I do, but don't you see? *I have no choice!*'

With her ear pressed to the wall, Claudia had no inkling that Mavor had come rushing out until she rounded the corner. There was no time to feign a stone in her sandal but, with her face swollen from tears and her auburn tresses flying wild, the Bird Priestess was deep in a world of her own.

'I . . . was looking for Swarbric,' Claudia blustered, walking forward to meet her. 'Is he home?'

'What?' For a couple of seconds, Mavor was unable to focus, but three hundred years of training don't run through the blood without leaving their mettle. 'No, my dear, no,' she said, mustering a smile. 'In fact, I came looking for him myself, but . . . but the door's locked.'

Claudia glanced at the entrance over Mavor's shoulder and tutted. 'Never mind, I'll just have to call back later, I suppose.'

Her eyes ranged over the priestess's rich russet robes. They were crumpled and creased, as though they'd been slept in, but through all the hundreds of crinkles she could not detect one spot of blood.

'Do you want to talk about what's upset you?' she asked. 'Is it Sarra?'

'Nothing's upset me, I was just next to some onions – what do you mean?' Mavor's face was with blank with bewilderment. 'What should Sarra have said to upset me?'

Claudia reeled. 'You . . . haven't heard?'

'Heard what, my dear?'

'Sarra was found early this morning in a glade beneath an oak,' she said gently. 'She'd been stabbed a number of times.'

What little colour was left in Mavor's cheeks drained

away. 'She's dead?' She blinked in incomprehension. 'Sarra's *dead*?'

When Claudia nodded, her shoulders began to tremble.

'Sweet Avita,' she muttered, hiding her face with her hands. 'Oh no, not this again, oh dear heaven, not this again.'

'Not what again?'

'This is terrible,' Mavor said, and there was no doubt she meant it. 'I don't know what he'll do when he finds out, I can't imagine—'

The rest of her sentence was drowned by four long blasts on a horn, but before Claudia could press her further, she was sprinting down the path like a hare with the hounds on its trail. It was a good morning for running, Claudia thought ruefully, and as a final blast on the horn told revellers that it was time to stop partying and prepare for the loosing of the midsummer arrows, she slowly walked up to the door and tried the latch. It wouldn't lift. She tried again in case it was stiff.

The door's locked, Mavor had said, but Mavor was lying. Caught off guard, she'd said the first thing that came into her head, and from then on, the door was in Claudia's sight all the time. She stared at the latch. Unless Mavor's companion had rushed out immediately after her and then took off down the other path, she'd have seen him – and how likely was that, if he'd taken such great pains to console her inside the hut? The odds were similar to the sun rising in the north, she decided.

Which meant that whoever Mavor was talking to a moment ago had locked himself inside and lay low.

On the Field of Celebration preparations were underway for the climax of the midsummer festivities, and the atmosphere was electric. It was the excitement that comes with all new beginnings, of course. An eagerness to interpret the omens and see what lies ahead for their future. But for Claudia, still in shock from discovering Pod bent over Sarra, it was hard to conceive that so much energy and life could be pulsating at a time when the corpse of a young girl lay cold on her bier. Shuddering, she glanced at the dais, where Beth stood smiling serenely, Dora reassured her squad of nervous novices

191

with a string of hilarious jokes, and where Fearn, Luisa and even Ailm now wore the brightest of smiles. How could they do it? she wondered. How could they stand there and pretend nothing had happened? *Why don't these bitches care?*

With a taste of bile at the back of her throat, Claudia nudged her way through the crowd, where fifty male slaves formed an orderly queue to collect a bow and an arrow apiece. Originally, she'd imagined that the reason the men weren't given their bows beforehand was because they couldn't be trusted with dangerous weapons. She'd had visions of mutiny, rebellion, priestesses held hostage, but now she understood. These weren't bows, they were treasures. Perfect specimens being entrusted to other perfect specimens, because even under cloud cover, their silver handgrips gleamed against the richly carved, well-polished yew.

'Aim true with this arrow, my friend.' Dora's voice boomed across the field as she addressed each archer in turn. 'It carries one of the Hundred-Handed's own favours, and through your strength and your accuracy, we will embed in the soil a part of ourselves. The cycle of life is eternal.'

Standing at the foot of the podium, tasked with dispensing the arrows, was Gurdo. His face showed no signs of strain as he laid one sacred offering after another in the men's outstretched palms, and she was just wondering where he'd managed to hide Pod when she noticed a familiar face close to the dais. Elusa? That blonde, almost white hair, was quite unmistakeable and something flipped in Claudia's stomach. Swarbric was right, Connal had gone – but not with his lover.

No more talk of escape, right? You've only been here a year, son, you're still learning.

A year, Swarbric said. A year in which a youth with fire in his belly had come to resent bitterly the chains he was forced to wear. A lump formed in her throat that would not go away. Swarbric, Swarbric, what have you done? Young and sentimental, he was chasing what he thought were runaway lovers, little knowing he was chasing a killer. What would happen? He'd gone armed with his short sword and dagger as always, but Connal, he thought, was a friend. A vulnerable youngster to take under his wing. Connal's knife would be in his ribs even while he embraced him . . .

Stupid, she told herself. You should have guessed—

Dammit, from the outset she'd considered rage as a motive for Clytie's murder. Sacrificed on an altar of despairing male principles, she had said, seeing the shape of the rock. So why didn't she realize? For gods' sake, why didn't she see what was in front of her own bloody eyes? A Briton in Gaul and enslaved to women, subjection hit at the very core of Connal's masculinity, and for a young man desperate to be with a girl in a society where everything was shared, including lovers, he was the perfect candidate for exploding anger. In a bid to stamp out the nits before they grew into lice, he'd killed one of the novices. He had disguised his motive by painting her face, and no doubt hoped to eliminate the rest of the nits when the opportunity arose. Or when his anger could not be contained—

I'm not some sodding bear that can be forced to dance or be beaten to within an inch of its life.

Ironically, Swarbric was the trigger. Frustrated by the knowledge that that's exactly what he was, that he was trapped and forced to perform, Connal exploded again. And this time he didn't try to disguise his anger. Sarra took the full brunt of his fury . . .

Her eyes were stinging, there was a lump in her throat. Oh, Swarbric, you bloody damned fool. Through the heads and shoulders of the cheering crowd, she scanned the archers as they lined up in front of Gurdo.

'Aim true with this arrow, my friend.'

Dora was addressing a long, lean hunk with a small goatee beard as though he was the only man in the world.

'The cycle of life is eternal – '

Orbilio was standing fifth from the back, but what the hell could he do? Claudia pushed her way forward.

'– carries one of the Hundred-Handed's own favours – ' the Oak Priestess had turned her attention to a young Arabian slave with rippling muscles and shoulder-length, oiled black curls – 'and through your strength and your accuracy—'

Claudia waved her arms to attract Marcus's attention. As the oiled black curls moved away, another archer stepped forward, one whose curls were short, dark and fuzzy. Look at me, dammit, she willed Orbilio. Look this way, for gods' . . . DARK AND FUZZY?

'– embed in the soil a part of—'

She peered through the crush, but her eyes hadn't deceived her. Dora was indeed addressing the young Briton and if there was any doubt left in Claudia's mind, it was the smile of pride on Elusa's face. But . . . She tried to think. But . . . if Connal was here and Elusa was here, what made Swarbric think they'd run away? Their conversation replayed at speed through her head.

They always find out, he had told Connal. *These trees have ears, they have eyes, the Hundred-Handed know everything. They pool secrets the same way they pool their knowledge of nature, the same bloody way they pool us, and what the trees don't give away, pillow talk does.*

Swarbric knew. Whether he'd known all along or found out through other means didn't matter. The point was, he knew Claudia had been eavesdropping on him and of course it wasn't Swarbric who suggested Connal had run off with Elusa, he merely said that he couldn't find him. It was left to Claudia to put the pieces together. Claudia who came to the conclusion that they'd eloped. Claudia who couldn't look past her stupid nose! And as another slave moved up to accept the sacred arrow, ice ran through her veins.

She had fallen straight into the German's trap. Too busy trying to pin the murder on Fearn, she had allowed Swarbric to manipulate her and let his charm blind her to common sense.

As the crowd cheered and applauded, she felt herself sway, sick to the stomach with guilt.

Thanks to her, the bastard had just escaped justice.

194

Twenty-Four

Lining up to collect his arrow, Orbilio weighted the ceremonial bow in his hand and took his hat off to the
craftsman who fashioned it. Each silver handgrip was skil-
fully engraved with an emblem to reflect the birch, the
moon, the fishes, whatever. Every aspect of nature was
covered. Last night lots had been drawn to determine which
slave fired which priestess's colours, and as he ran his finger
over the exquisite etching, he could almost feel the gorse
come to life in his hands. As an investigator, he did not
believe in coincidence, especially where crime was
concerned, but there had been no fiddling when it came to
the drawing of lots and he did believe in destiny. That it
was perhaps preordained that he should draw the bow of
Clytie's mother as he worked to unmask the monster that
took Clytie's life.

Not, to be truthful, that her death took priority at the
moment.

Yes of *course* he wanted to avenge the girl's death and
rid the world of a monster, but (back to coincidence) he
didn't believe it was chance that left Clytie dead on the
spring equinox and Sarra dead at midsummer. Unfortunately,
more lives were at stake now than a sick killer's victims.

The Scorpion was out of its cage.

What's the bastard up to? he wondered. What's he doing
here, at the College, why at midsummer, and why attach
himself to Orbilio? There was a distinct smell of fish in the
air, but despite the amount of time they'd spent together, he
was still no closer to understanding Manion's game. One
thing, though. The bastard was dangerous. He didn't trust
him an inch.

From the corner of his eye, he caught two hands windmilling above the heads of the crowd. That something appeared to be Claudia. He waved back.

There was only one explanation Marcus could think of to explain the Scorpion's presence. Rebellion.

'Gorse!' she yelled out. 'Gorse!'

'Thanks,' he mouthed back, holding up his bow, though he was surprised at such eager support. 'But you know me. Fearn's arrow today, Cupid's arrow tomorrow. Fancy pinning your colours to that?'

Forget the campaigning season, he thought. This was a man who'd been shunned by his tribe for speaking out against Rome but who didn't roll over under the shame. He went out and built up an army.

In Rome's eyes, it was nothing but a raggle-taggle bunch of boozers and losers, but at their head were two clever men. Together, Manion and his deputy, Ptian, had used crime to build up a rich seam of funds, and the money must have gone somewhere. Weapons, armour, food and supplies, they had to be as well organized as the crimes they set up and as smart as the false intelligence they'd sent back to Rome. However, with limited numbers, these so-called Saviours of Gaul couldn't possibly charge the legions head on. Orbilio's guess was that they'd use guerrilla tactics, striking when the enemy expected it least, and in ways it would not imagine.

'Not gorse, *horse!*' Claudia was making galloping actions. 'You need a *horse*,' she was shouting.

'I'm Taurus, not Sagittarius,' he laughed back, but it only served to deepen the scowl on her face.

Was it any wonder men did not understand women?

'Bit late, I'm afraid,' Manion puffed in his ear. 'Couple of things to sort out and time kind of ran away on me.' He made an intricate gesture with his bow in Claudia's direction. 'Have I missed much?'

Marcus doubted the Scorpion missed anything. 'Not so you'd notice,' he assured him with a smile.

'Hurry it along, you two, this isn't a mothers' meeting, you know.' Gurdo's temper wasn't improved by murder, it seemed. 'We fire at midday not bloody midnight.'

'Whoops.'

Manion jumped forward to collect the arrow tipped with

Fearn's gorse-coloured feathers. Orbilio took Luisa's red favours behind.

'These are the wrong way round,' he said.

'Does it matter?' Manion had already notched the shaft in its rest.

'Superstition among the Hundred-Handed says that to accept an arrow out of its allotted order brings bad luck.'

Though it didn't specify whether that bad luck befell the archer, the priestess or the aspect of nature that she protected.

'Want to swap back, Pretty Boy?'

'I'm not superstitious,' Marcus said, holding his gaze.

From the dais, Dora's voice boomed across the field as they turned round to take their positions to fire.

'Now, with the year at its zenith, we, the Hundred-Handed, give ourselves back to the earth that we came from, and with each favour, send out an arrow of peace. Are the archers ready?'

Fifty heads nodded, and at Gurdo's signal, fifty bowstrings were drawn back to their chests.

'Then let a simultaneous loosing of fifty arrows demonstrate the harmony of nature and of this order . . .'

A trumpet blew. Gurdo's hand came down. A rainbow of feathers flew into the sky. The crowd roared. It was over. The midsummer celebrations had come to an end. All boded well for the future.

Then a scream filled the air.

Piercing and protracted, it was a scream filled with agony. The whole field fell silent at once. Then a girl came rushing over, her face drained of colour, and Orbilio recognized her as the novice who'd won the dew competition. The crowd parted as Vanessia came forward.

'What on earth is it, child?' Dora asked, but with every step the girl took, the crowd drew back in horror.

Then he saw it.

In Vanessia's hands hung a bloodied black raven, from which one of the arrows protruded. Dora gasped. Beth gasped. All the priestesses and initiates gasped.

So did Marcus.

Mother of Tarquin, everyone in the Gaulish world knew that the souls of the priestesses were reborn as ravens. To kill one of these birds, no matter how, meant certain death, execution in the Pit of Reflection. He swallowed.

'Whose arrow is it?' someone rasped in his ear.

Orbilio couldn't answer.

He simply stared at its bright rowan-red feathers, sick in the knowledge that the arrow was his.

Twenty-Five

The very mention of the word June conjures up bright sun-kissed days and extended warm evenings, stars twinkling brightly and poppies nodding at the end of long velvety stems. It's when aubretia and thyme tumble down hills in thick purple cascades, when kingfishers dart, buzzards ride the thermals and mew, when brimstone butterflies vie with buttercups and flag irises for the honour of the brightest yellow. Midsummer is when leaves are at their greenest, grass at its lushest and skylarks are warbling over the meadows to take spirits soaring up there alongside them.

Now, it seemed, June was the season of death.

Or at least the condemning to death. July was when it would take place.

By the time dehydration and starvation finally claimed the pit's victim, the roses would be over, fairy rings would appear.

Marcus Cornelius would not be alive to see them.

There were no tears left. Her throat was raw from pleading, from threatening, she'd tried every tactic that she could think of, from bullying, hitting, scratching and biting to begging, bribing and blackmail.

Nothing penetrated the wall the Hundred-Handed put up. These were their grounds, these were their rules and they brooked no intervention.

Negotiation was not part of the deal.

'Listen, lady.' Gurdo sat by the empty shell that was Claudia Seferius in the cave and filled a stone grail with water. 'It doesn't matter if he's the Roman bloody Emperor, your friend killed a raven and the penalty for killing ravens is death.'

There was something about the smell of the water that made Claudia push it away.

'Drink it,' he insisted. 'It's black hellebore, which has already served Pod well today. It'll do you no harm to sleep deep at the moment.'

'I can't. I need to be there—'

'No, you don't,' Gurdo snapped. 'That's why I had you brought down here! You didn't want to watch while they threw him—'

'Yes, I did,' she wailed, hurling the grail at the wall. 'Don't you understand? It was me that brought him here in the first place, me that got him bloody well killed!'

'It was an accident, Lofty Legs, and accidents happen. You can't blame yourself any more than you can blame the raven for flying across that glade. There's nothing you can do about fate.'

Oh, Marcus, why didn't you listen to me? Why didn't you take that bloody horse from the stables and ride? Ride down and catch up with Swarbric?

Gurdo bent down to retrieve the vessel and filled it with water from the spring. 'You won't like what I'm going to say, but I'm going to say it anyway.' He let the trickle run over his hand. 'The best thing you can do for your friend is keep away from that place, do you hear me?'

'But—'

'But nothing, lady.' His mouth turned down in an inverted U. 'There's no trial, no appeal, you know that already. Nothing can change those priestesses' minds, and it doesn't matter whether they think the Pit is barbaric or not, this is one of the few issues on which there's no going back.' He paused and took a deep breath. 'Not that it matters. By now, they'll have thrown your friend down the cliff and that's why I say stay away.'

He knelt in front of her and placed his hands on her quivering shoulders.

'He'll have broken bones, internal bleeding, he'll be lying among the rotting remains of other poor sods,' he said, 'without food, without water and without anything to dull his pain.'

An animal sound came from somewhere close by. Claudia had no idea it was her.

'What he won't need is some woman weeping over him, making him feel even worse,' Gurdo continued steadily. 'Because physical pain is one thing, Lofty Legs. All you'd be doing is adding to it with emotional torture.'

At the bottom of the Pit, Marcus Cornelius felt something wet trickle down the side of his face and although he hadn't explored with his fingers yet, there was something badly wrong where his belt should have been.

It had happened so fast, that was the thing. One moment he was standing on the field, staring at the arrow sticking out of the raven. The next, rough hands had grabbed him, too many to fight, and he'd been carried yelling and kicking round the rock, up the hill, and flung into a fissure.

Vaguely he'd been aware of the priestesses' white faces, notably Beth's, which was carved of stone. But most of all he'd been aware of a wild animal howling, spitting, scratching, clawing at his captors as they climbed the hill, until half a dozen local Gauls pulled her off and carried her screaming off down to the river.

And now what?

High above, he could hear the song of a robin, but here it was blackness, hell come to life, and, among the rotting remains of other poor sods, knowing he was without food, without water, and with only a thin slit in the rocks through which he could see daylight, Marcus Cornelius rolled himself into a ball and cried like a baby.

His only consolation was that Claudia wasn't around to witness his ultimate humiliation.

'Orbilio, is that you skiving down there at the foot of that rock?'

Her voice sounded croaky, it must be the echo. He sniffed, cleared his throat and called back.

'Do you mind?' He blew his nose on his fingers. 'I'm mining for silver, if you please. It grows wild in these parts, I've been told.'

'Fiddlesticks, that's gold and you pluck it from trees.' There was a pause the length of two heartbeats. 'I'm going to get you out of there, you do you realize that?'

201

She'd have better luck picking nuggets from trees. 'I'm perfectly comfortable, thanks all the same.'

This time the pause was longer, and the voice was croakier still. It seemed an awfully long way away.

'Typical, Marcus. Always thinking of yourself, but I'll have you know there are fences to mend and pigs to muck out. The world can't wait while you pamper yourself, and don't tell me you didn't contrive this little charade so you'd add more bruises to your collection in the hope that the Hundred-Handed don't bed damaged goods.'

For a moment, he just couldn't speak.

'It's not the sex-slave part that bothers me,' he eventually called back. 'It's where they stick the tattoo.' He closed his eyes then opened them. 'Claudia.'

'M-Marcus?'

'Why did you come back?' He had to know. 'Why did you come back to Gaul?'

There was no reply for several minutes. He thought she must have gone away. 'Good grief, Orbilio, I wish you'd conserve your energies for something important, like climbing the rope I'll send down later, for instance.'

When he drew a deep breath, his ribs hurt.

'Don't you think it a bit odd that the entrance to this pit isn't guarded?' he said. 'There's no rope here long enough to reach, Claudia. There is no way up from this pit.'

'Then I'll ride straight to the Governor—'

'Claudia!' The pain that tore through him squeezed his eyes shut, but the pain had no physical source. 'Claudia, this is sacred ground. Even Rome won't go against their decision.'

For once nothing, not his wealth, his breeding, his family name or his rank, could extricate him from this, and whilst Rome might beat its breast over one of its sons – and who knows, maybe even erect a statue to him in some obscure square – Rome would not intervene in religious matters. It was imperial policy, he knew it and, judging from the time it took to reply, so did she.

'What am I going to do?' she whispered into the hole. 'Marcus, tell me what I must do.'

Pain washed over him like he'd never known. 'There's only one thing you can do for me, Claudia.'

'Anything, darling, just name it.'

There was a tightness in his chest. Nausea rose up to engulf him. 'Go away,' he rasped. 'Please.' He was fighting for breath. 'Just, please . . . please go away.'

He thought he heard crying, the racking of sobs. 'People keep telling me to do that, but I can't. I can't leave you down there on your own.'

'Yes, you can. You're strong, Claudia, stronger than you think, and if you . . . if you – ' he bit into his knuckle – 'if you care anything for me, you'll go. Now. Before it gets dark.'

'I—'

'Please, darling, don't make this harder. Just . . . just promise me, swear on the life of your mother, that you'll walk away and never come back.'

An eternity passed before she answered. His head pounded like rocks in a storm.

'You have no idea what my mother's life means when you ask me to swear an oath on it,' she said slowly. 'You asked why I came back here to Gaul, and I'll tell you, it was to come to terms with her suicide.' A sigh multiplied with its own echoes. 'I saw her choosing death over me, her only child, as rejection. She didn't even leave me a note. And since it was only last autumn that I came here to find my father, it took precious little to open old wounds. The death of a twelve-year-old child with her lifeblood drained out was enough to trigger a quest. Justice for her, answers for me. Sweet Janus, I needed them both.'

He said nothing. Just waited. And the pain where his belt should have been doubled. It was the only time she'd ever talked of her past.

'But that wasn't the reason, my darling. I could have taken a different path, one that did not bring me back, and all right, it might have meant killing a man, but hell.' She tried for a joke. 'He was only a Spaniard and they don't count.'

He couldn't laugh if he'd wanted.

'I came back,' she said, 'because of you.'

Nausea washed over him. To think he'd left Rome because he thought she didn't care. He pressed his fingers over his eyes. 'Do . . . do you love me?'

'You know I do, dammit.' He could almost see her scowl.

'Good.' He pressed harder. 'Now swear on the life of your dead mother that you'll walk away from this Pit and never come back.'

There was a long pause, he thought he heard sobbing. 'If that's what you want,' her voice was unrecognizable, 'very well. I swear I will walk away on the count of ten, and I will . . . I will never come back.'

He thought she might be waiting for him to protest, but he didn't. He dared not. Drumming up every ounce of courage, Marcus began the countdown aloud and to his credit, his voice didn't shake. When he reached eight, he stopped to hear her call down, 'Eight and a quarter,' but only silence filled the space in between them. By the time he reached nine, he knew she would answer. This was Claudia, for heaven's sake! But she made no reply, even when he called ten, then he couldn't control himself any longer. Ashamed of his weakness, he called her name softly. And then he shouted it loud. But Claudia Seferius had kept to her oath.

And this time, Marcus didn't care if the whole world heard his heart break.

Twenty-Six

'For every problem, my lady, there is always a solution,' Manion said, without lifting his eyes from the wood he was whittling. 'The only predicament comes when there's a choice.'

'Trust me, options are limited,' Claudia said.

They were beneath the point of the arrowhead rock, at the place where the tip was the sharpest. Above them, trees, mainly rowan and oak, clung for dear life to gaps in the stone, while holly and broom tumbled down in spiky profusion, but here at the bottom the boulders were mossy. For though the promontory faced the southern sun, in the dense shade of the forest, little daylight penetrated. And if Manion was surprised that she, a stranger, had found him in this secluded spot where he'd settled himself with back to the stone, that surprise did not show on his face. He simply continued to whittle the piece in his hand, blowing away the shavings with sensual care.

'What incentive are you offering?' he asked after a while, and she could smell his soft nutmeg scent.

'Freedom?'

If she was wrong about him placing himself in the auction, then bearing in mind that Swarbric had discovered a way out of here, between herself, her bodyguard and a few well-greased palms, escape shouldn't prove too much of a challenge. Once in Santonum, a change of clothing, a wig, and that average build, that nondescript face would instantly melt into a crowd. She would provide papers to say he was free.

'Freedom.' Manion rolled the word around on his tongue. 'Hm.'

He smoothed the wood on his soft deerskin pants. She couldn't imagine what he was carving.

'Much depends on your definition of the word,' he rumbled slowly. 'Considering that none of us can ever truly be free, it is only the degree of freedom that differs.' As he twisted the wood, light caught the ring that wrapped round his seal finger and bounced off in a bright silver shine. 'You think of slaves in terms of wanting their freedom, but talk to your bodyguard, Claudia. He could have bought himself out several times over, but has he?'

'You've spoken to Junius?'

'You sound surprised.' He stropped his knife with exaggerated care. 'I make it my business to know what goes on around me. That way, I know who my friends and my enemies are, as well as knowing who I can trust.'

Trust. The word ripped like a claw at her heart. *You fear abandonment, which is why you will not – perhaps cannot – trust a man enough to let him into your heart.* The pain intensified. Because of her, because she was stupid enough, selfish enough, not to admit how she felt, a man lay dying in the Pit of Reflection.

And after he'd died a lengthy, horrible, agonizing death, she'd be condemned to reflect for the rest of her life . . .

Die? Where did that defeatist notion spring from? Marcus wasn't going to die! She pursed her lips in determination. She'd put him in there and she would bloody well get him out!

'Back to freedom, however.' As the light caught his ring a second time, the engraving flashed. A serpent or something, she thought. 'Is a Roman wife free, simply because she was not bought at auction? Of course not. She is bought by a dowry and is the property of a man from the moment she's born to the moment she marries, and if she is widowed, passes like an heirloom to the nearest male relative which, with luck, is her son. The Hundred-Handed aren't free, they're enslaved to their order. You're not free, you're enslaved to your laws. But me.' He lifted his eyes to meet hers. They were as measureless as the seascape they resembled. 'I *am* free.'

He didn't even try to pretend, she thought. So what could it be in this College that he wanted so badly that he enslaved himself to them?

'Who are you?' she asked.

A soft snort of laughter escaped through his nose. 'Not so much who as what,' he replied, 'so I ask again. What incentive are you offering in return for my risking life and limb for a Roman patrician – oh, you didn't think I knew about that, either?' He tutted. 'Never underestimate a Gaul, not even your own bodyguard, Claudia. Junius has been very helpful to me.'

'He's *here*?' Dammit, she'd told him to wait in Santonum!

'Loyalty is a supple commodity,' Manion said. 'The boy is infatuated, I suppose you know that, he just could not keep away.' He indicated the woods with a vague gesture. 'Camped outside the grounds, to be close to his lady, it was easy enough to initiate contact.'

Amazed as she was that Junius had not only disobeyed orders, but had been hanging around the woods all this time, and as curious as she was about who might be the object of his affections (how could he possibly *know* any of these women?), there was no time for that at the moment.

'What do you want?' she asked bluntly.

Seascape eyes held hers for eternity. 'What I want is my life back,' he said, rising to his feet in one fluid gesture.

She had no idea what he meant, but it didn't involve refusing to help.

'Come back at midnight,' he said in a way that suggested he was accustomed to giving orders and having them obeyed. 'By then I shall have a strategy prepared and we will discuss terms, but in the meantime you will speak to no one of this.'

It wasn't much, but it was the only lifeline she had. Claudia nodded numbly and wondered, *what* terms?

'Midnight,' she echoed.

'Midnight,' he agreed. 'Oh, and catch!'

As he loped off up the hill, he tossed her the piece that he had been carving.

A scorpion, ready to strike.

They say things come in threes.

They were wrong.

She thought the situation was as bad as it could possibly get.

She was wrong.

It wasn't enough that Sarra had been slashed to ribbons this morning, or that no matter how hard the girl had fought back, her attacker was determined that she should die.

It wasn't enough that Claudia had personally helped Sarra's killer escape. Dammit, she'd even given the bastard her blessing.

And now, it seemed, it wasn't enough that Marcus Cornelius lay with god-knew-what injuries at the foot of a ravine from which there was no way out.

As Claudia made her way back to the precinct, she thought on the most dangerous man in the whole of Aquitania who had engineered his revenge on the woman who double-crossed him and was delighted for her to know it.

She rubbed at the throbbing behind her eyes. Sweet Janus, no wonder there was something familiar about Manion. Average height, average build, nondescript features, these were the very qualities that he turned to advantage, disguising himself beyond recognition. But a gesture here, a tilt of the head there, those things had lodged in her memory and explained why he'd refused to show her his ring yesterday. Why he'd removed it before his approach with the honeycomb. Manion planned to reveal his identity on his terms, not hers.

As cunning as he is ruthless, no one betrays him and lives.

Silly bitch. You even asked yourself while you ate honey-combs together, Why me? Why seek me out? But then once he was gone, you barely gave him a thought. Not one of her better decisions, she reflected, and dammit, even when Gabali stepped out of the shadows to ask how her investigations were going, she didn't suspect they were in league with each other.

Do not worry about the Scorpion, Merchant Seferius. You will be perfectly safe in Aquitania.

She'd simply taken this – the man who threw victims into the Pit, for gods' sake! – at face value. Concern for the daughter he loved.

Do not worry about the Scorpion, Merchant Seferius. You will be perfectly safe in Aquitania.

Was Clytie his daughter? The hell she was. Gabali went to Rome with the express purpose of luring Claudia back here so Manion could take his revenge and enjoy it—

I make it my business to know what goes on around me.

At the gatepost, she reeled and had to hang on for support. He was thorough, she'd give him that. Having found out about her past, he played on it in such a way that it twisted the knife even deeper. Using Clytie as his weapon, he forced Claudia to relive the most painful memories a child can experience. Her father's leaving. Her mother's death. The fact that neither parent had said goodbye. Fine. Painful as it was, all this she could have dealt with. As she said at the outset, Claudia Seferius played rough and she played dirty.

But to take it out on Orbilio . . .

Do you really prefer being on your own? She could almost hear his whisper in the late afternoon stillness. *Or are you just frightened of letting a man in? The right man, perhaps?*

He knew! He knew about her history with Marcus Cornelius. He knew about her crimes, her brushes with the Security Police, the chemistry that exploded between them.

Trust is when the same man is always behind you, to catch no matter how often you fall.

Who could have done this? she wondered bleakly. Who could have betrayed her innermost secrets?

Loyalty is a supple commodity.

Yes, of course, the bastard had openly bragged about it. She sighed. Junius would take a sword thrust for her, his loyalty went without question. But he'd travelled the world with her and shared several adventures and scrapes. It was only natural he'd make certain deductions. And if the Scorpion could fool her, when she was already vigilant, how simple it would be to manipulate the young Gaul. Same language, same culture, same subjugated background, he'd quickly pass himself off as a friend. Leaving Junius believing he'd done his mistress a favour by imparting her secrets!

For every problem, there is a solution. They were the Scorpion's very own words. *For every problem, there is a solution.*

Now it was a question of playing him at his own game and turning the tables in a way that would trap him. But how? Dear Diana, how he must have laughed when she came crawling to him for help. That's why he'd revealed himself with that carving. To let her know that Orbilio was doomed in that Pit and torture her even more. Bastard! He was perfectly happy to let Marcus die, simply because it would hurt her. No, wait—

Across the valley, a streak of white lightning flashed in a sky that had darkened to the colour of lead. The Scorpion knew that Marcus was Roman, and that he was a patrician to boot. He was also aware of the history between Claudia and him.

Was it really a twist of fate that had Orbilio's shot killing the raven? That business of Manion pushing in front at the last minute. Suppose he was late because he'd shot the bird earlier with a red-feathered arrow, tossed it in the clearing at the last moment, then jumped in to take Orbilio's place in the queue? Who would accept this as anything other than bloody bad luck? She pictured the glade. Fifty rainbow thorns in the ground. Fifty priestesses giving a piece of themselves back to nature. Some would lie embedded deeper than others, some flat on the grass where their force had been spent, with others at odd angles, perhaps flapping in the hot sticky breeze. But even if Claudia could prove there were fifty arrows in the clearing, not forty-nine, it was still too little, too late. The Hundred-Handed would argue that she'd planted the evidence; who could blame her, they'd murmur. It would not change their decision, and the very fact that the Pit was sited some distance from the College meant out of sight, out of mind.

The bitches were expert at closing their minds.

Somehow, though, there was a way out of this. Somehow there had to be a way to take whatever trickery the Scorpion was planning and turn it back on himself.

What I want is my life back, he'd said.

Revenge wouldn't give an outcast his life back, so what would? Rebellion was the obvious answer, and though she had no idea what manner of double-cross he was planning for midnight, two things were clear in her mind.

One. She could not rely on her bodyguard for assistance, the Scorpion would already have brainwashed the boy, and since she could not hope to save Marcus Cornelius by herself, she remained reliant on the very man who put him in there in the first place.

And two, once this was over she would personally send Manion to hell.

Twenty-Seven

As it happened, in the false bottom of Claudia's clothes chest was a blade so long and so thin that Manion could search her and still not find it. Which did not make the weapon any less deadly. Tossing the carved scorpion up in the air, she caught it in her left hand.

I make it my business to know what goes on around me. That way, I know who my friends and my enemies are, as well as knowing who I can trust.

His mistake, she thought, was to trust anybody. A smile played at the corner of her lips as the kernel of an idea began to form. The Scorpion had an ego, that went without saying. He had enormous belief in himself. To some extent, he was right to be proud of that achievement, and despite the circumstances, she had to admire the way he'd befriended her, a Roman in a closed Gaulish society, in a manner that was neither gushing nor overt but nevertheless ensured that, when crisis called, she had nowhere else to turn. But trust. That was the key—

Flinging open the door of her bedchamber, a giant bat shot up in the air. It took a full second before she realized that it was nothing more than a black robe with its shadow exaggerated by candlelight. Ailm straightened up from where she'd been bent forward over the table.

'Did I startle you?'

Straightened up? Claudia snatched the tablet out of her hand and scanned the words etched in the wax.

Are your clerk's fingers still in your money box?

The 'x' was missing, but if proof was needed that Ailm was the author, the stylus was still in her hand. Dear god! Claudia stared at the woman. As the priestess responsible for death on the pentagram, that was all she had to do! No

211

month fell under her special protection. She had no complicated bird life or animal behaviour to observe. No elements to keep track of and make meticulous records. Ailm's role was purely and simply to monitor the yew. A tree hardly renowned for its quick-changing properties!

'Sarra's not cold and you still write these venomous lies?' No wonder they were called poison pen.

'They're not lies,' Ailm snapped. 'People have a right to know what's happening around them. I simply alert them to the truth.'

'*Truth?* You told a pregnant woman that her loving, faithful husband was having an affair!'

'Don't tell me you don't know what men are like when they can't service their wives!' Ailm's eyes were hostile slits. 'They're animals, the lot of them, so they go looking elsewhere! That, my girl, is what men do.'

Hell hath no fury like a pentagram priestess scorned. Claudia had Fearn in mind when she first coined the phrase, but it looked like Ailm had also fallen in love and found it to be unrequited.

It was no excuse for what she did.

'What about the fisherman's widow who received a note at her husband's funeral, telling her that it was his drunkenness brought about his death?'

'What else could have made a small fishing boat capsize at sea?' Contrition wasn't one of the death priestess's virtues. 'People don't like to hear the truth, that's the trouble.'

'Really? What about this, then?' Claudia pushed the writing tablet in Ailm's face. 'Tell me where there's one single scrap of truth in this poison, because my clerks, I assure you, have no key to my money box.' She would die rather than have them see it was empty. 'Where's the honour in writing that, you poisonous self-centred bitch?'

'How dare you!' Ailm flung the tablet aside. 'You come in here and think you know everything, well you don't. You know nothing!'

'I know you're a vain, lazy cow,' Claudia hissed. 'I know you should be tending to Sarra's soul and saying prayers for her reincarnation, instead of spreading gossip and lies. But you're right, Ailm, I *don't* know everything. Because I sure as hell don't know how you wangled your way into the Hundred-Handed, though I do know you don't deserve the honour.'

'Oh, really? Then let me tell you this, Miss High-and-Mighty, *I* should have been Head of this College. Me! I should have been running the place, not that snooty cow, and you know why? She promised. The previous Birch Priestess gave me her word.'

Years of bitterness came tumbling out.

'When she fell ill, she said that in return for the favours I'd done her in the past, she'd take drugs to prolong her illness because at the time the Yew Priestess was also teetering at death's door. But what happens? When push comes to shove, the selfish old bitch didn't even *try* to hang on. Called me to her bedside, said Beth was the oldest, it was only fair she should take over, and me, I get saddled with the bloody yew.'

The Hundred-Handed don't strike me as the competitive type.

Stick around, Lofty Legs, and you'll see rivalry on every issue great, small and infinitesimal, you wouldn't believe what goes on inside that precinct.

She pictured the College thirteen years ago. Two pentagram priestesses both know they're dying. Two initiates step forward, ready to assume their names and step into their roles. One sees it as duty, the other as entitlement. A reward for being Goody-Two-Shoes. *She promised.* As the death spirits hover like bees at her bedside, the scales fall from the Birch Priestess's eyes. The initiate that she's been grooming as her successor has shown her true colours at last. She is nothing more than a shallow toady and who knows? Perhaps the priestess even hurries her own death, because she knows in her heart that the head of this order must be disciplined, she must be calm, but above all she must be constant . . .

'What's the penalty for writing this poison?' Claudia asked.

A sly grin crossed Ailm's exquisitely made-up face. Even in hate she remained beautiful.

'I'd be thrown out of the Hundred-Handed. I would have to work in the kitchens or maybe the bakehouse, and when

I died, my ashes would be scattered to the four winds, instead of spending eternity in a jar in the Cave of Resurrection, and of course my soul would not be reborn as a raven. But please make a note of the grammatical mood. Would is the operative word, my dear Claudia, because none of that will ever come to pass.'

She picked up the writing tablet and held it over the candle, melting her poison away.

'You do see, don't you? There is absolutely no evidence to connect these letters to me, and considering my sisters already believe you to be hysterical and irrational, they'd laugh your theory out of the house.' She smiled smugly. 'Make no mistake, Claudia Seferius. I *will* continue to tell people the truth.'

Bitch.

And anyway, Ailm was wrong.

Claudia changed into a simple light robe and strapped the stiletto to her inner thigh. Across the valley, the wind howled and whistled. White lightning lit up the sky, and this time it was followed by a loud crash of thunder. The gods were angry. They sought retribution. Claudia had sworn an oath on her mother's life and broken it in the same breath. On Olympus, reprisals beckoned. Fine, she thought wearily. But let's get Marcus out first, eh?

She looked at the notch on the candle marker. It told her that there were over three hours before she met with the Scorpion, and she had no intention of pacing this chamber until midnight. Not when she could use the time to clip the feathers on Ailm's poisonous quill. Toss out that inkwell of spite.

With lightning sparking high overhead, she had no need of a lantern as she slipped out of her room. From the long-houses lining the compound, laments joined the wailing of the wind as branches lashed against roofs. At least others mourned Sarra, if not Ailm, and she wondered how a priestess, one of the decision-makers at that, could be so cold towards one of her own. But Ailm's compassion had expired with Beth's predecessor on a deathbed of promise. Thirteen years of bitterness had turned hot blood to bile.

And there was irony here, Claudia thought, as the first drops of rain started to fall. That she could feel sympathy for the woman who'd been betrayed not once, but twice, and who now saw life only through eyes of betrayal.

Which was not to say Claudia would lose a wink of sleep when the unfeeling bitch was stripped of her status.

'No evidence?' she asked Jupiter, as he shook his thunder cloak overhead. 'We'll bloody well see about that.'

Rain made the path slippery and loosened the stones, but the raindrops were warm and the smell of the earth slammed into her nostrils. She tried not to think of Orbilio down in the pit, water pouring down the channels of stone, cold, wet, in pain and alone.

'Soon.' A knife twisted her gut. 'Soon, darling. Somehow I'll have you released from your torment, that I really do promise.'

But the words could not get past the lump in her throat. Poison might yet be his only escape—

Outside the Cave of Miracles she took care, but the Guardian of the Sacred Spring wasn't watching the path. He sat on a stool with his head in his hands, sweat darkening the shirt round his underarms, his ponytail limp with the heat. If she didn't know better, she'd have thought Gurdo was praying – but for what? she wondered. Pod? The boy would be coming round soon, he could not keep him in a drugged sleep for ever. But what then? Pod had found Clytie, Pod had found Sarra, and the man who adopted him wasn't stupid. His mind would be turning back a decade in time, to the day he found the boy wandering among the reed beds. A boy with spiky dark hair, a broad elfish grin, and no memory whatsoever—

Creeping past the cave mouth, Claudia half-expected the forbidden side to be blocked by a guard of priestesses, but it seemed resurrection was a lengthy process. Presumably it would only be once Sarra's body was cremated that any rituals would transfer to this cave. Inside, sheltered from the howls of the wind and the drumming rain, she strained both her eyes and her ears. But the spirits remained invisible, even in death, and their buzz was silent as ever, while deep underground the rumble of thunder echoed like the Minotaur's hoof.

She could turn back. Kill time in her room, pacing the floor. There was no need to do this, it could wait. But as long as her mind had nothing to occupy itself with, it tumbled with images of blood. Of broken bones. Of the rotting remains of animals that had fallen into the pit. Of the whimpers of previous victims . . .

She pushed deeper into the tunnel. Where the bloody hell was it? That scrap of paper that talked about millstones had to be a draft of the original letter. A draft Ailm had torn up because it wasn't nasty enough, and Claudia was sure it was around here that she'd found it. Ah, there you are! A fragment, but enough to confirm her suspicions that Ailm penned her poison down here, hiding the evidence where it would not be found. As the Death Priestess, she had the freedom to come and go as she pleased, no one would question her right to be here, not even Gurdo. But if the parchment and ink were squirrelled away, Ailm would need a place where the damp couldn't penetrate. Funnily enough, Claudia had a hunch about that, too.

Guided by the channel of softly trickling water, she felt her way through the Stygian blackness until she reached the great painted chamber, still mercifully illuminated by the glow from a score of candles. Once again she was struck by its beauty. Unlike the frescoes that adorned Rome, they lacked subtlety and style, and the colours were severely limited. But there was something deeply compelling about those stylized antelope, about the handprints of men and women long dead, and the sinuous lines of the lynx. High above, on ledges gouged out of the rock, the ashes of three hundred years watched over them from their communal urns. Yellow for gorse, purple for heather, red like Luisa's shiny bright rowans.

It was tempting to dismantle the cairn of white stones, but Beth had already tried that. Maybe she'd received a letter herself, but either way she knew about the poison-pen letters, because there was only one reason why the Head of the College would fail to reprimand an outsider from setting foot on sacred soil. Forget that nonsense about too many problems inside the College. That was false confidence, designed to distract Claudia from Beth's presence in the cave and the lie about visiting old friends. She'd been crouched down, behind that cairn, searching for the same thing Claudia was after today. Evidence. And she remembered the sighs that had echoed down the tunnel. Sighs, she realized now, that had been born of exasperation.

No evidence to connect these letters to me.

Wherever Ailm hid it, Beth hadn't found it, but the point is, Beth wasn't Ailm. Ailm would have hidden her secret in the one place Beth wouldn't dream of disturbing. Among the dead. Dragging the ladder against the ledge, Claudia picked up one of the candles and began to climb. It was wider up here than it looked from below, several feet deep in places. But with fifty funeral urns, each as high as her shoulder, where on earth to begin? Walking between the lines of colourful urns, running her hand over their painted imagery – birds, clouds, fruit trees, nuts – she wondered which one Ailm would have chosen. The resting place of her predecessors, perhaps? Claudia heaved off the heavy black lid and saw only ash staring back at her. Damn.

She promised.

Of course! Ailm would have hidden her secret inside the great silver urn, the one marked with the birch that she had seen as her birthright. By the flickering lamplight, Claudia flipped through draft after sickening draft.

Does your wife know about your trysts with that slut from the locksmith's?

Have you studied your son's profile? Have you studied yours?

The cask is best flavoured by the first fill of wine. This is why brides must be virgins. But can't you smell wine lees on your fiancée?

Page after page of stomach-churning venom, penned by a woman whose only means to fill the void in her life was to make others more miserable than herself. Claudia saw her rich peat-dark hair, her finely pleated robe and exquisite cosmetics. Resenting the other priestesses' busy days and multi-faceted lives, Ailm lavished attention on herself because

217

she had nothing else to do with her time. Another woman might pitch in with the chores, take up outdoor pursuits, even a succession of lovers. Instead, spite became Ailm's reason for living. Well, let's see how she takes to the kitchens! See how much time she has on her hands then!

From the corner of her eye, Claudia caught the glimpse of a shadow below. Saw silver robes flash in the lamplight.

'Good,' she told Beth, 'I'm glad you're here, because not only do I have the evidence to convict Ailm, I know what it is that you're hiding.'

So simple. All she'd had to do was look at the problem with sense and not sentiment and even before Claudia had reached this great painted chamber, she realized Swarbric hadn't killed Clytie.

'I know the reason Clytie died on the spring equinox,' she said steadily. 'I know why she died, I know why that particular rock was selected, I know why the body was moved, why her face was painted, and badly at that.'

Standing stiff, almost rigid, with her hands clasped behind her, the priestess's face was as blank as the stone that surrounded her. Round her neck hung a heavy bronze choker.

'But most of all, Beth, like you I know who took Clytie's life.' Her smile was sad. 'I know the secret you're hiding.'

Then three things happened at once.

First, as Claudia lifted her flame for a better view, she saw it was not a bronze choker round Beth's neck, but an arm. Holding a knife to her throat.

At the same time, the ladder was kicked away from the ledge.

And a man stepped out from the shadows.

Twenty-Eight

Stepping out of the shadows, the Whisperer smiled. Better and better, the Roman whore, too. Proof that the old gods were wise gods, and on his side. He cocked his ear to their low, insistent growls as they rumbled through the tunnels and caves. To their wails and keening cries. The gods were calling out to the Druids for blood. Blood to redress the balance and turn back the tide of neglect. His smile broadened. Who was he to disobey their demands?

'It is time,' he said, testing the rope that bound the bitch's hands behind her back. 'Tonight, at midnight, the battle cry will echo over this land, the earth will drink of the blood of the innocent and there will be carnage like no one has seen.'

He jerked her head back by her chestnut hair.

'Throats will be slit from here,' he touched her earlobe with the tip of his knife and ran it slowly under her chin, 'to here,' he said softly. 'Hands will be hacked off at the wrists, eyes gouged out, tongues will loll in the gutter, then let's see what language you speak, when you're bleeding to death and in pain.'

'Kill me, maim me, this is only one part of life's cycle,' she said, fixing him with her cold brown eyes. 'Do what you like with my body, for my soul is out of your reach.'

He laughed. 'Oh, Beth, Beth, do you seriously think I'm going to kill you?'

He threw her to the ground like the rubbish she was.

'The others, yes. Like that blonde cow this morning, oh, Beth, you should have seen her face! Saw me charging down naked, thought I was going to rape her, the conceited, stuck-up, arrogant cow!'

He shook his head as he tied the bandana around his neck.

'I wouldn't sully myself with one of you bitches, not in a million, two million years. I was naked so no blood would show on my clothing – and oak, Beth. What a masterstroke, to kill her under an oak, don't you think? Using your own beliefs to confuse you. Sowing another seed of fear, making sure you'd not feel safe on your own land. Isn't fear a wonderful weapon?'

'You do not scare me,' she replied steadily, even though he knew she'd cracked her knee when she fell.

'No?' He blew on his ring, then buffed the silver to a shine on his pants. 'Maybe when you see Dora crucified on her own oak, you'll feel differently, or Mavor's head rolling to a stop at your feet. The novices, ah, perhaps that'll change your mind, when I set them alight and use them as torches, or how about seeing babies hacked to death in their crib?'

'Your brutality only serves to reassure me that you will not be reborn again. Your soul will be demolished by the three-headed dragon. Your evil will end with your death.'

'Evil?' He was astonished that she could even think such a thing. 'This is not wickedness for its own sake, you fool. This is expedience, woman. Necessity.'

With the carnage of innocents, Rome would be set buzzing. Blinded by anger and grief, they won't have time to form an organized response. Got you, you bloody bastards.

'Surprise is my weapon, surprise and fear. For in panic and disarray, their armies will be led into traps, cut down in places they hadn't predicted, and the winter is Gaul's ally's, not Rome's.'

By spring, there would not be a legionary left in Aquitania.

'The Druids will be returned to their rightful position, men will have power over their own bloody families and Gaul will be the proud nation that it once was. That is not evil, Beth. That is justice. And *you*.'

He lifted his eyes to the bitch on the ledge.

'Maybe I won't take you as my whore after all. I'll leave you up there to rot, slowly, a symbol of Rome's influence in Gaul. Day by day growing weaker. Withering away, frightened, alone, with only ghosts of the past for companionship. Won't that be nice?'

'What will be nice is watching you paraded in chains round the streets of Santonum, while your own people mock you, because you know what you are? You're a coward.'

'Coward?' He could hardly believe it. 'I am no coward, you acid-tongued bitch. I am Ptian!'

'*Ptian?*' She was genuinely surprised. 'The Scorpion's deputy? I – I thought you were just one of the guards.'

'For three years I have been all things to all people. Three fucking years, kowtowing to this one, kowtowing to that one, smiling when my heart has been pained, nodding when what I really want to do is put a knife through their ribs, but no longer.' He squared his shoulders in pride. 'Ptian has stepped out of the shadows.'

'Ptian?' she scoffed. 'That's not a name, that's the noise someone makes when they spit.'

She spat and made it sound like his name.

'Be careful,' he warned. 'Do not insult me, for the name of Ptian will live forever among my people. Ptian will save Gaul from itself. With the right military leader and a sound intelligence network, the old order will be restored. Ptian will make kings of the Druids, for he is a warrior, a general, a leader of men. He is—'

'A snivelling coward who kills women, and why? Because he's too puny to take on a man.'

'Why, you—' Kicking the rubbish that was Beth out of his way, he reached for his bow. 'No one calls me weak, you bitch! I am no coward!'

'What else should I call someone who sneaks up on defenceless young girls because he knows he'd lose to anything stronger?'

'Bitch.' The hand that notched the arrow trembled with rage. 'You bloody bitch.'

'And hides in the shadows, too scared to come out. That's why you kill women, Ptian.' She spat his name in saliva. 'You didn't rape her, for the simple reason that you can't. You're half woman yourself, you spineless freak.'

Fuck. Missed. As he notched another arrow, a foot kicked at his shin. He grabbed the priestess by the scruff of her silver robe and landed a punch on her jaw. Beth dropped like the scum that she was.

'Feel better?' the bitch on the ledge sneered. 'Does it feel good, hitting women twice your age who are tied up and defenceless?'

Fuck and double fuck. He watched his arrow bounce off an urn to drop harmlessly among the bear skulls.

'I won't waste good weapons on useless trash,' he snarled. 'You can jump the twenty feet and break both your legs or you can stay up there and starve, I don't care!'

'Can't even shoot me, dear god, what a loser.'

The scorn in her voice ripped through his brain. Bitch. He would show her. He would look that bitch right in the eye as he shot her. He moved close to the shelf. Forced his hands to stop shaking. The leg, he decided. The thigh. That would fucking well hurt. He clenched his fingers round the hand-grip. Drew back the string. As he lifted his bow, a candle tumbled towards him. He laughed as he ducked. Did she think she could burn him with that stupid thing? The flame was extinguished within the first second. Pathetic. Bloody pathetic.

The Whisperer was still laughing when the lid of the silver urn crashed down on him.

Since the stone splintered his ribs, crushing his lungs and his liver, he wasn't laughing for long.

Claudia had no idea how long she sat on the shelf, listening first to the death rattle twenty feet below and then, when it finally stopped, hearing nothing but the echoes of thunder.

Had he killed Beth with that punch? She didn't think so, but there was no movement from that heap of fine silver linen. Only an ominous trickle of blood.

One by one, the candles round the chamber started to gutter. The wind, perhaps, or simply the dying of wicks. How long before someone came to replace them? Hours? Days? She looked at the handprints that speckled the walls and realized that, if Ptian's rebels won, it could be centuries before anyone came this way again.

The battle cry was going up tonight, the call that would signal rebellion, and suddenly Claudia understood the importance of midnight. Midnight is what the Scorpion had planned all along. He wanted her to hear it, be part of it, to witness the slaughter then take the story to Rome, let them know what his army had done. What it is capable of in the future. That's what he meant by getting his life back. He was challenging Rome to come out here and fight, knowing that by spring the Druids would have backed the rebel army, the tribes would have united, and that millions of warriors were no match for Rome.

That was the Scorpion's revenge on the woman who double-crossed him.

Not death in the sense that she had envisaged. His revenge was a living death in which she was doomed to constantly re-live the horror. Whenever she looked at a child in the street, he knew she'd see the mangled corpses of novices. That was what he was condemning her to. Waking up every night with the screams of the tortured ringing in her ears, unable to block out the carnage that she'd been forced to watch. Every night, every day, she would be tormented by Marcus starving to death in that godless pit, knowing she was *this* close but could not save him . . .

Tears flowed. Candles snuffed. Thunder echoed along the tunnels.

The gods were enjoying their retribution.

If there was any bright spot in this terrible mess, she supposed it was that the Scorpion's deputy had not lived to gloat over the bloodbath. She had at least done that much for the Hundred-Handed, for Gaul, for herself, for Rome. But they would all be like him, that was the trouble. Embittered rabble who'd been shunned by society because their own people couldn't stand their whingeing and whines. Scum too lazy to put in an honest day's work, they wanted everything on a plate. They were bullies and boors, dim-witted and craven, soured by everything except their self-importance.

And the bastards were armed to the teeth.

Time passed. More flames died. Then finally she heard a moan.

'*Beth?*'

The silver heap stirred. A chestnut head lifted. 'Claudia?'

'Beth, are you all right?'

'I . . . think so.' She wriggled herself into an upright position and licked the trickle of blood that ran down a cheek that was swollen and red. 'What happened? Where did Ptian go?'

'Straight to hell.'

Beth followed the direction of her finger and groaned. 'Holy mother, what has become of us? What are we come to,' she whispered.

Claudia stared. These women! They never ceased to amaze her. A monster lies dead and Beth feels *sorry* for him?

'What time is it,' she asked, 'can you see?'

'Time?'

'Is it midnight yet?'

Sensing the urgency, Beth shuffled over to one of the tall marker candles. 'Very close, why? He can't give the battle cry now.'

Claudia tossed down the knife she'd strapped to her thigh. It was her back-up plan, had the lid missed its target. And while Beth sliced through the rope that bound her wrists, she explained about the signal that would ignite Gaul. It would be lit by Manion, not by Ptian.

'I'll try to stop it,' she said, as Beth dragged the ladder against the ledge. 'But there's a chance I won't be able to, that it's already too late, you must run and round up the women. Take them into the woods then make for Santonum. Rome is not as unprepared as they think.'

That was a lie, she had no idea how prepared the legions might or might not be. But once again, if Aquitania was on the brink of insurgency, Marcus Cornelius Orbilio would not have left his post.

Marcus Cornelius Orbilio was not a gambling man.

Scrambling down the ladder, she gagged at the mangled mess beneath the giant stone lid. She had seen him around the place many times. One of the volunteers who patrolled the men's palisade, but without the bandana, of course, which would have drawn attention to himself. It was why he'd been able to kill Sarra so easily. An opportunist thug, who thought himself clever. The name still made her spit.

'You need tighter security checks in the future,' she began, but Beth was removing the silver ring from his finger and tears flowed down her face. 'Save your sympathy,' she snapped. 'The bastard didn't deserve it.'

224

The ring was a phoenix, she saw in the lamplight. The bird that rose triumphant from the ashes. Ptian had taken this as his emblem. How ironic that it was ashes that finally killed him.

'That's not the point,' Beth sobbed, closing the lids on his sightless eyes. 'Whatever his faults, you see—'

She broke up and looked up at her.

'Ptian is still my son.'

In the centre of the world, between earth, sky and sea, at the point where the realms of the universe meet, Rumour greeted old friends. The news they brought to the halls of echoing brass was sad. One of their most frequent tellers-of-tales would visit no more. The man who whispered into the ears of the Druids was dead.

Together, they mourned his passing in murmurs.

Countless doors and numerous windows carried the murmurs away.

Where they faded and died on the wind.

Flying down the path to meet Manion, Claudia thought it was not death spirits that hovered like bees, it was tragedy that danced in the air.

The Hundred-Handed are slaves to their system every bit as much as we are, Swarbric had said.

For three centuries, the Hundred-Handed have provided spiritual guidance for small, isolated communities who rely on this forest for their very survival. This time the words were Orbilio's. *In leading by example, the priestesses set high moral standards—*

Poor Beth.

I am not against love, how could I be? Love is the pivot upon which the world turns.

Claudia had been thinking in terms of marriage, of couples, of men kicked out at forty to start afresh, when Beth had been referring to an altogether different kind of love. That of a mother for her own child.

The Hundred-Handed do care, she realized. But they were born into a society that valued others higher than themselves, and Swarbric was wrong. They weren't in thrall to their own system. They selflessly dedicated themselves to those who looked to them for spiritual guidance.

Our system is far from ideal, Beth had said, adding that she would lay down her life to preserve it, flaws and all, in order to retain the respect of the people they served. *We cannot teach them that nature is constant if the very College that serves it keeps changing.*

Except Beth had had to sacrifice more than her life. She'd had to sell her own son and endure the worst pain any woman could suffer. Every day, she would wake, fearing for his welfare. Was he eating enough? Was he sick? Did his new family love him like she would have done? Did they beat him? Every single day, she'd have lived with this ache in her heart.

Only to have her worst fears realized.

Bitter at being abandoned, Ptian grew up hating women and she was responsible for making him the monster he was, at least that's the guilt that she carried. And at last Claudia understood why Beth allowed Gurdo to keep Pod. Pod symbolized the son she'd been forced to sell and by letting the Guardian of the Spring keep his mysterious foundling, she might, in some small way, make reparation. It was the same reason that she'd kept Clytie's death secret—

'Right on time,' a voice said from the darkness, and Claudia smelled nutmeg even through the torrential rain, and twin points of lightning flashed in eyes that were neither blue nor green.

'For what?' she retorted. 'Rebellion?'

'No,' he corrected, with a broad grin. 'Victory.'

He stepped out from the shelter of an overhang of rock. 'How well do you know your own history, Claudia?'

So calm, she thought. So bloody confident. And that was the thing. The Scorpion trusted his own confidence and success. Big mistake.

'Me,' he said, 'I've read a lot about Rome and its conquests lately. There was so much to learn, too.' His smile widened. 'How three generations of civil war ripped it apart, yet through all that scheming and backbiting, Julius Caesar still managed to conquer most of Gaul.'

She said nothing.

'Then, after his assassination when the rifts ran even deeper, I read how Rome went on to conquer Egypt.'

'And Spain, and Galatia, and Raetia.'

'My point exactly,' he said evenly. 'Which is why I want what is best for my people.'

'Oh, you'll feel victory, Manion. You'll feel it slice through your belly in the form of cold steel, slow, agonizing, it'll take you three days to die.'

He moved closer, and his seascape eyes danced. 'Surely, after all the confidences we've shared,' he whispered, 'you wouldn't allow that to happen?'

'No.' Claudia's smile was as cold as the Arctic. 'I have herbs that'll stretch it to four.'

Without hesitation, her knife plunged into his heart.

Twenty-Nine

The track to the pit was slippery from mud and hazardous with stones loosened by rain. Claudia noticed none of these things. All she could think was, He'll be all right. Manion was dead, his battle cry died with him, and with neither leader nor deputy, rebellion stood no chance. The monster was nothing without its head.

'I'm here,' she shouted over the storm. 'Orbilio, can you hear me, it's over!'

Now she'd seen the true picture, Beth could raise no objection to him leaving the Pit. Nothing stood in his way.

'It's just a question of finding a rope long enough, and it may be tomorrow, it may be the next day, but I'll send down some food and . . . Marcus?'

'C-Claudia?'

The voice was faint. She could hardly hear it. More a rasp, a rattle—

Oh, god.

'Marcus, are you all right?'

A low groan was all that came back. Sweet Janus, no. No. Not after all this . . .

'Marcus, hold on.' She tried not to let panic affect her voice. 'I'm going to fetch help.'

'Too . . . late,' he wheezed.

'No, no, Gurdo has herbs, he'll be able to treat you, we'll have you out of there in a jiffy.'

'Can't,' he rasped. 'Compli – *ah* – cations.'

She wanted to scream.

She wanted to die.

She would follow him even to Hades.

And around the abyss, the storm crackled and howled, and trees bent in the wind.

'Marcus! Marcus, you can't leave me now, do you hear? I won't let you go, I love you too much.'

'Say . . . say again. Let me hear it before I . . . before I . . .'

No, you can't bloody die. I won't let you.

'I said I love you, you fool, I've always loved you.' Rain mixed with the tears. 'Manion was right, I wouldn't let you in, because everyone close to me left and the hurt of rejection was too much to go through again. But I understand now. Clytie's death showed me that. Oh, darling, I'm sorry, I'm so sorry, but hold on! You must! I'll go and fetch help—'

'Don't go! *P-please.*' The pause was agonizing. 'What . . . what did Clytie's death tell you?' he wheezed.

'Everything,' she cried, and suddenly it all came tumbling out. A twelve-year-old girl dies on the spring equinox from wrists that had been slashed on the very rock where she played with her friends . . .

'You were right about motive being the key,' she sobbed.

First, one had to get inside the skin of the victim. A self-righteous little prig, Gurdo had called her, adding that she was a pain in the arse. Even Sarra, as gentle and sweet as she was, felt that Clytie put her in a difficult position.

Because she didn't share her friends' desire to climb rocks, swing from ropes or go poking around in caves and things, she'd come to me ostensibly to get thread to sew up a tear in Aridella's robe or a new ribbon because Lin had lost hers, but basically Clytie was lonely and wanted someone to talk to, she said.

The clue lay in the word ostensibly.

At some point in the conversation it would slip out why she wanted these things – and once that happened, I was duty bound to put the girls on report.

Clytie was lonely, indeed she was . . .

At the Disciplinary, she would rush forward and speak up for her friends, apologizing for landing them in it, but the trouble was, the damage was already done and Beth was left with no choice. She had to punish the girls.

Clytie was the neatest, the tidiest, the cleanest, the cleverest of the four novices, but none of this seemed to matter. It was the flaxen-haired tomboys who were the priestesses' darlings. They would happily turn a blind eye to their scrapes and beside them, Clytie was invisible.

'It wasn't accidental that she "let drop" their escapades.'

She deliberately told tales on her friends, knowing they'd be reported to Beth, but hey presto, this was her chance to shine. She would vouch for her friends! Throw herself at their mercy! Clytie the Heroine would ride to the rescue!

Except there *was* no rescue. Nothing changed. The flaxen-haired trio did not alter their ways, they were too full of life to cow down. Instead, they resented her tittle-tattling. Perhaps they argued? Perhaps they pretended to shun her, to teach her a lesson? Whatever happened between them, it came to a head on the spring equinox.

Just because we deliver a baby, it doesn't follow that we bond differently with that child than we do from any other.

Unless, of course, you are that child—

'Unloved, unwanted, Clytie must have been consumed by grief,' Claudia sobbed.

The last straw would have been the letter. The draft Claudia had found in the urn. The scribbled evidence that would finally convict Ailm.

Clever enough to tell tales, but not clever enough to qualify, are we?

It was too much.

'On the night her mother took centre stage on the dais, Clytie went down to the river and slashed her wrists.'

Right from the start, Claudia was reminded of her own mother's death, was haunted by her suicide. And though she'd come to Gaul to lay the ghosts of her past, she still couldn't see beyond the pain of betrayal.

Clytie wasn't murdered. Not in that sense. But a young girl on the brink of womanhood had received one disappointment too many, and though Beth hadn't told her that she would not qualify for the Hundred-Handed, Ailm couldn't resist 'telling the truth'.

'She chose that particular rock because she wanted her friends to find her.'

Like her mother, Claudia realized too late, she wanted

to be found by someone she loved. Someone who would understand . . .

'But the girls didn't know this.' How could they? It had taken her a lifetime herself. 'They panicked.'

They're children, not adults, and because Clytie had killed herself on their own special rock, they thought she'd done it to get them into trouble. Instead of running for help, they remembered hearing about women who were killed in Santonum and who had had their faces painted.

'They tried to disguise Clytie's suicide.'

Having applied the cosmetics, they pulled her off the rock and left her beside the river, her hair fanned out, her arms outstretched, knowing that either Pod or Gurdo would find her.

'I should have seen it,' Claudia sobbed. 'It was so bloody *obvious*.'

The peaceful death, just like her mother's . . .

'It's because I didn't think clearly that you're in this mess, and I'm sorry, but please don't die on me, Marcus.'

'I love you, too,' he croaked back. 'Oh, god, Claudia, I love you so much and if I . . . if I . . .'

'Will you stop bloody iffing!' she screamed. 'I've already killed two men tonight, so if you think I'm going to let you sit on that ferry to Hades alongside Ptian—'

'You killed Ptian?'

The voice came from behind, a deep baritone, and it smelled of sandalwood unguent.

'*ORBILIO?*'

She stared at him. Stared at the abyss. Stared at him once again. Not a ghost. Not a hallucination. The bastard was there in the flesh.

'You said you were dying!'

'I said it was too late.' His face twisted. 'I just omitted the part about getting me out of the Pit, I was already out.'

But—

'You said there were complications. You said—'

He took a step forward. The rain had plastered his hair to his face, but his eyes were as dark as the storm. 'And you said you loved me,' he rasped.

'You bastard.'

231

'Claudia, I'm sorry.' A pulse beat at the side of his neck. 'But it was the only way I could get you to say it.'

'Say what? The first thing that came into my head, so a dying man wouldn't feel he was alone?'

He tricked her and so help her, she'd never forgive him.

'Do you really think I give *this* for you?' she hissed, snapping her fingers.

'Do not be too hard on him, Merchant Seferius.' A second figure stepped forward and rain or not, you could still kohl your eyes in the shine in his hair. 'Your policeman was only trying to bring my daughter's killer to book.'

'Gabali?'

Janus, Croesus, how many more people had heard her make a fool of herself? Had he hired a team of bloody claqueurs and sold tickets? Then she looked at the Spaniard's face, sunken with grief, at the stipples that stood out on his cheeks.

'Clytie *was* your daughter!'

Penetrating brown eyes bored through his thin pointed features. 'How could you doubt it?' he asked, and his voice was hoarse with emotion. 'And now you tell me that she killed herself because nobody loved her.'

'No.' Claudia could barely speak the words. 'She killed herself because she had nothing to live for and, believe me, Gabali, there is a difference.'

She would never know what made her mother slit her wrists that afternoon. Was suicide a notion she'd contemplated once, twice, a hundred times before? Was it a spur-of-the-moment decision? An impulse driven by wine? Maybe, like Claudia, it was the not-knowing that finally eroded her strength. Of seeing the man she had married and with whom she'd raised a child march off to war and never come home. Being nothing more than a lowly orderly, his absence, even death, was not worth recording. For four years her mother would have lived with the uncertainty of not knowing if it was her drunkenness that drove him away.

'Suicide occurs when the burdens of life are too heavy to bear and death seems the only way out,' she told Gabali. 'It's not rational, but that's the point. And it certainly isn't because no one loves them.'

It's just that that person's love isn't enough.

A shame Claudia had carried too long—

'I hope you are right, Merchant Seferius. I hope to the gods you are right, but with all my heart I thank you for getting to the truth, and I thank you, Marcus, for suggesting I go to her for help.'

'*WHAT?*'

'If I lied to you, I apologize,' he said. 'But the Hundred-Handed—'

'*Lied to me?*'

'– refused to even meet with me when I turned to them for justice—'

'*Gabali, you threatened me with—*'

'– and if they would not help, nor the local judiciary, Manion said my only recourse then was the Security Police.'

Claudia's anger found a new outlet. 'Manion said?'

'I did not lie when I said I worked for the Scorpion,' he said in his soft Andalus accent, and did nobody care about the storm crashing around them? 'I merely omitted that, from time to time, I also undertake certain contracts for your friend here, contracts that might be too sensitive, leastways politically, for Rome.'

'*You work for Orbilio?*'

It must have been the wind screaming through the branches, because he didn't seem to hear her.

'Through my contacts with the College, I wangled Ptian a job as a guard, then engineered Manion a place in the slave auction, even though he was expecting an attempt on his life. That was why he joined the queue at the last minute, switching places with your friend here—'

'He is not a friend, and he certainly isn't mine,' Claudia hissed.

'– to throw the sniper off guard, but the attempt was more subtle than that.'

'The raven.' She refused to even look at Orbilio. 'But if it wasn't Manion who shot that bird, who on earth wanted the Scorpion dead?'

'Ptian, of course.' Ptian had no intention of sharing power, he explained. 'He wanted to be known as the man who led Aquitania to freedom, so he killed a raven with an arrow

233

flying Manion's colours in a plan that should have been fool-proof.'

Foolproof? Then Claudia remembered the way Ptian had blown on his ring, buffing it up on his pants like Manion. The ring was silver – like Manion's. Engraved – like Manion's. Doubtless one of many characteristics that Ptian had copied to mould himself into what he assumed was the embodiment of a rebel leader. Were we only able to see ourselves as other people see us, she reflected wryly. Because then he'd see that he was nothing but a shallow imitation, a thug and a bully, without character of his own. But bloated on self-importance mixed with smugness and a certain native cunning, Ptian would have considered himself the intelligent one, not Manion. *He* was the hero, the man to lead Gaul, and no wonder the emblem on his ring was the phoenix. It symbolized a new leader rising from the ashes of subjugation. But Ptian was also a coward. If he was to kill Manion, he had to be sure to succeed.

No one crosses the Scorpion and lives.

No indeed. Just as no one thrown into this pit ever comes out, not even their bones.

'You anticipated the attempt on Manion's life to be through trickery not direct action,' she told Gabali. 'That's why you brought a long rope.'

And who better to smuggle one in than the man who used to throw victims into the Pit?

'*Si.*' Gabali's smile lacked warmth. 'To think like an assassin, it is best to be an assassin. To shoot the Scorpion in public would draw too much attention and risked killing the wrong man.'

'Yet Manion believed Ptian would still take the gamble?'

'He was closing in on him and needed to stop him. Ptian knew this—'

'Wait.' Too many things had happened in too short a time. Her head pounded from overload. 'Wait. He needed to *stop* him?'

'Manion knows that sedition is not the answer. Unlike Ptian, he truly appreciates how immense your empire stretches, how powerful its authority, how mighty its retribution, whereas Ptian continually underestimated its strength and chose to disregard its . . .'

Claudia had ceased to listen.

I've read a lot about Rome and its conquests lately. There was so much to learn, too.

'Gabali, when Manion talked about the civil wars that tore us apart, yet said how Caesar still managed to conquer much of Gaul, he wasn't suggesting Aquitania could follow suit at all, was he?'

He was telling her that he understood how powerful the Empire was.

'Here.' Orbilio wrapped his strong arm around her. 'You're shivering.'

But not with the cold, and though she tried to shake his arm off, the strength had leached from her body.

'And the fact that we annexed Egypt while still bitterly divided didn't mean Gaul could do the same,' she said dully.

Gabali's face changed from anguished to something approaching alarm as he picked up the tone of her words. 'No, Merchant Seferius, it did not.'

'I want what's best for my people, he said, and when he said victory, I thought he meant over us, but dear god, he meant victory over Ptian. Sweet Janus, Orbilio, don't you see what I've done?' She could hardly speak from teeth that wouldn't stop chattering. 'Manion was the second man I killed tonight.'

May the gods have mercy, she'd just murdered an innocent man.

Thirty

O nce words are written down, they become frozen, Beth had said, and once something freezes it dies.

But like nature and the seasons, change is as inevitable as it is anticipated, and in the way that an acorn grows into an oak or a tadpole turns into a frog, so she understood that the Hundred-Handed must also change, or the order would die.

It had taken tragedy upon tragedy for her to see this, but as she sat at the birth point on the pentagram table, cradling her swollen bruised jaw, she understood that her role went beyond simply overseeing the propitious start of new years and new lives. It was to encourage the birth of new ideas.

She had been wrong to suppress the truth about Clytie. The pentagram priestesses had known almost from the start that she had killed herself on that rock. The heavy-handed, almost clownish cosmetics on her face smacked of a child's handiwork, and the arrangement of her body revealed an innocence which no copycat killer would have thought of. She had immediately instituted a search and found a stick in which Clytie had notched her reasons for killing herself, a stick so thin that it had blown into the bushes in the wind. But a stick nonetheless. And for their sins, the pentagram covered it up.

They agreed that by keeping it quiet, the tragedy would blow over, and agreed with the Death Priestess that no blame should be attached to the three little conspirators for moving her body.

The pentagram priestesses were wrong.

We are all of us accountable for our actions, Beth thought, even a twelve-year-old child, and it matters not a jot whether that decision is wrong or it's right, that decision is not ours. It was Clytie's. She should at least have told Gabali the truth when he came searching for answers, but she remembered the fierce love he'd held for Mavor and the passion she'd shared with him, and equally the passion of unrequited love that beat in the heart of Fearn. Better, the pentagram priestesses agreed, that Gabali was fobbed off and the quicker Mavor would get over him. Once again, they miscalculated.

Gabali's instincts as a father would not let it go. His capacity to love was too strong.

Whereas Beth's own instincts had failed her on every level . . .

She had listened to Fearn – who abused her authority as one of the pentagram in an effort to split Gabali from Mavor, even at the expense of the death of her own child – without delving deeper into Fearn's reasons.

She'd allowed herself to be swayed by Ailm, who single-handedly insisted that Vanessia, Aridella and Lin should not be punished, instead of asking herself why Ailm, who systematically refused to cast a deciding vote, should fight so vehemently on this one particular issue.

Then there was the notched stick, which she found by her bed. Labelling her a cheat and a liar, it insinuated that she'd manipulated the previous Head of the College when she was dying in order to gain her promotion. Beth knew there was only one person who would think such a thing, but instead of confronting Ailm or enquiring whether she'd sent similar poison to others, she'd shrugged it off. Kind or spiteful, all words are simply breath, she had argued, and breath is gone with the wind.

So many mistakes, she reflected, balling her hands into fists. So many mistakes when she'd defied her own instincts to listen to others, believing their hearts were pure when they were not, and even her instincts as a mother had failed her. She closed her eyes. How little she imagined twenty-seven years ago, when she begged that Ptian be sold to family close by that she might keep an eye on him as he grew up, the poison that would brew in his heart. Stories filtered back of bullying other children and tormenting cats, but this was a phase, she convinced herself. He'd grow out of it. Instead he moved to wife-beating, child abuse, drunkenness and worse, but rather than face the fact that Ptian was violent by nature, she used her influence to tip the balance in being shunned by his people. Isolation would teach him humility and contrition, she thought. Instead, he was on the verge of unleashing unimaginable horrors.

But. She sighed. Ptian was dead and his corroded soul fed to the dragon.

Now what?

Placing her hands flat on the table, Beth opened her eyes and stared not at Luisa and Dora, but at the two empty chairs either side of her. It had taken the very brink of slaughter and bloodshed for her to come to her senses. Crisis had cleared her mind.

She regretted it had taken Clytie's suicide, Sarra's murder and the death of her own son before she finally understood what she'd been born for. To lead. To lead the Hundred-Handed not through the daily routines and the seasons, but the changes life itself brings.

Instate a fairer ballot, Ailm had snapped when asked to cast the deciding vote on the issue of witchcraft.

Fair? With the shocking events in the past twenty-four hours, Beth no longer understood the meaning of fair. But she did understand that, instead of casting three votes at the pentagram, she needed to change the law. From now on the Head of the College would still guide the proceedings, but hers would be the final vote. Hers and hers alone.

So even though Oak and Rowan were in favour of expelling Yew from the Hundred-Handed, when they felt Gorse should keep her place, Beth used her powers for the first time.

'Fearn had allowed personal issues to dictate College matters,' she argued. 'Such an abuse could not be tolerated. And the three girls must be punished for the sin they'd committed.'

Yes, of course, they were scared, but they were scared for themselves not for Clytie, who had killed herself on the stone where they played. Worse, they gave no thought to the consequences of someone else having the shock of finding her body, much less the potential ravages of animals or the fear that would be unleashed at the prospect of a vicious killer on the loose. Children or not, rightly or wrongly, fair or unjust, those girls bore as much culpability as Ailm in the matter of Clytie's suicide.

We must show strength by believing in ourselves and standing by our convictions, Beth had told Claudia down in the cavern.

Whatever the cost?

How well she remembered the lead in her heart as she finally gave her reply. *Yes*, she had said. *Whatever the cost.*

And now she understood that, whether written or spoken, words don't freeze and die. They burn in the memory for eternity, and let the Druids keep up their symbols of notches on wood. The keys of wisdom, as they were called. The sun was setting on the day of the Druids, and whether the Hundred-Handed would survive for another three centuries or just another three years, so long as people continued to flock to them for spiritual guidance, that guidance would continue to be in line with nature.

And thus change.

'Step forward, Mavor,' she called aloud.

Two initiates would take the vacant places at the table tomorrow, but right now, this was business that could not wait. The door to the Voting Hall opened with a slight creak, and candlelight bounced off her wild auburn curls.

'There are those among us who are pushing for marriage among our order,' Beth said. 'But I cannot allow this in our College.'

'Hear, hear,' Dora boomed.

'However.' Beth took care to look only at Mavor. 'We know you have been meeting Gabali, when you are well aware that he was forbidden from entering our sacred grounds. We know that he asked you to hide the rope that would help the victim escape from the Pit of Reflection, even though you were not happy to do so. We know, moreover, that he asked you to hide it in Swarbric's hut, where you and he have been conducting your illegal assignations. And—'

She glanced at the space where Fearn should have been sitting. Love, she thought sadly. Love had so much to answer for . . .

'– and we know that you are pregnant.'

Mavor went white. 'How?'

'My dear, we have all had children,' Dora said gently. 'The signs are as plain as the clouds in the sky.'

'You do understand that Gabali must leave and that if he sets foot on this land again, he will be thrown into the Pit?'

'Which this time will be guarded,' Luisa added.

'However,' Beth said, before Mavor could speak, 'the Hundred-Handed have decided' – her smile was thin – 'if any of our order is not happy and wishes to leave, she is free to do so.'

Left unchecked, change could gallop out of control. Her job was to hold the reins and see that it advanced one pace at a time.

'These are the rules laid down by the pentagram: that any among us, priestess or initiate, may leave on condition she swears an oath never to speak of this College again, and on the strict understanding that she can never come back.'

For a beat of three only emotion pulsed between them, then Beth cleared her throat.

'Do you stay or do you go?'

Tears flowed down Mavor's cheeks and her shoulders heaved. 'Beth, I love this place with all my heart, you know that, and I love the work that I do, but it is not enough.'

'With Gabali do you think it will be enough?'

'I don't know, but I'm willing to try, and perhaps with a child . . .' Her words trailed off. 'Thank you, thank you all so very much – oh, but what about Swarbric? Please don't punish him for my sins, I beg you.'

'We will not,' Dora said crisply. 'We have graver issues to discuss with that young man. Kindly send him in as you leave.'

Still handsome, still confident, despite the mop of sodden grey hair and dripping pantaloons, Swarbric swaggered into the hall, his thumb hooked in his belt adjacent to the empty scabbard where his dagger should have been. Disarmed, but never disarming, Beth thought.

'Ladies.'

He bowed low.

Beth wasted no time.

'Swarbric, forgetting for a moment your complicity in an affair between a priestess and a male who was forbidden to set foot on our sacred ground again, you forsook your trust as Guardian of the Sacred Gate.'

She paused, but he made no attempt to apologize or explain.

'And even though it was to save two foolish lovers who didn't need saving and that, having found the fishing boat tied up next to a hut in which Pod was recovering from a fever, you returned to your post of your own free will, the pentagram is still of the opinion that we should strip you of your special privileges. How do you answer?'

There was a twinkle in his eye as he flashed his famous disarming grin.

'Ladies,' he breathed, advancing towards the table, 'I think you should just strip me and see what happens next.'

Despite themselves, the pentagram burst out laughing.

'You are incorrigible, Swarbric,' Dora spluttered.

'Which of course is why we all love you,' Luisa chuckled.

It was left to Beth – naturally – to pass sentence on the deserter. Outside, thunder rolled and rain drummed on the heavy thatched roof. The storm which had been building all day was spilling its anger on Gaul. Her sigh came from the heart.

'Oh, for pity's sake, Swarbric. Get back to your post, before I find myself promoting you.'

Thirty-One

Claudia stood on the footbridge while the fury of tempest whipped up the stream, swirled the treetops around and sent branches crashing down to the earth. Down the valley, the wind howled like a mother bereaved. Like a wild beast tormented by pain. Rocks tumbled down the arrowhead like pebbles.

She thought of the men and women who'd taken shelter in the caves, making their home in the cavern and leaving their art and their handprints for posterity. She saw them snug under the skins of the bears that they worshipped, a fire keeping them warm through the cold winter nights, water keeping them clean. A safe place. A holy place. A place where the spirits of the living were locked for eternity, but not in the form of souls or ghosts. It was their energy that remained trapped in the cave, as their dynamism and drive lingered on through millennia . . . And now she had tainted their memory with blood.

Not Ptian's.

If Beth's dragon existed, he was welcome to the feast.

Claudia was thinking of Manion. Of the fiery young man who'd spoken up against Rome and was shunned by his tribe for stirring up trouble. In his fervour to rid his country of the oppressors, he'd seen revolt as the only solution, and when revolution needs funding and crime pays handsome dividends, he'd seen a way to liberate Gaul. Gathering together hundreds of equally disenchanted outcasts, he formed a militia and armed it with the proceeds of crime. And in doing so, realized he'd created a monster.

These things Gabali told her as they made their way back from the Pit.

That it was this revelation that made Manion study his

enemy, Rome, and see that a small bunch of warriors, no matter how zealous, could not hope to take on the might of the Empire and win. It would only end in bloodshed and heartache, with villages razed in retribution, whole tribes taken as prisoners of war, women sold into slavery, men put down the mines, any surviving militia executed for sport. Ptian had refused to listen. He decried Manion's arguments as cowardice and capitulation, citing this erosion of passion as yet another reason to rid Aquitania of its oppressors. At which point, Manion realized that here was a young buck looking to oust the herd's leader. From now on he'd need to watch his back.

But Ptian had learned well from the master. The phoenix proved as slippery as the scorpion when it came to being pinned down.

But using Gabali's acquaintance with the College, Manion exploited Ptian's misogyny by contriving for him a job in the very heart of the society he hated. He'd weighed the risks carefully, Gabali explained, knowing that Ptian's obsession might well explode in bloodshed. But it was the only way Manion could set a trap on his own terms, using himself as the bait, and he'd attached himself to Orbilio as the first step to rehabilitation. Gabali was a link to them both.

Maybe not, as Claudia first said, an innocent man. But a reformed man, who'd dedicated himself to ridding Gaul of rebels with the same passion he'd used to incite them. A man who regretted his past and wanted to make amends.

What I want is my life back.

Instead, she took it away . . .

Her finger went to her mouth, to the place where Manion had wiped away the drizzle of honey, and as she felt once more the sensuousness of his touch. While in her hand, a carved scorpion burned—

'Listen, lady, if you're going to stand around in the rain, have the decency to do it out of sight of my cave. Moping depresses the patient.'

She stared down at the malevolent scowl and hoped no one would tell him what a good soul he was, it would kill him.

'Yes, how is Pod?' she asked.

Gurdo grunted. 'As far as the College is concerned, it's a fever, but if you think I'm going to catch pneu-bloody-monia talking about him in the rain, think again, Lofty Legs.'

Grabbing her arm, he dragged her along the path to the cave.

'Pod'll be fine.' He had to shout over the howl of the wind. 'He hardly knew Sarra, it was more puppy love, he'll get over her, given time, though between you and me, Lofty Legs, that boy had me worried. First Clytie, then Sarra.'

When he shook his head, drips flew off his ponytail, splattering Claudia's arm.

'I don't know what happened to the lad before I found him wandering the reed beds, but it was nasty, that much I can tell you. Enough to wipe his memory clean and trigger a breakdown when he found those poor cows, but – ' he shrugged – 'could have been worse, I suppose.'

So that was what put a spring in his step. Knowing Pod wasn't a killer.

'Here.' In the cave, he threw a blanket round Claudia's wet shoulders and shoved her without ceremony towards a heap of blankets piled in the corner. The blankets smelled faintly of nutmeg. 'Now say you're sorry.'

'Sorry? What for?'

'For not learning anatomy,' Manion croaked from the covers. 'That was my rib you jabbed with that blade. But not, thank the gods, my black heart.'

Thirty-Two

After the rain comes the sun, and with the sun came the heat. Steam rose from the paths like tropical jungle, birds bathed in the puddles and cows munched on grass flooded by rivers that broke their banks in the surge.

Beneath the dripping oak, Swarbric flourished his short sword as though he'd never been parted from it at a flaxen-haired trio, who squealed as they pulled out their skirts from their knicker cloths and promised never to do it again.

At the gate, Gabali lifted Mavor into his arms and threw her, laughing, into his gig.

Pod laid white roses in a glade for his true love.

Fearn broke her heart as hers drove away, and with that fat redheaded wanton as well.

In the Voting Hall, two new priestesses were sworn in at the pentagram.

In the kitchens, Ailm picked up a heather broom and started to sweep, defying with a glare any one to speak of her fall.

While a young girl with blonde, almost white hair, mixed scented oils in the Hall of Purification and dreamed of smuggling out a fuzzy-headed young slave under cover of night. If, of course, Connal would have her.

And a young man with a wound in his chest and seascape eyes took the first step towards getting his life back.

'You could have told me Gabali was working for you,' Claudia snapped.

They were standing by the cascade, which, swollen by the storm, came roaring out of the rock, its droplets making rainbows in the midsummer sun. Above the pool, swallows performed acrobatic parabolas and high overhead a black kite cast a silent shadow.

'Yes, I could,' Orbilio said quietly. He was no longer in shirt and pantaloons, but wore his long patrician toga that smelled faintly of rosemary, and his feet were encased in patrician boots. 'But you don't stop, Claudia. You continue to perpetrate these crimes and the bottom line is, people suffer.'

'Rubbish. No one gets hurt by my odd . . . indiscretion.'

'Fraud is never a victimless crime, because someone some-where always loses out, and even if the victim can afford it financially, there's an emotional price to be paid. You have to learn the difference between right and wrong.'

'This was to teach me a lesson?'

He spiked his hair out of his eyes. 'It's not as though you need the bloody money—'

'I'm broke.'

'You're irresponsible, Claudia, that's why! A good accountant, some sensible policies and—'

'Oh, well, if you're going to start talking about being sensible—'

'Stop it.' He spun round to face her and his face was carved out of stone. 'You can't go on making a joke of it,' he said brusquely. 'Sooner or later you have to face up to the fact you don't have the skills to manage a business of this magnitude. Claudia, you have to start trusting people.'

Trust is when the same man is always behind you, to catch no matter how often you fall.

She stared into the torrent. He had always been there. He had always caught her . . .

'Once you accept that you need help and put some faith in your accountants, your scribes, your agents, your managers, your business will boom.'

What? And have them screw fifty per cent of the profits? Did she look like she had the word lunatic tattooed on her forehead?

'I'll think about it,' she said.

'Don't think too long,' he growled. 'I can only protect you so far, and believe me, the army is full of hungry young lions eager to make their first kill. That's why I decoyed you out here to Gaul. It took several weeks before I found an excuse in the form of poor little Clytie, but knowing

246

about your mother's suicide, I knew you wouldn't resist the challenge.'

'Gabali phrased the word challenge somewhat differently, as I recall.'

'Between you and me, I think he rather enjoyed that.' Marcus flashed her a grin. 'But the point is, you and I have to make a decision. We can't go on as we are, and now that you said outright that you love me—'

Something flipped over beneath her ribs. 'I explained that.'

'Yes, you did.' He rubbed his jaw for a count of ten. 'You know your problem?'

'No, but I have a feeling you're going to enjoy telling me.'

'You like being broke. You enjoy living on the edge. You're totally addicted to the thrills.'

'So?'

'So—'

He leaned down, cupped her face in his hands and kissed her until she could hold her breath no more and was forced to kiss him back.

'So take the biggest risk you've ever taken in your life,' he rasped. 'Marry me. What do you say?'

She looked at him, dark and strong, always there, always capable. An honest man, a good man, a man she could trust and rely on. Life in the marriage bed would always be fun, he was handsome and passionate, and sweet Janus, she loved him with every aching beat of her heart.

'What I say is go to hell.' Disentangling herself from a thorn bush would be less painful than disentangling herself from his arms, but she managed. 'You deceived me, you lied to me—'

'I explained why.'

The burn of his lips almost undid her. She scrubbed the memory off with the back of her hand, while her soul had turned to lead.

'Orbilio, if you think the means justifies the end, think again.'

'Sometimes it does, I needed to force your hand, so help me, there was no other way.'

She smelled the sandalwood of his skin, tasted his fresh minty breath. Wanted to die in them both.

'No alternative to lying and cheating? Go to hell!'

'Claudia, no. Don't go—'

His hand lashed out, but she was faster, and although he raced up the path after her, she once was a dancer, remember.

'N-o-o-o,' he screamed as she ran inside the gate. 'For gods' sakes, Claudia, don't do this to me. Don't, please don't, do this to us.'

But she was inside the precinct, where no man may tread. With her hands clamped over her ears.

Around the cave, the spirits hovered like invisible bees, and the bees made honeycombs for young men so that they might wipe off the drizzle from the lips of young women, and then lick their thumbs slowly.

The house of Rumour buzzed with their sound.